SWORD AND FIST:

A Guidebook to Fighters and Monks

Credits

Design: Jason Carl
Additional Design and Development: Andy Collins, Monte Cook, Bruce Cordell, Dale Donovan, David Eckelberry, David Noonan, Jonathan Tweet, James Wyatt
Editor: Dale Donovan
Creative Director: Ed Stark
Cover Illustration: Jeff Easley
Interior Illustration: Wayne Reynolds, Lars Grant-West
Art Director: Dawn Murin
Graphic Designers: Sean Glenn, Sherry Floyd
Cartographer: Dennis Kauth
Typography: Erin Dorries
Project Managers: Larry Weiner, Josh Fischer
Production Manager: Chas DeLong
Legal Counsel: Brian Lewis

The halfling skiprock and the duelist prestige class both originally appeared in DRAGON® Magazine #275. Our thanks go to the DRAGON staff for their cooperation.

Based on the original DUNGEONS & DRAGONS® rules created by E. Gary Gygax and Dave Arneson, and the new DUNGEONS & DRAGONS game designed by Jonathan Tweet, Monte Cook, Skip Williams, Richard Baker, and Peter Adkison.

This Wizards of the Coast game product contains no Open Game Content. No portion of this work may be reproduced in any form without written permission. To learn more about the Open Gaming License and the d20 System License, please visit www.wizards.com/d20.

U.S., CANADA,
ASIA, PACIFIC, & LATIN AMERICA
Wizards of the Coast, Inc.
P.O. Box 707
Renton WA 98057-0707
(Questions?) 1-800-324-6496

620-T11829-002-EN
9 8 7 6 5 4 3

EUROPEAN HEADQUARTERS
Wizards of the Coast, Belgium
P.B. 2031
2600 Berchem
Belgium
+32-70-23-32-77

TABLE OF CONTENTS

TABLES

INTRODUCTION

Few moments in fantasy are more thrilling than the climactic battle of good versus evil. When the arrows fly, the dragon breathes fire, and death lurks around every corner, then do the warriors step forth to do battle, with blades or bare fists, to end the evil and win the day. Clerics, wizards, and rogues notwithstanding: warriors win battles. Let glorious victory fall upon the shoulders of those few: the fighters and the monks!

Among the eleven character classes available in the *Player's Handbook,* the fighter and the monk both begin their adventuring careers with only their own martial prowess to protect them against the dangers common to their chosen way of life. They survive by combining martial talent with unique battlefield knowledge, and this combination makes them the undisputed masters of physical confrontation. Combat is their stock in trade, and muscle, speed, and stamina are their primary tools. Monks and fighters cannot rely on ready access to arcane or divine spells to achieve their goals: They must make their way in the world without such conveniences.

It is with this in mind that we examine these two character classes in depth, and provide you with new information that allows you to maximize their potential and your enjoyment when playing them.

WHAT THIS BOOK IS, AND IS NOT

All the material herein is brand-new and pertains to the new edition of the DUNGEONS & DRAGONS® game. You will find new feats, rules, and prestige classes, as well as useful advice and for getting the most out of your fighter or monk.

Nothing here supersedes or replaces the rules or information in the *Player's Handbook.* This supplement is designed to mesh with the rules system presented in the *Player's Handbook* and the other core rulebooks, the DUNGEON MASTER's *Guide* and the *Monster Manual.*

Like the new rules themselves, this book provides options and not restrictions for playing the D&D game. Take and use what you like, modify whatever you feel requires it, and ignore the rest. Players should ask their DMs about incorporating any elements of this book beforehand. DMs can use the rules, classes, and magic items for nonplayer characters as well as for player characters.

HOW TO USE THIS BOOK

This book's primary goal is to help you customize your fighter or monk player character. The *Player's Handbook* provides all the information you need to create a new 1st-level fighter or monk character, while *Sword and Fist* contains information that allows you to personalize that character, broaden his range of capabilities, and enhance the role he plays in your adventuring party. When creating a brand-new character, you will find *The Hero Builder's Guidebook* an invaluable resource in defining and detailing your character's background and life before taking up this exciting but dangerous line of work.

The information in this book is intended for players and DMs, and pertains equally to both—all the material applies to both PCs and NPCs. When place names are given, these names refer to the D&D world, as defined in the *D&D Gazetteer.* DMs using other campaign settings can simply replace these names with others of their choosing.

Chapter 1 presents an array of new feats designed to help fighters and monks do what they do best: fight.

Chapter 2 offers new prestige classes that fighters and monks can strive toward.

Chapter 3 gives several organizations that fighters and monks can join in the course of the campaign, in order to foster a sense of camaraderie with similar characters, to grant the character an additional means of support, and to provide adventure hooks for the character and the party.

Chapter 4 provides advice on taking best advantage of the rules as well as giving new, optional combat rules to add depth to game combat and extended examples of combat.

Chapter 5 expands the range of weapons, armor, equipment, and magic items available to your character, plus detailing eight sites or locales, complete with NPCs and construction costs, that PCs can explore, attack, buy, or build for themselves.

CHAPTER I: FEATS AND SKILLS

Feats are an exciting new element of the D&D® game. This chapter presents even more new combat options, designed with your fighters and monks in mind (though anyone who qualifies can take them). These new feats have prerequisites, such as an ability score minimum or a minimum base attack bonus. Asterisked feats below are available as fighter bonus feats.

VIRTUAL FEATS

If you effectively have a feat as a class feature or special ability, then you can use that virtual feat as a prerequisite for other feats. What does this mean? If you have, for example, some class feature or ability that says, "This is the same as Mobility," then you are considered to have the Mobility feat for the purposes of acquiring the Spring Attack feat. If you ever lose the virtual prerequisite, you also lose access to any feats you acquired through its existence.

NEW FEATS

"Have I got a surprise for you. Come closer, I'll show you what it is."

—Regdar

Blindsight, 5-foot Radius [General]

You sense opponents in the darkness.

Prerequisites: Base attack bonus +4, Blind-Fight, Wisdom 19+.

Benefit: Using senses such as acute hearing and sensitivity to vibrations, you detect the location of opponents who are no more than 5 feet away from you. *Invisibility* and *darkness* are irrelevant, though you cannot discern noncorporeal beings. Except for the decreased range, this feat is identical with the exceptional ability blindsight defined in the *Monster Manual*.

Circle Kick [General]

You kick multiple opponents with the same attack action.

Prerequisites: Base attack bonus +3, Improved Unarmed Strike, Dex 15+.

Benefit: When you perform the full attack action, you can give up your regular attacks and instead make a single unarmed attack. If this attack hits, you can make a single unarmed attack against a different opponent that is within the area you threaten. You use your full attack bonus for the second attack.

Close-Quarters Fighting* [General]

You are skilled at fighting at close range and resisting grapple attacks.

Prerequisite: Base attack bonus +3.

Benefit: You are entitled to make an attack of opportunity even if the attacking creature has the improved grab ability. When an enemy attempts to grapple you, any damage you

inflict with a successful attack of opportunity provoked by the grapple attempt is added to your ensuing grapple check to avoid being grappled.

This feat does not provide you with additional attacks of opportunity in a round, so if you do not have an attack of opportunity available when your enemy attempts to grapple you, you do not get any benefit from Close-Quarters Fighting.

For example, a dire bear strikes you with a claw attack. If you don't have this feat, the dire bear's improved grab ability allows it to immediately attempt a grapple check, provoking no attack of opportunity from you. However, with Close-Quarters Fighting, you are entitled to an attack of opportunity. If you hit and score 8 points of damage, you may add +8 (plus your attack bonus, Strength bonus, and size modifier) to your grapple check to resist the dire bear's grapple attempt.

Death Blow* [General]

You waste no time in dealing with downed foes.

Prerequisites: Base attack bonus +2, Improved Initiative.

Benefit: You can perform a coup de grace attack against a helpless defender as a standard action.

Normal: Performing a coup de grace is a full-round action.

Dirty Fighting [General]

You know the brutal and effective fighting tactics of the streets and back alleys.

Prerequisites: Base attack bonus +2.

Benefit: When you perform the full attack action, you can give up your regular attacks and instead make a single attack. If this attack hits, you deal an additional +1d4 points of damage.

Dual Strike* [General]

Your combat teamwork makes you a more dangerous foe.

Prerequisites: Base attack bonus +3, Combat Reflexes.

Benefit: If you and an ally both have this feat and are flanking an opponent, you both get a +4 bonus on your attack roll.

Normal: The standard flanking attack roll bonus is +2.

Eagle Claw Attack [General]

Your unarmed attacks shatter objects.

Prerequisites: Base attack bonus +2, Improved Unarmed Strike, Sunder, Dex 15+.

Benefit: You can strike an opponent's weapon or shield with an unarmed strike.

Normal: You cannot choose the Strike a Weapon attack option with an unarmed attack.

Special: Weapon hardness and hit point ratings are given on Table 8–13: Common Weapon and Shield Hardness Ratings and Hit Points in the *Player's Handbook*.

Expert Tactician* [General]

Your tactical skill works to your advantage.

Prerequisite: Base attack bonus +3.

Benefit: This feat allows you to make one melee attack (or anything that can be done as a melee attack) against one foe who is within melee reach and denied her Dexterity bonus against your melee attacks for any reason. You take your extra attack when it's your turn, either before or after your regular action. If several foes are within melee reach and denied their Dexterity bonus, you can attack only one of them with this feat.

Extra Stunning Attacks [General]

You gain extra stunning attacks when fighting unarmed.

Prerequisites: Base attack bonus +2, Stunning Fist.

Benefit: You gain the ability to make three extra stunning attacks per day. You may take this feat multiple times.

Eyes in the Back of Your Head [General]

Your superior battle sense helps minimize the threat of flanking attacks.

Prerequisites: Base attack bonus +3, Wis 19+.

Benefit: Attackers do not gain the usual +2 attack bonus when flanking you. This feat grants no effect whenever you are attacked without benefit of your Dexterity modifier to AC, such as when you are flat-footed.

Normal: When you are flanked, the flanking opponents receive a +2 attack roll bonus against you.

Feign Weakness [General]

You capitalize on your foe's perceptions of your unarmed status.

Prerequisites: Base attack bonus +2, Improved Unarmed Strike.

Benefit: If you make a successful Bluff check against your opponent's Sense Motive check, you lure the foe into attempting an attack of opportunity because he thinks you are unarmed. But you are armed, and you make your attack against your drawn-out foe who is caught flat-footed, before he takes his attack of opportunity.

You also may attempt this feat with a Tiny or Small weapon with which you are proficient by attempting to hide it until the last second, but you incur a −2 or −6 penalty on your Bluff check, respectively. You can use this feat with a disguised weapon, such as a war fan, at no penalty on the Bluff check. Using Feign Weakness is a standard action, just like a feint, except that if you succeed you get to make your attack immediately. You can only Feign Weakness once per encounter. After one use, your opponents are too wary to fall for this maneuver again.

Fists of Iron [General]

You have learned the secrets of imbuing your unarmed attacks with extra force.

Prerequisites: Base attack bonus +2, Improved Unarmed Strike.

Benefit: Declare that you are using this feat before you make your attack roll (thus, a missed attack roll ruins the attempt). You deal an extra 1d4 points of damage when you make a successful unarmed attack. You may use this feat a number of times per day equal to 3 + your Wisdom modifier.

Hold the Line* [General]
You are trained in defensive techniques against charging opponents.

Prerequisites: Base attack bonus +2, Combat Reflexes.

Benefit: You may make an attack of opportunity against an opponent who charges you when he enters an area you threaten. Your attack of opportunity happens immediately before the charge attack is resolved.

Improved Overrun* [General]
You are trained in knocking over opponents that are smaller than you.

Prerequisites: Expertise, Improved Bull Rush, Improved Trip, Str 13+, Power Attack.

Benefit: When you attempt to overrun an opponent who is at least one size category smaller than you, the target cannot avoid you. If you knock down your opponent, you immediately get an attack of opportunity against that opponent, gaining the standard +4 bonus on attack rolls against prone targets.

Normal: The target of your overrun attack chooses to avoid you or block you.

Improved Sunder* [General]
You are adept at placing your attacks precisely where you want them to land.

Prerequisites: Base attack bonus +2, Sunder.

Benefit: When you strike an opponent's weapon, you inflict double damage.

Knock-Down* [General]
Your mighty blows can knock foes off their feet.

Prerequisites: Base attack bonus +2, Improved Trip, Str 15+.

Benefit: Whenever you deal 10 or more points of damage to your opponent in melee with a single attack,

you may make a trip attack as a free action against the same target. Use of this feat cannot be combined with Improved Trip to generate an extra attack, and successful use of this feat does not grant an extra attack through the Cleave or Great Cleave feats.

Lightning Fists [General]
Your skill and agility allow you to attempt a series of blindingly fast blows.

Prerequisites: Monk level 4th+, Dex 15+.

Benefit: You can make two extra attacks in a round. All attacks made this round suffer a –5 attack penalty. This feat requires the full attack action. You cannot use Lightning Fists and flurry of blows at the same time.

Mantis Leap [General]
You deliver a powerful attack after making a jump.

Prerequisites: Monk level 7th+, 5 ranks in Jump.

Benefit: Designate an opponent who is within the maximum distance you can reach with a successful Jump check. Make a normal Jump check; if your check is successful, you can make a normal charge attack against the opponent you designated as part of the same action. If your charge attack is successful, you inflict normal damage, plus your Strength modifier multiplied by 2 regardless of whether you're using one- or two-handed weapons.

Monkey Grip [General]
You use a wider variety of sizes of weapons.

Prerequisites: Base attack bonus +3, Weapon Focus with the appropriate weapon, Str 13+.

Benefit: You can use one melee weapon that is one size larger than you in one hand. For example, a halfling with the Monkey Grip feat can use a longsword in one hand. You suffer a –2 penalty on your attack roll when using this feat. This feat can be taken multiple times, each time with a different weapon.

Normal: Only weapons of your size or smaller can normally be wielded with one hand.

Off-Hand Parry* [General]
You use your off-hand weapon to defend against melee attacks.

Prerequisites: Base attack bonus +3, Ambidexterity, Dex 13+, Two-Weapon Fighting, proficiency with weapon.

Benefit: When fighting with two weapons and using the full attack action, on your action decide to attack normally or to sacrifice all your off-hand attacks for the round in exchange for a +2 dodge bonus to your AC. If you take this option, you also suffer the standard penalties on your attack, as if fighting with two weapons. If you are also using a buckler, its AC bonus stacks. You can use only bladed or hafted weapons of a size category smaller than you with this feat.

Pain Touch [General]

You cause intense pain in an opponent with a successful stunning attack.

Prerequisites: Base attack bonus +2, Stunning Fist, Wis 19+.

Benefit: Victims of a successful stunning attack are subject to such debilitating pain that they are nauseated for 1 round after being stunned for 1 round as usual. A stunning attack involves a monk's stunning attack power or the use of the Stunning Fist feat. Creatures that are immune to stunning attacks are also immune to this feat, as are any creatures that are more than one size category larger than the feat user.

Pin Shield* [General]

You know how to get inside your opponent's guard by pinning his shield out of the way.

Prerequisites: Base attack bonus +4, Two-Weapon Fighting.

Benefit: This feat can only be used against an opponent who is using a shield and who is within one size category of you. Make an off-hand attack against an opponent's shield using the normal rules for striking a weapon (see the *Player's Handbook*, Chapter 8). If your attack roll is successful, you momentarily pin your opponent's shield with your off-hand weapon, and you may make an immediate attack of opportunity against your opponent with your primary weapon at your full attack bonus. Your foe gains no AC benefit from her shield for this attack. You cannot use this feat if you are fighting with only one weapon.

Power Lunge* [General]

Your ferocious attack may catch an opponent unprepared.

Prerequisites: Base attack bonus +3, Power Attack.

Benefit: A successful attack roll during a charge allows you to inflict double your normal Strength modifier in addition to the attack's damage regardless of whether you're using one- or two-handed weapons. You provoke an attack of opportunity from the opponent you charged.

Prone Attack* [General]

You attack from a prone position without penalty.

Prerequisites: Base attack bonus +2, Dex 15+, Lightning Reflexes.

Benefit: You can make an attack from the prone position and suffer no penalty to your attack roll. If your attack roll is successful, you may regain your feet immediately as a free action.

Rapid Reload* [General]

You reload a crossbow more quickly than normal.

Prerequisites: Base attack bonus +2, proficiency with the crossbow used.

Benefit: You can reload a hand crossbow or light crossbow as a free action that provokes an attack of opportunity. You may reload a heavy crossbow as a move-equivalent action that provokes an attack of opportunity. You can use this feat once per round.

Normal: Loading a hand or light crossbow is a move-equivalent action, and loading a heavy crossbow is a full-round action.

Remain Conscious [General]

You have a tenacity of will that supports you even when things look bleak.

Prerequisites: Base attack bonus +2, Endurance, Iron Will, Toughness.

Benefit: When your hit points are reduced to 0, you may take one partial action on your turn every round until you reach −10 hit points.

Sharp-Shooting* [General]

Your skill with ranged weapons lets you score hits others would miss due to an opponent's cover.

Prerequisites: Base attack bonus +3, Point Blank Shot, Precise Shot.

Benefit: You gain a +2 bonus to your ranged attack rolls against targets with some degree of cover. This feat has no effect against foes with no cover or total cover.

Shield Expert* [General]

You use a shield as an off-hand weapon while retaining its armor bonus.

Prerequisite: Base attack bonus +3, shield proficiency.

Benefit: You may make an off-hand attack with your shield while retaining the shield's AC bonus for that round. For the purposes of determining attack penalties, shields are considered light weapons.

Normal: Using a shield as a weapon prevents you from gaining its AC bonus for the round.

Snatch Arrows* [General]

You are adept at grabbing incoming arrows, as well as crossbow bolts, spears, and other projectile or thrown weapons.

Prerequisites: Base attack bonus +3, Deflect Arrows, Dex 15+, Improved Unarmed Strike.

Benefit: You must have at least one hand free (holding nothing) to use this feat. When using the Deflect Arrows feat, you may catch the weapon instead of just deflecting it. Thrown weapons such as spears or axes can be thrown back at the original attacker as an immediate free action or kept. Projectile weapons such as arrows or bolts can be fired back normally on your next turn or later, if you possess the proper kind of bow or crossbow.

Throw Anything [General]

In your hands, any weapon becomes a deadly ranged weapon.

Prerequisites: Base attack bonus +2, Dex 15+.

Benefit: You can throw any weapon you can use, regardless of whether it is intended to be used as a ranged weapon. The range increment of weapons used in conjunction with this feat is 10 feet.

Zen Archery [General]

Your intuition guides your hand when you use a ranged weapon.

Prerequisites: Base attack bonus +3, Wis 13+.

Benefit: The character can use her Wisdom modifier instead of her Dexterity Modifier when making a ranged attack at a target within 30 feet.

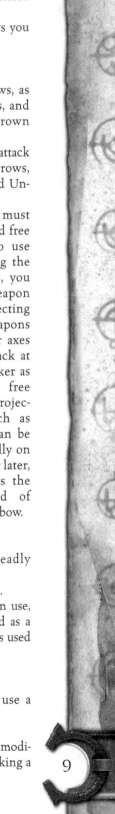

SKILLS

"You underestimate me because I do not encase myself in metal. I have no need for it; I possess skills you can never comprehend."

—Ember

Skills are a vital component when building a successful and hardy adventurer. When your monk or fighter gains additional skill points as he progresses in levels, you might be tempted to gloss over the process of selecting and assigning skills. We have a handy tip for you: Do not make that mistake. Choosing your skills carefully often means the difference between success and failure, or even between life and death for your character.

Like the skills in the *Player's Handbook*, those presented here represent a variety of abilities, and you get better at them as you go up in level and can devote more skill points to them.

NEW KNOWLEDGE SKILLS

Like the Craft and Profession skills in the *Player's Handbook*, Knowledge actually encompasses a number of unrelated skills. Knowledge represents a study of some body of lore, possibly an academic or even scientific discipline. Below are a few new fields of study. With your DM's approval, you can invent other new areas of knowledge.

- Hearth wisdom (folklore, myths, origins of place names, folk remedies for common ailments).
- Literature (stories, plays, ballads, epic poetry, legends).
- Mathematics (basic math, geometry, algebra).
- Politics (government bureaucracies, petitions, bribes, subterfuge, art of compromise).
- Streetwise (drinking, flirting, gambling, tailing).
- War (siege engines, sapping, siege tactics and strategy).

SAME SKILLS, NEW USES

Skills play a vital role in the success of your character's adventures and exploits. Without them, you would be unable to accomplish a variety of tasks from the simple (spotting a boat on the ocean horizon) to the crucial (climbing a dungeon wall to escape a rampaging owlbear). We designed the skill system, however, so you can use almost any skill in more than just one way, in ways beyond the obvious application. Some suggestions follow for getting more out of the skills in the *Player's Handbook*.

Bluff (Cha)

Normal Use: Sometimes you need to persuade someone that your unlikely or even improbable statements are true and that you can be trusted. This can be helpful in numerous situations, and not merely when you need to fence those magic items that you liberated from the mad wizard's tower.

New Use: *Seduction.* You can use Bluff to convince members of the opposite sex to believe that your romantic intentions are sincere, persuading him or her to do you a small, temporary favor (such as looking the other way as you climb up the wall and into the window, or giving you the password that allows you to pass safely by the guards). This action cannot be used during combat.

Diplomacy (Cha)

Normal Use: Sometimes it is important that others find you pleasant, cooperative, or socially acceptable—even if you are not. You might think your fighter character looks ruggedly handsome in his blood-stained chainmail and travel-ragged cloak, but the Master of the Revels may not agree unless you can convince him to allow you into the king's ballroom despite your unkempt appearance.

New Use: *Know how to address someone.* Even the most skilled dragon slayer cannot afford to antagonize those individuals who occupy positions of power and authority. Nobles and other dignitaries usually expect to be addressed correctly. Knowing when to call a wealthy patron "Your grace" rather than "Your ladyship" can help make the scale of reactions tip in your favor.

Gather Information (Cha)

Normal Use: This skill helps you find out if any rumors or legends exist surrounding that dungeon you are considering looting by asking those around who might have such information to share.

New Use: *Find out who is* really *in charge.* You need help from the Temple of the Four Winds, but do not know whom to ask. Should you approach the Grand Master himself, or should you ask one of his many underlings for aid? Proper use of this skill can help you find out who makes important decisions.

New Use: *Who's who.* Wily adventurers always know whom they deal with before committing to an agreement. Was the cloaked stranger who just hired your adventuring party really the duke's steward, and if so, does he really have his master's trust?

Sense Motive (Wis)

Normal Use: This skill comes in very handy when someone uses the Bluff skill against you. You make an opposed skill check, and if you succeed, you are not bluffed.

New Use: *Combat prediction.* You get a good though general idea of an opponent's combat skill. This use of the skill requires you to spend a minimum of 3 rounds observing an opponent who is engaged in combat. You can take no other actions in that time other than moving your normal movement rate. You must keep your subject in view at all times. The DC is 20 +1 for every experience level your opponent has attained. If successful, you gain a +4 bonus on your first attack roll against the observed opponent. This attack must come within 24 hours of the observation or the bonus is lost. You cannot gain this bonus against the same opponent twice unless the character's level has changed since you last observed him.

New Use: *Decipher strategy.* You assess a combat situation and determine its true purpose. You must observe the combat for a minimum of 3 rounds before making the skill check. The DC is 15 +1 for every opponent you face. If successful, you determine your opponents' true motive (cut you to pieces, lure you away from or drive you toward a particular spot, rescue a captive, and so on).

CHAPTER 2: PRESTIGE CLASSES

"How do you do that?"

—Regdar

Introduced in the DUNGEON MASTER'S GUIDE, prestige classes are character classes that PCs must qualify for before taking. Requirements for entry are listed in each prestige class's section. Unless noted otherwise, follow all normal multiclass rules when adding prestige classes to your PCs.

CAVALIER

Representing the ultimate in mounted warfare, the cavalier is the quintessential knight in shining armor. The charge of the cavalier is among the most devastating battlefield offensive weapons any culture can hope to field.

Most cavaliers belong to the upper social class or nobility of a society. The cavalier dedicates his life to the service of a higher authority, such as a noble or sovereign, deity, military or religious order, or a special cause. His is a hereditary honor that comes with the price of lifelong service to his monarch, country, or other object of service. The cavalier is expected to participate in any wars or other armed conflict in which his lord or cause is engaged. Cavaliers in service

to other nobles often serve their master beyond the battlefield as well, performing such duties as their skills, and their noble lord, see fit.

The cavalier often pursues such selfless goals as the eradication of evil and chaos from the world, and justice for all the subjects of his land. He can also be a bully and a braggart who uses his status and privileges to pursue only his own self-aggrandizement.

Hit Die: d10.

Requirements

To qualify to become a cavalier, a character must fulfill the following criteria.

Alignment: Lawful.
Base Attack Bonus: +8.
Feats: Spirited Charge, Weapon Focus (lance), Weapon Focus (any sword), Mounted Combat, Ride-By Attack.
Handle Animal: 4 ranks.
Knowledge (Nobility and Royalty): 4 ranks.
Ride: 6 ranks.
Equipment: Masterwork heavy armor and masterwork large shield.

Class Skills

The cavalier's class skills (and the key ability for each skill) are Diplomacy (Cha), Intimidate (Cha), Knowledge (nobility and royalty) (Int), Profession (Int), and Ride (Dex). See Chapter 4: Skills in the *Player's Handbook* for skill descriptions.

Skill Points at Each Level: 2 + Int modifier.

TABLE 2–1: THE CAVALIER

Class Level	Base Attack Bonus	Fort Save	Ref Save	Will Save	Special
1st	+1	+2	+0	+2	Mounted weapon bonus lance +1, Ride bonus +2, tall in the saddle +1
2nd	+2	+3	+0	+3	Deadly charge 1/day, mounted weapon bonus sword +1
3rd	+3	+3	+1	+3	Burst of speed, mounted weapon bonus lance +2, tall in the saddle +2
4th	+4	+4	+1	+4	Deadly charge 2/day, mounted weapon bonus sword +2, Ride bonus +4
5th	+5	+4	+1	+4	Mounted weapon bonus lance +3, tall in the saddle +3
6th	+6	+5	+2	+5	Deadly charge 3/day, full mounted attack, mounted weapon bonus sword +3
7th	+7	+5	+2	+5	Mounted weapon bonus lance +4, Ride bonus +6, tall in the saddle +4
8th	+8	+6	+2	+6	Deadly charge 4/day, mounted weapon bonus sword +5
9th	+9	+6	+3	+6	Mounted weapon bonus lance +5, Ride bonus +8, tall in the saddle +5
10th	+10	+7	+3	+7	Deadly charge 5/day

Class Features

Weapon and Armor Proficiency: The cavalier is proficient with all simple and martial weapons, all types of armor, and shields.

Knowledge (Nobility and Royalty): The cavalier gains a +2 bonus to this skill automatically at first level.

Tall in the Saddle: The cavalier gains a bonus to his Ride skill check whenever he uses the Mounted Combat feat to negate a hit his mount takes in combat.

Deadly Charge: When mounted and using the charge action, you deal triple damage with a melee weapon (or quadruple damage with a lance), up to the number of times per day indicated. This ability supersedes the Spirited Charge feat.

Mounted Weapon Bonus: The cavalier gains a bonus to his attack roll when using the designated weapon while mounted.

Ride Bonus: The cavalier gains a competence bonus to Ride checks.

Burst of Speed (Ex): At 3rd level, the cavalier can urge his mount to greater than normal speeds. This ability doubles the distance of the mount's normal charge movement. This ability can be used once per day without penalty to the mount. Each additional use of the ability in a single day requires the mount to make a Will save (DC 20) immediately after the conclusion of the additional charge; failure results in the mount taking 2d6 points of damage.

Full Mounted Attack: At 6th level, the mounted cavalier can take a full attack action if the mount makes no more than a single move (assuming an opponent exists to be attacked), rather than a single attack as a partial action.

DEVOTED DEFENDER

The devoted defender is a professional guardian. She is an individual who is skilled at protecting a designated client from harm, often by taking her charge's place as the target of threats and attacks. In return for these services, the devoted defender usually receives compensation in the form of coin, room and board, and sometimes in resources such as access to magic healing, but the exact details of the agreement are between the individual devoted defender and her employer. It is not uncommon for a noble or other important personage to number at least one

TABLE 2–2: THE DEVOTED DEFENDER

Class Level	Base Attack Bonus	Fort Save	Ref Save	Will Save	AC Bonus	Special
1st	+1	+2	+2	+0	+1	Harm's way
2nd	+2	+3	+3	+0	+1	Defensive strike
3rd	+3	+3	+3	+1	+2	Deflect attack +1
4th	+4	+4	+4	+1	+2	Defensive strike +1
5th	+5	+4	+4	+1	+3	Deflect attack +2
6th	+6	+5	+5	+2	+3	Defensive strike +2
7th	+7	+5	+5	+2	+4	Deflect attack +3
8th	+8	+6	+6	+2	+4	Defensive strike +3
9th	+9	+6	+6	+3	+5	Deflect attack +4
10th	+10	+7	+7	+3	+5	Defensive strike +4

AC Bonus: The defensive bonus to the character's Armor Class, added to the character's normal AC bonus. This bonus applies *only* when the devoted defender is actively engaged in protecting her client from an attack; otherwise, use the character's normal AC bonus.

devoted defender among his personal retinue, and sometimes to make a devoted defender the chief of his security services.

Most devoted defenders are fighters, but any character who becomes a devoted defender benefits from the attack, save and Armor Class bonuses. Monks sometimes become devoted defenders, as do clerics, when they are assigned to protect important individuals within their order or clergy. NPC devoted defenders are mostly fighters who either left military service and turned to security work to make a living.

Hit Die: d12.

Requirements

To qualify to become a devoted defender, a character must fulfill the following criteria.

Base Attack Bonus: +5.

Feats: Weapon Focus (any melee weapon), Alertness.

Search: 4 ranks.

Sense Motive: 4 ranks.

Spot: 4 ranks.

Class Skills

The devoted defender's class skills (and the key ability for each skill) are Climb (Str), Innuendo (Wis), Jump (Str), Listen (Wis), Profession (Int), Sense Motive (Wis), Search (Int), and Spot (Wis). See Chapter 4: Skills in the *Player's Handbook* for skill descriptions.

Skill Points at Each Level: 2 + Int modifier.

Class Features

Weapon and Armor Proficiency: The devoted defender is proficient with all simple and martial weapons, all types of armor, and shields.

Armor Class Bonus: The devoted defender concentrates on defense, both for herself and her charge. She receives this dodge bonus to AC as a result of that focus.

Harm's Way (Ex): Beginning at 1st level, the devoted defender may elect to place herself in the path of

danger in order to protect her single charge. Any time that you are within 5 feet of your charge, and your charge suffers an attack, you may switch places with your charge and receive the attack in his place. You must declare this before the attack roll is made. You select your charge when you roll initiative, and it is a free action to do so. You may not change your charge for the duration of that combat.

Defensive Strike (Ex): You can make an attack of opportunity against any adjacent opponent who attacks your charge in melee. You gain a +1 bonus to this attack for every two levels after 2nd.

Deflect Attack (Ex): Beginning at 3rd level, the devoted defender can attempt to parry a melee attack against her charge. She must be within 5 feet of her charge to attempt this and holding a melee weapon or shield to deflect the attack. Once per round when your charge is attacked, you may make an opposed attack roll. You gain a competence bonus to your attack roll as indicated on the table. If you beat the attacker, you deflect the blow. You must be aware of the attack beforehand and not flat-footed.

DRUNKEN MASTER

Martial arts students face a bewildering array of martial arts schools, each with its own adherents and detractors. But few schools are as unusual—or as controversial—as Drunken Boxing. By weaving and staggering about as if inebriated, drunken boxers avoid many blows. Likewise, their stumbling, lurching attacks catch their opponents off guard. Moreover, when they actually imbibe alcohol, drunken masters can perform truly prodigious feats of strength and bravery.

None of this garners them much respect among other martial arts schools, because drunken boxing exacts a toll on its users. Drunken masters remain intoxicated for hours after a fight, and they are often found half-asleep in taverns, mumbling incoherently. This flies in the face of other schools' ascetic principles. But rival schools must be wary—they never know when the tipsy lout at the bar is just a harmless thug, and when it is a nigh-unstoppable drunken master.

Monks form the backbone of the drunken boxing school. They lose some face with their original school or monastery for becoming a drunken master, but a brilliant display of drunken fighting can sometimes silence critics in one's former school. Members of other character classes are chosen as drunken boxers only rarely, although students often tell the tale of a barbarian from the north who became a phenomenal drunken master.

Prospective students are studied at a distance by drunken masters, then treated to a display of drunken boxing's power. If the student expresses enthusiasm for learning the new techniques, a group of drunken masters take him or her from tavern to tavern, getting rip-roaring drunk, causing trouble, and passing along the first secrets of the technique. Those who survive the revelry are new drunken masters.

NPC drunken masters are often found in taverns and bars. They rarely pick fights there, but are quick to come to the aid of someone overmatched in a tavern brawl. Most keep a low profile, although some are famous—or infamous—for the deeds they have performed while under the influence.

Hit Die: d8

Requirements

To qualify to become a drunken master, a character must fulfill all the following criteria.

Base Attack Bonus: +4.

Base Unarmed Attack Bonus: +4.
Feats: Great Fortitude, Dodge.
Tumble: 6 ranks.
Other: Evasion ability, must be chosen by existing drunken masters and survive night of revelry among them without being incarcerated, poisoned, or extraordinarily embarrassed.

Class Skills

The drunken master's class skills (and the key ability for each skill) are Balance (Dex), Bluff (Cha), Climb (Str), Craft (Int), Escape Artist (Dex), Hide (Dex), Jump (Str), Listen (Wis), Move Silently (Dex), Perform (Cha), Profession (Wis), Swim (Str), and Tumble (Dex). See Chapter 4: Skills in the *Player's Handbook* for skill descriptions.

Skill Points at Each Level: 4 + Int modifier.

Class Features

Drink Like a Demon (Ex): Your body handles alcohol differently from other people's. You can drink a large tankard of ale, a bottle of wine, or a corresponding amount of stronger alcohol as a move-equivalent action. Every bottle or tankard of alcohol you consume during combat reduces your Dexterity, Wisdom, and Intelligence by 1 point each, but increases your Strength or Constitution (your choice) by 1 point. However, your Reflex save bonus, Dexterity bonus to Tumble, and AC bonus remain at their original levels regardless of your new Dexterity modifier. Your body metabolizes one drink per hour, reducing both the penalties and the bonus accordingly. You only gain the Strength and Constitution bonuses for alcohol drunk during a fight, and the bonuses only last until the end of the combat. (The penalties disappear more gradually.) What

TABLE 2–3: THE DRUNKEN MASTER

Class Level	Base Attack Bonus	Fort Save	Ref Save	Will Save	Special
1st	+1	+2	+2	+0	Speed 50 ft., drink like a demon, bottle proficiency, unarmed damage 1d8
2nd	+2	+3	+3	+0	Stagger
3rd	+3	+3	+3	+1	Speed 60 ft., swaying waist
4th	+4	+4	+4	+1	AC bonus +1, improvised weapons
5th	+5	+4	+4	+1	Drunken rage, unarmed damage 1d10
6th	+6	+5	+5	+2	Speed 70 ft., lurch
7th	+7	+5	+5	+2	Drunken embrace
8th*	+8	+6	+6	+2	*For medicinal purposes*
9th*	+9	+6	+6	+3	AC bonus +2, speed 80 ft., corkscrew rush, unarmed damage 1d12
10th*	+10	+7	+7	+3	*Breath of flame*

Base Attack Bonus: Note that, like a monk, a drunken master makes unarmed iterative attacks at a –3 penalty, not the usual –5 penalty.

*Drunken masters cannot attack more than five times per round.

quantity of alcohol constitutes a "drink" is deliberately left undefined.

Bottle Proficiency: You can use bottles and large tankards as weapons using your unarmed base attack bonus, including your more favorable number of attacks per round. Bottles do 1d6 points of bludgeoning damage with their first blow, then 1d4 points of slashing damage thereafter. Tankards do 1d6 points of bludgeoning damage. Furthermore, you can make these attacks without spilling most of the liquid inside.

Stagger: By tripping, stumbling, and staggering, you can make a charge attack that surprises your opponents. This has two beneficial aspects: First, your charges need not be in straight lines, and you still move up to twice your speed. Second, make a Tumble check (DC 15) when you begin your charge. If you succeed, your movement through threatened squares provokes no attacks of opportunity.

Swaying Waist: You weave and bob about as you attack. You gain a +2 dodge bonus to AC against any one opponent you choose during your turn. This supersedes the Dodge feat, but functions like it in all other ways.

Improvised Weapons: You can use furniture, farm implements, or nearly anything else at hand to attack your foes. Anything from a ladder to a haunch of meat to a barstool is a weapon once you imbue it with your *ki* using this ability. Regardless of the exact item, the weapon does 1d6 points of damage at your more advantageous number of attacks per round. Most items do bludgeoning damage, although shish-kabob skewers, for example, would do piercing damage. Long items (such as ladders) have reach according to their length, and items with many protrusions (such as chairs) give you a +2 bonus on Disarm attempts. Finally, large items with broad, flat surfaces (such as tables) can be upended to become improvised tower shields.

Drunken Rage (Ex): You can rage just as a barbarian does, with a duration equal to your (new) Constitution modifier plus the number of drinks you have consumed. You gain +4 to Strength, +4 to Constitution, a +2 morale bonus on Will saves, and a −2 penalty to AC. This ability supersedes the Strength and Constitution bonuses from drink like a demon.

Lurch: Your lurching movements let you make one feinting in combat Bluff check (opposed by Sense Motive) per round as a move-equivalent action. You gain a +4 competence bonus to Bluff checks made for this purpose.

Drunken Embrace (Ex): You can grapple an opponent without provoking an attack of opportunity, and you gain a +4 competence bonus on all opposed grapple checks.

For Medicinal Purposes **(Sp):** By combining your *ki* power with alcohol, you can convert an alcoholic drink to a *potion of cure moderate wounds* up to three times per day. The alcohol activates the *ki* in your body, so the *cure* only works on you. Alcohol drunk in this way neither impairs nor improves your ability scores.

Corkscrew Rush: You leap forward, twisting your body in midair as you head-butt an opponent. This is a charge attack that, in addition to dealing normal damage, automatically initiates a bull rush attack (without provoking an attack of opportunity). Furthermore, you are considered to have the Power Attack feat for the purposes of a corkscrew rush, and if you hit your opponent, you stun your foe unless she makes a Will save (DC 17 + the drunken master's Wisdom modifier). However, if your attack misses, you land prone in front of your opponent.

Breath of Flame **(Sp):** You can use your *ki* to ignite the alcohol within you and spew it forth from your mouth in a breath of flame. Breath of flame deals 3d12 points of fire damage to all within the 20-foot cone (Reflex save DC 18 for half). Each time you use breath of flame, it consumes one drink's worth of alcohol within you, reducing both penalties and bonuses to your ability scores.

DUELIST

In a world with heavily armored knights on huge, galloping chargers and powerful mages wielding mind-churning spells, there's no place for the daring swashbuckler who relies on his wits and reflexes to survive, right? Wrong. The duelist proves that precision and skill are viable alternatives to massive weapons and agility is a viable alternative to heavy armor.

The duelist is a nimble, intelligent fighter trained in making precise attacks with light weapons, such as the dagger. Also known as the swashbuckler, the duelist always takes full advantage of his quick reflexes and wits in a fight. Rather than wearing bulky armor, duelists feel the best way to protect themselves is to not get hit at all.

Duelists are most often fighters or rangers, but almost as often are rogues or bards. Wizards, sorcerers and monks make surprisingly good duelists due to the lack of the class's reliance on armor. They benefit greatly from the weapon skill the duelist offers. Paladins and barbarians who deviate a good deal from their archetypes become duelists. Elves are more likely to become duelists than dwarves, and halfling and gnome duelists are not uncommon. Half-orc duelists are very rare.

TABLE 2–4: THE DUELIST

Class Level	Base Attack Bonus	Fort Save	Ref Save	Will Save	Special
1st	+1	+0	+2	+0	Canny defense
2nd	+2	+0	+3	+0	Precise strike +1d6
3rd	+3	+1	+3	+1	Enhanced mobility
4th	+4	+1	+4	+1	Grace
5th	+5	+1	+4	+1	Acrobatic attack
6th	+6	+2	+5	+2	Precise strike +2d6
7th	+7	+2	+5	+2	Elaborate parry
8th	+8	+2	+6	+2	Improved reflexes
9th	+9	+3	+6	+3	Deflect Arrows
10th	+10	+3	+7	+3	Precise strike +3d6

NPC duelists are usually loners looking for adventure or a get-rich-quick scheme. Occasionally they work in very small, tight-knit groups, fighting with team-based tactics.

Hit Die: d10.

Requirements

To qualify to become a duelist, a character must fulfill all the following criteria.

Base Attack Bonus: +6.
Perform: 3 ranks.
Tumble: 5 ranks.
Feats: Dodge, Weapon Proficiency (rapier), Ambidexterity, Mobility.

Class Skills

The duelist's class skills (and the key ability for each skill) are Balance (Dex), Bluff (Cha), Escape Artist (Dex) Innuendo (Wis), Jump (Str), Listen (Wis), Perform (Cha), Sense Motive (Wis), Spot (Wis), Tumble (Dex). See Chapter 4: Skills in the *Player's Handbook* for skill descriptions.

Skill Points at Each Level: 4 + Int modifier.

Class Features

Weapon and Armor Proficiency: The duelist is proficient with all simple and martial weapons, but no type of armor. The only shield they are proficient with is the buckler.

Canny Defense: When not wearing armor, duelists add their Intelligence bonus (if any) to their Dexterity bonus to modify Armor Class while wielding a melee weapon. If the duelist is caught flat-footed or otherwise denied his Dexterity bonus, he also loses this bonus.

Precise Strike: At 2nd level, the duelist gains the extraordinary ability to strike precisely with a one-handed piercing weapon, gaining a bonus 1d6 damage added to her normal damage roll. When making a precise strike, the duelist cannot attack with a weapon in her other hand, although she can defend with it (or, if she has the proficiency, a buckler). A duelist's precise strike only works against living creatures with discernable anatomies. Any creature that is immune to critical hits (including undead, constructs, oozes, plants, and incorporeal creatures) is not vulnerable to a precise strike, and any item or ability that protects a creature from critical hits (such as armor with *fortification*) also protects a creature from a precise strike. Every four duelist levels gained thereafter, she increases the extra damage by +1d6.

Enhanced Mobility: When unarmored, the duelist gains an additional +4 bonus to AC against attacks of opportunity caused when he moves out of or within a threatened area.

Grace: At 4th level, the duelist gains an additional +2 competence bonus to all Reflex saving throws. This ability functions for the duelist only when wearing no armor.

Acrobatic Attack: At 5th level, if the duelist attacks by jumping at least 5 feet toward his opponent, jumping down at least 5 feet onto his opponent or swinging on a rope or similar object into his opponent, he gains a +2 to attack and damage rolls. Make a Jump check; if the result is less than 5 feet, you cannot use this ability on this attack. If the distance is greater than that between the duelist and the opponent, the duelist can limit the distance to that of the opponent as a free action. This is an extraordinary ability.

Elaborate Parry: At 7th level, if the duelist chooses to fight defensively or use all-out defense in melee combat, she gains an additional +1 dodge bonus to her AC for each class level of duelist she has advanced. This is an extraordinary ability.

Improved Reaction: At 8th level, the duelist gains a +2 to initiative rolls. This ability stacks with Improved Initiative.

Deflect Arrows: The duelist gains the Deflect Arrows feat (see the *Player's Handbook*) only when he uses his one-handed piercing weapon.

FIST OF HEXTOR

While many view the Fists of Hextor simply as effective if brutal mercenaries, they are in fact templars sworn to the service of their unforgiving deity. The world is a dark and unforgiving place, or so says the Church of Hextor, wherein the strong survive by ruling the weak and forging order from the chaos. To support its dogma, the Church established this elite company of templars and made them available for hire to those whose causes complemented the Church's ultimate goals (and who could, naturally, afford to pay the hefty tithes necessary to maintain a crack unit of well-armed and well-trained men and women). The Fists are infamous for their efficient brutality: Nowhere will an employer in need of military aid locate mercenaries more dedicated to ensuring that the rule of law prevails over the forces of anarchy and confusion.

Most Fists of Hextor are fighters, monks or clerics, but ex-barbarians, ex-paladins, rangers, and wizards are all counted among their number. The chief qualifications for membership are (apart from veneration of Hextor, Champion of Evil and Scourge of Battle) a willingness to utilize cruelty and harsh measures to crush dissent, a belief that power is the greatest reward life offers, and a willingness to endure all manner of hardship in service to these ideals.

NPC Fists of Hextor are usually mercenary soldiers engaged in some martial enterprise on behalf of the nearest temple dedicated to Hextor. Sometimes small groups or even solitary Fists are encountered, though these too are often carrying out a specific task or mission for the Church.

Hit Die: d10.

Requirements

To qualify to become a Fist, a character must fulfill all the following criteria.

Alignment: Lawful evil, neutral evil, or lawful neutral.
Base Attack Bonus: +5.
Feats: Power Attack, Cleave, Spiked gauntlet weapon proficiency.
Intimidate: 4 ranks.
Spot: 4 ranks.
Knowledge (religion): 4 ranks.
Other: Must worship Hextor, and must survive the ritual ceremony of induction into the Fists of Hextor (see Organizations on page 44 of this book).

Class Skills

The Fist of Hextor's class skills (and the key ability for each skill) are Climb (Str), Intimidate (Cha), Knowledge (religion) (Int), Profession (Int), Ride (Dex), Sense Motive (Wis), and Spot (Wis). See Chapter 4: Skills in the *Player's Handbook* for skill descriptions.

Skill Points at Each Level: 2 + Int modifier.

Class Features

Weapon and Armor Proficiency: All Fists of Hextor are proficient with all simple and martial weapons, with all types of armor, and with shields.

Brutal Strike (Ex): The Church of Hextor trains its templars to fight with ruthless efficiency. Every action, the Fist may add this bonus either to one attack roll or one damage roll, but not both. You must declare where the bonus applies at the start of your action.

Strength Boost (Ex): Starting at 2nd level, the Fist can call upon Hextor for a +4 Strength bonus once per day. The Fist may boost his Strength one additional time per day for every three levels above 2nd. This bonus lasts for 4 rounds plus the Fist's level.

Frightful Presence (Ex): When a Fist of Hextor reaches 3rd level, he gains the extraordinary ability to instill *fear* in others as a free action once per day. The Fist must make some dramatic action in the round in which he uses the ability, and it only affects those who

TABLE 2–5: THE FIST OF HEXTOR

Class Level	Base Attack Bonus	Fort Save	Ref Save	Will Save	Special
1st	+1	+2	+0	+0	Brutal strike +1
2nd	+2	+3	+0	+0	Strength boost 1/day
3rd	+3	+3	+1	+1	Frightful presence 1/day
4th	+4	+4	+1	+1	Brutal strike +2
5th	+5	+4	+1	+1	Strength boost 2/day
6th	+6	+5	+2	+2	Frightful presence 2/day
7th	+7	+5	+2	+2	Brutal strike +3
8th	+8	+6	+2	+2	Strength boost 3/day
9th	+9	+6	+3	+3	Frightful presence 3/day
10th	+10	+7	+3	+3	Brutal strike +4

see (or possibly hear, depending on the dramatic act) the Fist. The ability has a range of 5 feet per level. All those (except for other Fists) within range are frightened for 5d6 rounds. Those who succeed at a Will saving throw are merely shaken. The DC for the Will save is 10 + the Fist's level + the Fist's Charisma modifier. This extraordinary ability creates a mind-affecting fear effect. The Fist may use this one additional time per day for every three levels above 3rd.

GHOSTWALKER

A mysterious figure becomes visible at the edge of town. Unheralded and unnoticed until his first step onto the dried-mud street, the stranger's only companion is soundlessness. He draws the wordless gaze of children who cease their play and scurry to seek a hidden place to watch him, unseen. From behind shuttered windows and closed doors, parents and shopkeepers end their conversations as their eyes follow his slow steps. The din of the blacksmith dies, and the sudden whinny of a horse is blasphemously loud. No one saw this one before he seemed to appear out of the summer's haze, but they know their lives will change before he has gone.

The ghostwalker is not a role that fits many heroes. The ghostwalker wanders from place to place, typically alone as he goes about his business. Just what drives the ghostwalker to roam from one town to another depends on the individual. Many are monks who have left behind their cloisters, because they could no longer engage in a life of contemplation or because they rebelled against the ordered, sheltered life within a world of chaos. One ghostwalker may be out to right an ancient wrong, another to take vengeance on a distant foe, and yet another to atone for some tragic mistake. Some ghostwalkers represent a source of merciless justice as they right wrongs and punish the villainous. Others are more compassionate as they progress from one community to another, helping those in need. Ghostwalkers do exist who seep into communities determined to spread their selfish desires and villainy like a cancer. Their abilities

point to some underlying, mysterious mysticism that surrounds and accompanies these wanderers, and they often appear just when and where they are needed.

Most ghostwalkers are warriors, whether their background describes them to be fighters, monks, or rangers. Former barbarians, fallen paladins, rogues, and some bards also take to the dusty roads of a wandering life. Wizards, clerics, druids, and sorcerers are rarely seen as ghostwalkers, but have been known to exist.

Hit Die: d10.

Requirements

To qualify to become a ghostwalker, a character must fulfill the following criteria.

Alignment: Lawful good, lawful evil, chaotic good, chaotic evil, or true neutral.
Base Attack Bonus: +6.
Feats: Endurance, Iron Will, Toughness.
Intimidate: 4 ranks.
Move Silently: 4 ranks.

Class Skills

The ghostwalker's class skills (and the key ability for each skill) are Bluff (Cha), Diplomacy (Cha), Gather Information (Cha), Intuit Direction (Wis), Knowledge (law) (Int), Profession (Wis), Spot (Wis), Listen (Wis), Move Silently (Dex), and Sense Motive (Wis). See Chapter 4: Skills in the *Player's Handbook* for skill descriptions.

Skill Points at Each Level: 4 + Int modifier.

Class Features

Weapon and Armor Proficiency: The ghostwalker is proficient with all simple and martial weapons, light and medium types of armor, and shields.

Painful Reckoning: If the ghostwalker loses more than 50% of his normal hit-point total in one encounter (and survives), he gains this circumstance bonus to his AC, attack, and damage rolls when he faces the specific foe(s) that he fought in the initial encounter. This bonus stacks with all other bonuses except itself. The

TABLE 2-6: THE GHOSTWALKER

Class Level	Base Attack Bonus	Fort Save	Ref Save	Will Save	Special
1st	+1	+2	+0	+2	Painful reckoning +1, resolute aura, anonymity
2nd	+2	+3	+0	+3	*Feign death*, painful reckoning +2
3rd	+3	+3	+1	+3	Superior Iron Will, painful reckoning +3
4th	+4	+4	+1	+4	*Etherealness* 1/day, painful reckoning +4
5th	+5	+4	+1	+4	*Shadow walk*, painful reckoning +5
6th	+6	+5	+2	+5	Painful reckoning +6
7th	+7	+5	+2	+5	*Etherealness* 2/day, painful reckoning +7
8th	+8	+6	+2	+6	Painful reckoning +8
9th	+9	+6	+3	+6	Painful reckoning +9
10th	+10	+7	+3	+7	*Etherealness* 3/day, painful reckoning +10

Armor Class bonus applies against touch attacks and when the ghostwalker is denied his Dexterity bonus.

Resolute Aura (Ex): Whether fearful or respectful, humanoids around the ghostwalker typically pause and obey when confronted. Ghostwalkers add their number of ghostwalker levels to all Intimidate checks. Therefore, a 5th-level ghostwalker has a +5 bonus to all Intimidate checks.

Anonymity: The ghostwalker benefits from anonymity, but should his name ever become known to his foes, his powers are weakened. On those enemies who know his name, his resolute aura no longer functions. If they are hostile, he cannot feign death, become ethereal, or shadow walk in their presence (to a distance of 100 feet), and his painful reckoning bonus, if any, is halved against them.

Feign Death (Sp): Once per day, the ghostwalker can enter a cataleptic state that is impossible to distinguish from actual death—usually for ending an encounter. The effect lasts for 10 rounds per level of the ghostwalker. Although he can smell, hear, and knows what is going on, no feeling or sight of any sort is possible for the ghostwalker; any wounding of his body is not felt, and any damage taken is only one-half normal. Paralysis, poison, and energy drain do not effect the ghostwalker in this state, but poison injected into the body becomes effective when the effect ends.

Superior Iron Will: This ability provides an additional +2 bonus to Will saves. It stacks with the Iron Will feat.

Etherealness (Su): Calling on the obscure, mystic forces that drive him to wander the world, the ghostwalker has the power to become ethereal, as per the spell *ethereal jaunt*. The effect persists for 1 round per level of the ghostwalker. This is a supernatural ability.

Shadow Walk (Su): The ghostwalker can shadow walk, as per the spell. The character travels at a rate of one mile in (11 – the number of ghostwalker levels) minutes. The maximum time that the ghostwalker can shadow walk is 1 hour per level per day. The ghostwalker can shadow walk three times per day. In addition, while in this state, the ghostwalker heals at the rate of 3 hit points per ghostwalker level per hour. This is a supernatural ability.

GLADIATOR

Some are mere slaves, sent into a squalid pit to fight against insurmountable odds. Others are wealthy professionals with an entourage of managers, agents, and trainers. Rich or poor, all gladiators face death whenever they step into the arena.

Gladiators are trained warriors who fight in front of spectators in arenas large and small. Usually they face other gladiators in single combat, but larger arenas sometimes offer group battles. Some even feature man vs. monster matches, pitting one or more gladiators

against a beast captured from the wilderness. The spectators cheer wildly for their favorite gladiators, and many bet vast sums on a combat's outcome. No one wagers more than the gladiator herself does, for often a match ends only when the loser dies.

Most gladiators were once fighters or barbarians, but rogues and monks sometimes find their way to the arena floor (much to the chagrin of their surprised opponents). In some rare cases, arenas feature "spell-caster duels" or pit a warrior against a wizard, making sure that the spellcaster's repertoire is suitably flashy and unlikely to harm the spectators. Becoming a gladiator is a simple matter, say the veterans of the pits. "Survive your first match, and you can call yourself a gladiator. Lot of good it will do you. . ."

NPC gladiators usually ply their trade in caravans that travel from arena to arena, although some are employed as regulars in the vast coliseums of large cities. Sometimes more famous gladiators are hired to act as bodyguards for aristocrats, and veteran gladiators assess new prospects and train would-be gladiators for their first fights in the ring.

Hit Die: d10.

Requirements

To qualify to become a gladiator, a character must fulfill all the following criteria.

Base Attack Bonus: +5.

Perform or Intimidate: 4 ranks. (Crowds respond best to the most attractive and most menacing combatants.)

Feats: Must have at least two feats from the list of fighter bonus feats. You do not have to earn them as a fighter, but they must appear on that list.

Class Skills

The gladiator's class skills (and the key ability for each skill) are Bluff (Cha), Climb (Str), Craft (Int), Handle Animal (Cha), Intimidate (Cha), Jump (Str), Perform (Cha), Ride (Dex), and Tumble (Dex). See Chapter 4: Skills in the *Player's Handbook* for skill descriptions.

Skill Points at Each Level: 4 + Int modifier.

Class Features

Improved Feint: The gladiator has learned sneaky tactics such as kicking dirt in a foe's face, pretending to be badly wounded, or forcing an opponent to stare into the sun. You can use the feinting in combat Bluff technique on page 64 of the *Player's Handbook* as a move-equivalent action.

Study Opponent: You are adept at spotting weaknesses in your foes' fighting styles. If you take a all-out defense action, you gain a dodge bonus to your AC against any opponent who attacks you in melee combat that round. The dodge bonus begins the round

TABLE 2–7: THE GLADIATOR

Class Level	Base Attack Bonus	Fort Save	Ref Save	Will Save	Special
1st	+1	+2	+0	+0	Improved feint
2nd	+2	+3	+0	+0	Study opponent +1
3rd	+3	+3	+1	+1	Exhaust opponent
4th	+4	+4	+1	+1	Roar of the crowd
5th	+5	+4	+1	+1	Study opponent +2
6th	+6	+5	+2	+2	Improved coup de grace
7th	+7	+5	+2	+2	Poison use
8th	+8	+6	+2	+2	Study opponent +3
9th	+9	+6	+3	+3	Make them bleed
10th	+10	+7	+3	+3	The crowd goes wild

after that opponent attacks you and lasts for the duration of the fight.

Exhaust Opponent (Ex): As combat continues, you can tire out your foe. You must attack the same opponent for at least 3 consecutive rounds. After your third set of attacks, your opponent must make a Fortitude save to avoid taking 1d6 subdual damage from exhaustion. The DC for this save starts at 15 and increases by 1 for every round beyond the third you continue to attack the same foe. Many gladiators fight defensively while employing this attack. If you do not attack for one round, the count resets to zero.

Roar of the Crowd: You can appeal to spectators with flourishes, trash-talking, and fancy moves. As a move-equivalent action, make a Perform check (DC 15). If you succeed, you get a +1 morale bonus to attacks and damage for the duration of the fight. Spectators must be noncombatants, and there must be at least a half-dozen of them.

Improved Coup de Grace: You dispatch fallen foes quickly, or with great flair. You may use a melee weapon to deliver a coup de grace attack as a standard action. If you are being showy, you take a full-round action to deliver the coup de grace attack, but gain a +2 morale bonus to attack for the rest of the combat.

Poison Use: You are trained in the use of poison just as assassins are. Ask your DM for details; the poison rules are found in the *DUNGEON MASTER's Guide*.

Make Them Bleed (Ex): You are skilled at dealing wounds that cause extra blood loss. When you deal damage with a slashing weapon, the wound bleeds for one point of damage per round thereafter until a Heal check (DC 15) is made, any *cure* spell is applied, or 10 rounds minus the opponent's Constitution modifier elapse. Multiple wounds are cumulative, but creatures without discernible anatomies such as constructs, undead, and plants are immune to this effect.

The Crowd Goes Wild: With each blow you strike, the spectators cheer more loudly. If you have already engaged the spectators with roar of the crowd, you gain a +2 morale bonus to damage on your first successful blow. This bonus increases by +2 for each successive consecutive blow that deals damage to your opponent. The bonus resets to +2 if you miss.

HALFLING OUTRIDER

The semi-nomadic culture of the halfling race often results in sudden encounters with peril. To safeguard themselves, many halfling communities turn to their outriders, an elite champion whose task it is to warn his fellows of, and protect them from, danger. The outrider is naturally skilled in the arts of riding and scouting.

Most halfling outriders are fighters, rangers, druids or rogues. All classes, however, can benefit from the AC bonus and defensive riding capabilities of the class.

NPC halfling outriders are usually found performing their duties in the field, or relaxing in their off-duty hours. The presence of an outrider whether afield or at rest indicates that a halfling community cannot be far away.

However, some outriders feel the pull of adventure more strongly. These leave behind their hearths and homes for a life of excitement on the road.

Hit die: d10.

Requirements

To qualify to become halfling outrider, a character must fulfill all the following criteria.

Base Attack Bonus: +5.
Race: Halfling.
Listen: 4 ranks.
Ride: 6 ranks.
Spot: 4 ranks.
Feats: Mounted Combat, Mounted Archery.

Class Skills

The halfling outrider's class skills (and the key ability for each skill) are Animal Empathy (Wis), Handle Animal (Cha), Listen (Wis), Ride (Dex), Search (Int), and Spot (Wis). See Chapter 4: Skills in the *Player's Handbook* for skill descriptions.

Skill Points at Each Level: 2 + Int modifier.

Class Features

Weapon and Armor Proficiency: The halfling outrider is proficient with all simple and martial weapons, light armor, and shields.

Mount: Halfling outriders gain a mount appropriate to the resources of their halfling community at 1st level. Most halfling communities attempt to provide their outriders with warponies, though some have been known to make do with lesser steeds, and a few boast more exotic animals. The outrider is not required to pay for the mount, nor its tack, harness and accoutrements.

Alertness: The halfling outrider gains Alertness as a bonus feat.

Ride Bonus: The halfling outrider gains a +2 competence bonus on all Ride checks.

Defensive Ride (Ex): The nature of the halfling outrider's responsibilities has taught him the tricks of defensive riding, provided that he does nothing else (he cannot attack when riding defensively).

He gains +2 Dexterity and a +4 AC dodge bonus. In addition, his mount gains: ×2 speed, a +2 bonus on all Will saves, and a +4 AC dodge bonus.

A defensive ride lasts for 3 rounds, plus the character's (newly improved) Dexterity modifier. The outrider may end the defensive ride voluntarily. At the end of the ride, both the outrider and his mount are winded and suffer a –2 Strength penalty until they are able to rest for at a minimum of 10 minutes. The outrider can only embark on a defensive ride a certain number of times per day (determined by level). Beginning the ride is a free action, but the outrider can only do so on his action.

Deflect Attack (Ex): Beginning at 3rd level, the outrider can attempt to parry a melee attack against his mount. He must be holding a melee weapon or shield to deflect the attack. Once per round when your mount would normally be hit with a melee weapon, you may make a Reflex saving throw against DC 20. (If the melee weapon has a magical bonus to attack, the DC increases by that amount.) You gain a competence bonus to your Reflex save as indicated on the chart. If you succeed, you deflect the blow as a free action. You must be aware of the attack beforehand and not flat-footed.

Table 2–8: The Halfling Outrider

Class Level	Base Attack Bonus	AC Bonus	Fort Save	Ref Save	Will Save	Special
1st	+1	+1	+0	+2	+0	Alertness, Ride bonus
2nd	+2	+1	+0	+3	+0	Defensive ride 1/day
3rd	+3	+2	+1	+3	+1	Deflect attack +1
4th	+4	+2	+1	+4	+1	Defensive ride 2/day
5th	+5	+3	+1	+4	+1	Leap from the saddle
6th	+6	+3	+2	+5	+2	Defensive ride 3/day
7th	+7	+4	+2	+5	+2	Deflect attack +2
8th	+8	+4	+2	+6	+2	Defensive ride 4/day
9th	+9	+5	+3	+6	+3	Deflect attack +3
10th	+10	+5	+3	+7	+3	Defensive ride 5/day

AC Bonus: This is a nonmagical deflection bonus applied to the character's Armor Class regardless of armor worn only when mounted.

Leap from the Saddle (Ex): When your mount is moving no faster than twice its Speed, you can dismount with a successful Handle Animal check (DC 20) and land adjacent to your mount as a free action. If an opponent is in an area you threaten (after you dismount), you can make a charge attack against that opponent. This requires the full attack action.

KNIGHT PROTECTOR OF THE GREAT KINGDOM

The few, the proud, the Knight Protectors are warriors dedicated to restoring the ideals of knightly chivalry before they fade forever. The Protectors see moral decay everywhere they look in the world around them, brought on by a lapse in ethical behavior following the collapse of the once-proud Great Kingdom. The Protectors are the last remnants of a formerly great order of knights who pledged their existence to defending that now-defunct nation. Few of this ancient lineage remain alive today, and all that remains of the Great Kingdom is its name and a scattered few inheritor countries. But those who take up the mantle of Knight Protector today still hope for the return of the Great Kingdom, and believe they can hasten its restoration and repair society's ills by living their lives as paragons of their venerable chivalric code.

Like paladins, knight protectors adhere to a rigid code of behavior that expresses such values as honor, honesty, chivalry, and courage. Unlike paladins, the Protector's first duty is to this code and the vanished nation for which it stands, rather than to a deity or holy order. The Protector is expected to display these ideals in all aspects of his behavior, and throughout all his actions and deeds, however arduous they may be. A Knight who unwillingly or unknowingly violates this code, or violates it willingly in the belief that doing so contributes to an act of greater good, may redeem himself by undertaking and completing a quest or other dangerous mission

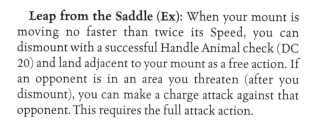

WAR 2000

assigned by the order's leadership. A Protector who willingly and knowingly violates this code for no adequate reason is removed from the order, and may no longer advance in levels as a Knight Protector.

Hit Die: d10.

Requirements

To qualify to become a Knight Protector of the Great Kingdom, a character must fulfill all the following criteria.

Base Attack Bonus: +4.
Race: Dwarf, elf, half-elf, human.
Diplomacy: 6 ranks.
Knowledge (Nobility and Royalty): 4 ranks.
Ride: 6 ranks.
Feats: Power Attack, Cleave, Mounted Combat, Great Cleave.
Heavy armor proficiency.
Alignment: Lawful.
Other: Gain membership in the order.

Class Skills

The Knight Protector's class skills (and the key ability for each skill) are Diplomacy (Cha), Intimidate (Cha), Knowledge (Nobility and royalty) (Int), Ride (Dex), and Spot (Wis). See Chapter 4: Skills in the *Player's Handbook* for skill descriptions.

Skill Points at Each Level: 2 + Int modifier.

Class Features

Weapon and Armor Proficiency: Knight Protectors are proficient with all simple and martial weapons, with all types of armor, and with shields.

Defensive Blow: Whenever the Knight Protector is engaged in a melee combat situation where the Knight seeks to protect a creature who is weaker than the Knight Protector (fewer HD or total levels) or who is helpless, the Knight Protector gains the listed morale bonus to his attack and weapon damage rolls.

Shining Beacon (Su): The Knight Protector is the physical and spiritual embodiment of high ideals. All his allies gain a +4 morale bonus on saves versus

---

The Code of the Knight Protector

Code of Conduct: The Knight Protector must be of a lawful alignment, and must adhere to the order's Code of Conduct (see below).

Support: The order supports its own. The Knight Protector can expect to receive normal arms and armor, room and board, a mount and its accoutrements from the order for as long as he remains in its ranks and adheres to the Code.

The Code:

Courage and enterprise in obedience to the Order.

Defense of any mission unto death.

Respect for all peers and equals; courtesy to all lessers.

Combat is glory; battle is the true test of self-worth; war is the flowering of the chivalric ideal.

Personal glory above all in battle.

Death to those who oppose the Great Kingdom.

Death before dishonor.

TABLE 2–9: THE KNIGHT PROTECTOR

Class Level	Base Attack Bonus	Fort Save	Ref Save	Will Save	Special
1st	+1	+0	+0	+2	Defensive blow +2, shining beacon
2nd	+2	+0	+0	+3	Best effort +2, Iron Will
3rd	+3	+1	+1	+3	Supreme Cleave
4th	+4	+1	+1	+4	Defensive blow +3
5th	+5	+1	+1	+4	Best effort+3
6th	+6	+2	+2	+5	No mercy +1
7th	+7	+2	+2	+5	Defensive blow +4
8th	+8	+2	+2	+6	Best effort +4
9th	+9	+3	+3	+6	No mercy +2
10th	+10	+3	+3	+7	Best effort +5, defensive blow +5

fear effects when they stand within 10 feet of the Knight Protector. If the Knight is *held*, unconscious, or otherwise rendered helpless, his allies lose this bonus.

Best Effort (Ex): The daunting nature of the Knight Protector's goals often requires special focus of effort. Beginning at 2nd level, a Knight Protector gains a bonus to any one skill check he makes, once per day. You must declare that you are using this ability before you make the skill check.

Iron Will: At 2nd level, the Knight gains the feat Iron Will.

Supreme Cleave: Beginning at 3rd level, the Knight can take a 5-foot step between attacks when using the Cleave or Great Cleave feat. A character can take only one 5-foot step each round, and then only if the character has not moved or already taken a 5-foot step during the round.

No Mercy: At 6th level, the Knight Protector gains the ability to make extra attacks of opportunity. The knight protector may make a number of extra attacks of opportunity against opponents equal to the number of the bonus and use the Knight's full attack bonus.

LASHER

The lasher prestige class uses the whip as an extension of herself. A whip in the hands of a lasher is like unto a live thing, obeying the character's every command. Lasher training goes far beyond simple exotic weapon proficiency, and not all who take up the discipline survive to its end. Lashers prefer to use a whip or a whip dagger (exotic weapons, both). Their ability with the whip makes them deadly warriors to be reckoned with.

Fighters, ex-paladins, rangers, ex-druids and barbarians are drawn to the art of the lash, which transforms an interesting tool into a deadly weapon. Rogues, monks, and bardic lashers find the understated profile of a whip a plus in many of their activities. Sorcerers, wizards, and clerics are least likely to be drawn to the art of the lash.

As NPCs, lashers are individuals who love to display the crack and snap of their whip skills. Though they consider the use of the whip an art form, they recognize it is a martial art used primarily for combat.

Hit Die: d10.

Requirements

To qualify to become a lasher, a character must fulfill the following criteria.

Base Attack Bonus: +5.
Rope Use: 2 ranks.
Craft (leatherworking): 2 ranks.
Weapon Focus: Whip.
Exotic Weapon Proficiency: Whip.
Special: The lasher must own a whip or whip dagger (see Chapter 5). Usually, a lasher owns both types of whip (and, if wealthy enough, mighty versions of both types).

Class Skills

The lasher's class skills (and the key ability for each skill) are Balance (Dex), Craft (Int), Escape Artist (Dex), Intimidate (Cha), Jump (Str), Spot (Wis), and Use Rope (Dex). See Chapter 4: Skills in the *Player's Handbook* for skill descriptions.

Skill Points at Each Level: 2 + Int modifier.

Class Features

Weapon and Armor Proficiency: A lasher's weapon training focuses on the whip. Lashers are proficient with no armor and no shields.

Whip Sneak Attack: If a lasher catches an opponent unable to defend himself effectively from her attack anywhere within range (up to 15 ft.), she can use a whip or whip dagger to strike a vital spot for extra damage (a lasher does not gain a sneak attack with other weapons). Any time the lasher's target would be denied his Dexterity bonus to AC (whether he actually has a Dexterity bonus or not) or when the lasher flanks the target, the lasher's attack deals +1d6

TABLE 2–10: THE LASHER

Class Level	Base Attack Bonus	Fort Save	Ref Save	Will Save	Special
1st	+1	+0	+2	+0	Whip sneak attack +1d6, close combat, wound, whip lash
2nd	+2	+0	+3	+0	Improved trip, third hand
3rd	+3	+1	+3	+1	Crack of fate
4th	+4	+1	+4	+1	Lashing whip
5th	+5	+1	+4	+1	Sneak attack +2d6
6th	+6	+2	+5	+2	Improved Disarm
7th	+7	+2	+5	+2	Stunning snap
8th	+8	+2	+6	+2	Crack of doom
9th	+9	+3	+6	+3	Sneak attack +3d6
10th	+10	+3	+7	+3	Death spiral

points of damage. This extra damage increases by a +1d6 points every fourth level (+2d6 at 5th level, and +3d6 at 9th level). Should the lasher score a critical hit with a sneak attack, this extra damage is not multiplied. This ability stacks with any other sneak attack ability.

With a regular whip (but not a whip dagger), the lasher can make a sneak attack that deals subdual damage instead of normal damage (see Wound below).

A lasher can only sneak attack living creatures with discernible anatomies—undead, constructs, oozes, plants, and incorporeal creatures lack vital areas to attack. Additionally, any creature immune to critical hits is similarly immune to sneak attacks. Also, the lasher must also be able to see the target well enough to pick out a vital spot and must be able to reach a vital spot. The lasher cannot sneak attack while striking at a creature with concealment or by striking the limbs of a creature whose vitals are beyond reach.

If a lasher gets a general sneak attack bonus from another source (such as rogue levels), the bonuses to damage stack.

Close Combat: At 1st level, the lasher can attack an opponent in a threatened square with a whip or whip dagger and not provoke an attack of opportunity.

Wound: At 1st level, a lasher can use a normal whip to deal regular damage to an opponent, instead of subdual damage, at her option. This allows the lasher to inflict damage on creatures with an armor bonus of +1 or better or a natural armor bonus of +3 or better. If using the whip to deal subdual damage, it deals no damage to creatures with a +1 or more armor bonus or +3 or more natural armor (as usual). Lashers using a whip dagger always deal regular damage to opponents.

Whip Lash: The lasher can make attacks of opportunity with his whip or whip dagger against foes within 5 feet as if it were a melee weapon.

Improved Trip: At 2nd level, the lasher gains the Improved Trip feat, if using a whip or whip dagger to perform the trip. She need not have taken the Expertise feat, normally a prerequisite, before this.

Third Hand: At 2nd level, a lasher's precision with the whip or whip dagger allows her to use it almost like a third hand—a third hand at the end of a flexible 15-foot-long arm—as a standard action. Depositing a lashed object into your hand is a move-equivalent action. *Note:* A lasher generally uses a normal whip to perform abilities granted by third hand, because a whip dagger deals its damage to the object or individual grasped, while a regular whip does not. Sometimes, this is not a problem, especially if the item grasped has hardness, but other times inflicting damage by using third hand is a bad idea. Thus, most lashers carry two whips. A lasher successfully performs a task if her attack roll equals or exceeds the DC for a given task:

- Punch a button, snuff a candle flame, flick a coin lying along the ground, etc. as a move-equivalent action. Range 15 feet, DC 15.
- Retrieve an unattended object of up to 20 pounds, and deposit into your off hand as a move-equivalent action. Range 15 feet, DC 20.
- Firmly wrap the end of your whip around a pole, spike, or other likely projection up to 15 feet away as a move-equivalent action. The DC is 22. If used to wrap around a projection at the top of a wall, reduce the DC to climb the wall by 5. If the point of attachment is optimal on a ceiling fixture, you could swing over a chasm of up to 25 feet wide. You can also wrap items heavier than 20 pounds, but you cannot automatically flick them into your off hand (but you could drag them). You can unwrap the end of your whip from the entangled object as a free action.
- When the victim of a precipitous fall, you can give up your Reflex save in an attempt to use your whip to snag a likely projection, pillar, rafter, etc., within 15 feet of the edge of the pit, cliff, bridge, etc. Generally, an unattached item (such as a statue, table, etc.) must weight twice as much as you for you to arrest your fall, otherwise you merely pull it after you. You may attempt to snag a friend or foe standing near the edge

of the precipice as you fall. You make a ranged touch attack against another creature's AC (the friend does not apply his Dexterity bonus while an unwilling friend or a foe applies their Dexterity modifier to AC), If you hit, you wrap your whip around the target, who must make a successful Strength check against DC 20 to arrest both you and himself. An unsuccessful Strength check sends both you and your target into the precipice. You can unwrap the end of your whip from the entangled object as a free action.

Crack of Fate: At 3rd level, a lasher can take one extra attack per round with a whip or whip dagger. The attack is at the lasher's highest base attack bonus, but each attack (the extra one and normal ones) suffers a –2 penalty. The lasher must use the full attack action to use crack of fate.

Lashing Whip: At fourth level, the lasher adds a +2 damage bonus to her whip and/or whip dagger. If using a whip, she adds +2 subdual damage or +2 regular damage, at her option. If the lasher has already gained weapon specialization from another class (fighter, for example), the damage bonus stacks.

Improved Disarm: At 6th level, the lasher gains the Improved Disarm feat, if using a whip or whip dagger to perform the disarm action. She need not have taken the Expertise feat, normally a prerequisite, before this. If the lasher successfully disarms a foe, she can attempt use her third hand ability to deposit the weapon of up to 20 pounds in her off hand if she makes the appropriate check, as a move-equivalent action. Treat the lasher's whip as a Medium-size weapon for purposes of disarming an opponent.

Stunning Snap: A lasher can use a whip or whip dagger to stun a creature instead of inflicting subdual or normal damage. The lasher can use this ability once per round, but no more than once per level per day. The lasher must declare she is using a stun attack before making an attack roll. (A missed attack roll ruins the attempt.) A foe struck by a whip or whip dagger must make a Fortitude saving throw (DC 10 + the lasher's level + Strength modifier), in addition to receiving normal damage (subdual or standard). If the saving throw fails, the opponent is stunned for one round. A stunned character cannot act and loses any Dexterity bonus to AC, while attackers get a +2 bonus on attack rolls against a stunned opponent. Constructs, oozes, plants, undead, incorporeal creatures, and creatures immune to critical hits cannot be stunned by the lasher's stunning attack.

Crack of Doom: At 8th level, a lasher can take two extra attacks per round with a whip or whip dagger. This ability supersedes crack of fate (the abilities do not stack). The attack is at the lasher's highest base attack bonus, but each attack (the extra one and normal ones) suffers a –4 penalty. The lasher must use the full attack action to use crack of doom

Death Spiral (Su): At 10th level, the lasher gains transcendental understanding of her whip or whip dagger. Once per day, she can spin the whip over her head with supernatural speed. All foes within a 15-foot radius of the lasher must make a Reflex save against a DC equal to the lasher's attack roll. Opponents who fail are stunned for 1d4+1 rounds. Stunned opponents must make a successful Fortitude save (DC 18) or become helpless for 1d4–1 rounds (minimum 1 round). Allies (as selected by the lasher) in range are spared the effects of the death spiral. The death spiral is a supernatural ability.

MASTER OF CHAINS

The master of chains is a combatant specializing in the use of chains—specifically the spiked chain—as a weapon. They usually have a sinister aura about them, and are never completely good. They use chains as tools of terror and intimidation as much as weapons. Along with their use of chains, they are good with locks as well.

Fighters are best equipped to become masters of chains, although rogues, rangers, and barbarians make excellent members of this rare, frightening group as well.

A master of chains often creates a lair underground filled with chains on the ground and hanging from the

TABLE 2-11: THE MASTER OF CHAINS

Class Level	Base Attack Bonus	Fort Save	Ref Save	Will Save	Special
1st	+1	+0	+2	+0	Scare
2nd	+2	+0	+3	+0	Climb fighting
3rd	+3	+1	+3	+1	Superior Weapon Focus
4th	+4	+1	+4	+1	Chain bind
5th	+5	+1	+4	+1	Chain armor, double chain
6th	+6	+2	+5	+2	Deflect attacks
7th	+7	+2	+5	+2	Superior Weapon Specialization
8th	+8	+2	+6	+2	Superior barbed chain
9th	+9	+3	+6	+3	Swinging attack
10th	+10	+3	+7	+3	Chain mastery

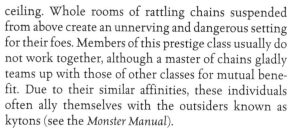

ceiling. Whole rooms of rattling chains suspended from above create an unnerving and dangerous setting for their foes. Members of this prestige class usually do not work together, although a master of chains gladly teams up with those of other classes for mutual benefit. Due to their similar affinities, these individuals often ally themselves with the outsiders known as kytons (see the *Monster Manual*).

Hit Die: d10.

Requirements

To qualify to become a master of chains, a character must fulfill all the following criteria.

Alignment: Any nongood.

Escape Artist: 6 ranks.

Open Lock: 4 ranks.

Intimidate: 4 ranks.

Feats: Exotic Weapon Proficiency (spiked chain), Expertise, Improved Trip, Improved Disarm, Weapon Focus (spiked chain), Weapon Specialization (spiked chain).

Ability Score: Int 13+ (required for Expertise).

Class Skills

The master of chains' class skills (and the key ability for each skill) are Balance (Dex), Climb (Str), Craft (metalworking) (Int), Escape Artist (Dex), Hide (Dex), Intimidate (Cha), and Open Lock (Dex). See Chapter 4: Skills in the *Player's Handbook* for skill descriptions.

Skill Points at Each Level: 4 + Int modifier.

Class Features

Weapon and Armor Proficiency: The master of chains is proficient with no weapons, and no type of armor or shield.

Scare (Su): By rattling his chains as a standard action, the master can induce *fear* in a creature as the spell of the same name, using his class level as the caster level (see the *Player's Handbook*). The master can use this supernatural ability only once per day.

Climb Fighting: If master of chains is climbing on a rope or a chain, he suffers no penalty to attacks and foes gain no bonus to attack him, rather than the master of chains losing his Dexterity modifier while climbing and his enemy gaining a +2 on attack rolls against the master of chains. If the master of chains is hanging from a chain that has the ability to swing more than five feet, he can use that to his advantage and gain a +2 dodge AC bonus.

Superior Weapon Focus: Stacking on top of any existing Weapon Focus bonus, this ability grants a master of chains an additional +1 to attack rolls with a spiked chain.

Chain Bind: At 4th level, the master of chains can use his weapon and a quick application of a lock (the whole process requiring a full-round action) to bind a single Small, Medium, or Large creature. This should be treated as an attack with a net, except that the Escape Artist check to escape has a DC of 25, and the burst DC is 30. A chain at least 10 feet long is required to accomplish this. If it is a spiked chain, the entangled creature suffers 1 point of damage per round while entangled unless they remain motionless.

Chain Armor: At 5th level, a master of chains can wrap himself in chains (as long as he has at least 20 feet of chain) to provide him with a +5 armor bonus to AC. For him, there is only a −2 maneuver penalty, no max Dex modifier, and a 30% arcane spell failure chance. Speed is not affected.

Double Chain: At 5th level, the master of chains can choose to use a spiked chain as a double weapon instead of a weapon with reach. (Each round, he can switch how he uses it.)

Extra Lash: At 6th level, a master of chains inflicts an additional +1d6 points of damage with a spiked chain, slashing the foe with extra slack in the chain. He must use the full attack action to use this ability.

Deflect Attacks: As a move-equivalent action, a 6th-level master of chains can use a spinning chain to provide a +4 deflection AC bonus against all attacks coming in from a chosen 180-degree arc. This is an extraordinary ability.

Superior Weapon Specialization: Stacking on top of any existing weapon specialization bonus, this adds an additional +2 to all damage rolls made with a chain or spiked chain.

Superior Spiked Chain: At 8th level, the master of chains can modify his spiked chain so that it leaves cruel barbs behind in the targets it strikes. Using the chain in this way causes victims to bleed 1 hit point per round until a successful Heal check is used to bind the wounds (DC 15) or until magical healing is applied to them. It costs 25 gp to modify a chain in this manner, and 10 gp to add new spikes once the modified chain has been used five times. (After five uses, the modified chain can be used as a normal spiked chain.) Only 8th level and above masters of chains can make and use these specially modified weapons properly—in anyone else's hands they are simply spiked chains.

Swinging Attack: At 9th level, as a full-round action, the master of chains can wrap the end of his chain around an overhead object (something that can sustain his weight) and swing at any target within 10 feet. The foe so attacked is treated as flat-footed and the master gains a +2 attack bonus and inflicts +3d6 damage with this single attack (only one attack is allowed).

Chain Mastery (Su): As a supernatural ability, the master of chains can animate a chain (as the spell *animate rope*, but with chains) of up to 50 feet in length for 10 rounds. The master of chains can use this ability three times per day plus a number of times equal to his Charisma bonus.

MASTER SAMURAI

The master samurai is a military retainer of a feudal overlord; he practices a martial code of behavior that emphasizes the value of personal honor over life itself. In some cultures he is part of the warrior aristocracy.

The details of the master samurai code are quite specific. Master samurai are required and expected to demonstrate absolute obedience to their feudal overlord, even if his lord's commands might result in the master samurai's certain death. He remains ready to die for his lord or his honor at a moment's notice, and to avenge to the death any slight to either. His personal honor demands that he repay all debts fairly. Perhaps the most important tenet of this code is the expectation that the master samurai never commit a dishonorable act or demonstrate the slightest fear of personal injury or death. Master samurai who fail to live up to these strictures face personal shame so overwhelming that they prefer to destroy themselves rather than live under its shadow.

Fighters, rangers, and paladins make excellent master samurai, and they find that its class abilities enhance their own combat potential. Monks also make good master samurai: The discipline of bushido is a natural reflection of the monk's desire to study a philosophy or belief with single-minded determination. Wizards and sorcerers may find it difficult to qualify for master samurai, but those who do enjoy the martial enhancements available to them.

Hit Die: d10.

Requirements

To qualify to become a master samurai, a character must fulfill all the following criteria.

Base Attack Bonus: +5.
Knowledge (nobility and royalty): 4 ranks.
Ride: 4 ranks.
Intimidate: 4 ranks.
Feats: Cleave, Improved Initiative, Mounted Archery, Mounted Combat, Power Attack, Weapon Focus (bastard sword).

Class Skills

The master samurai's class skills (and the key ability for each skill) are Intimidate (Cha), Jump (Str), Knowledge (code of martial honor) (Int), Knowledge (nobility and royalty) (Int), Ride (Dex), and Tumble (Dex). See Chapter 4: Skills in the *Player's Handbook* for skill descriptions.

Skill Points at Each Level: 2 + Int modifier.

Table 2–12: The Master Samurai

Class Level	Base Attack Bonus	Fort Save	Ref Save	Will Save	Special
1st	+1	+0	+2	+2	Tumble bonus, Great Cleave
2nd	+2	+0	+3	+3	Blades of fury, Supreme Cleave
3rd	+3	+1	+3	+3	Supreme Mobility
4th	+4	+1	+4	+4	Blades of death
5th	+5	+1	+4	+4	*Ki* strength 1/day
6th	+6	+2	+5	+5	*Ki* attack 1/day
7th	+7	+2	+5	+5	*Ki* strength 2/day
8th	+8	+2	+6	+6	*Ki* attack 2/day
9th	+9	+3	+6	+6	*Ki* strength 3/day
10th	+10	+3	+7	+7	*Ki* attack 3/day

Class Features

Weapon and Armor Proficiency: Master samurai are proficient with all simple and martial weapons, with all types of armor, and with shields.

Code of Conduct: The master samurai must be of a lawful alignment, and must adhere to the martial code of honor (see sidebar). If the master samurai violates this code, he may be required to atone by performing some arduous or disagreeable task; if the violation was particularly egregious, he may be invited to commit ritual suicide. In some cultures, when a feudal overlord is killed, defeated, or disgraced, his master samurai retainers are expected to follow him into death.

Support: Master samurai can expect to receive all the necessary requirements of life from their feudal overlord, including room and board, transportation, normal (including masterwork) arms, and armor. Those master samurai who do not serve a lord are called ronin and do not receive the support benefit.

Tumble: At 1st level, the master samurai gains a +2 competence bonus to Tumble skill checks.

Great Cleave: At 1st level, the master samurai receives this feat for free.

Supreme Cleave: At 2nd level, the master samurai gains the ability to take a 5-foot step before making a Cleave or Great Cleave attack. A character can take only one 5-foot step each round, and then only if the character has not moved or already taken a 5-foot step during the round.

Blades of Fury: When a master samurai delays his attack with the katana until after he is attacked in the round, he takes advantage of the opening and can add a +2 bonus to his attack and damage rolls. In other words, you delay your action until after you are attacked in melee combat.

Blades of Death: When the master samurai fights with the katana two-handed, he adds double his Strength modifier to damage rolls instead of 1.5 times his Strength modifier..

Supreme Mobility: The master samurai gains a +6 dodge bonus to his AC against attacks of opportunity provoked by moving into or out of a threatened area. Note: A condition that makes you lose your Dex bonus to Armor Class (if any) also makes you lose dodge bonuses. This dodge bonus supersedes that of Mobility.

Ki Strength (Ex): Beginning at 5th level, the master samurai learns to channel *ki*, a source of inner energy and strength shared by all living creatures. You can add +2 to your Strength score for a number of rounds equal to your Wisdom bonus.

Ki Attack (Ex): Beginning at 6th level, the master samurai gains the supernatural ability to imbue his melee attacks with *ki* energy for one successful attack as a free action. The damage from such an attack can harms even a creature with damage reduction. When using this ability, consider the master samurai's weapon to be a magic weapon with a bonus equal to the character's Wis modifier for of harming a creature with damage reduction. Once activated, this bonus remains until the master samurai hits once with the weapon charged with *ki*.

The Master Samurai's Code

The master samurai is obedient to his lord.

It is a master samurai's right to protest against bad judgments or orders from his lord and death is the final protest a master samurai can make.

The master samurai is ready to die at any time.

There is no failure, only success or death.

To die in the service of one's lord is the greatest service a master samurai can perform.

Dishonor to one's lord or family is dishonor to the master samurai.

All debts, of honor or vengeance, are repaid.

An enemy deserves no mercy.

Cowardice is dishonorable.

NINJA OF THE CRESCENT MOON

Some monks seek only enlightenment. Others are tempted by more shadowy pursuits.

The Ninja of the Crescent Moon is a mercenary clan whose members engage in sabotage and other covert missions for an outlandish fee—if the job meets their own inscrutable moral code. The ninja are a thorn in the side of both evil tyrants and just nobles, and no one outside the upper hierarchy knows what their real aims are. Their bases and safehouses are unknown to any outside the Crescent Moon, and would-be patrons contact them only through a long chain of contacts.

But once the Ninja of the Crescent Moon are hired, they generally complete the job by the next crescent moon (hence the name). The black-garbed ninja typically infiltrate their target, reveal themselves in a whirlwind of violence, then slip away into the shadows of the night.

Most ninja were once monks who heard the whispered promise of the ninja's esoteric secrets. Curious, they began to research the Crescent Moon, following half-remembered rumors to their source. Any monk (or occasionally rogue or fighter) who manages to track the ninja back to their source are typically offered membership. Those who turn the Crescent Moon down are marked for death.

NPC ninja appear seemingly from nowhere, striking without mercy. They are often hired to steal a valuable item, kill a powerful rival, or infiltrate a besieged fortress as a precursor to an attack.

Hit Die: d8.

Requirements

To qualify to become a ninja, a character must fulfill all the following criteria.

Base Attack Bonus: +6.

Feats: Improved Unarmed Strike, Deflect Arrows, Quick-Draw.

Move Silently 10 ranks.

Hide 10 ranks.

Other: Evasion class feature, must contact Crescent Moon leadership.

Class Skills

The ninja's class skills (and the key ability for each skill) are Alchemy (Int), Balance (Dex), Climb (Str),

TABLE 2–13: NINJA OF THE CRESCENT MOON

Class Level	Base Attack Bonus	Fort Save	Ref Save	Will Save	Special
1st	+0	+0	+2	+0	Monk-like armor bonuses, sneak attack +1d6
2nd	+1	+0	+3	+0	Improved evasion, *kuji-kiri*
3rd	+2	+1	+3	+1	Poison use, sneak attack +2d6
4th	+3	+1	+4	+1	AC bonus +1, fast climb, silencing attack
5th	+3	+1	+4	+1	Fast sneak, sneak attack +3d6
6th	+4	+2	+5	+2	*Invisibility*, opportunist
7th	+5	+2	+5	+2	*Gaseous form*, sneak attack +4d6
8th	+6/+1	+2	+6	+2	Improved *kuji-kiri*
9th	+6/+1	+3	+6	+3	AC bonus +2, blindsight, sneak attack +5d6
10th	+7/+2	+3	+7	+3	Always sneaky, *ethereal jaunt*

Base Attack Bonus: Note that, like a monk, this class makes unarmed iterative attacks at a –3 penalty, not the usual –5 penalty.

Craft (Int), Escape Artist (Dex), Hide (Dex), Jump (Str), Listen (Wis), Move Silently (Dex), Swim (Str), and Tumble (Dex). See Chapter 4: Skills in the *Player's Handbook* for skill descriptions.

Skill Points at Each Level: 4 + Int modifier.

Class Features

Weapon and Armor Proficiency: The ninja gains no additional weapon or armor proficiencies.

Monklike AC Bonuses: When the ninja is wearing no armor or shield, he receives the AC bonus listed in Table 3–10 in the *Player's Handbook*. This bonus stacks with any AC bonus he previously received as a monk. Furthermore, the ninja applies Dexterity and Wisdom bonuses to AC if unarmored.

Sneak Attack: If a ninja can catch an opponent when she is unable to defend herself effectively from his attack, he can strike a vital spot for extra damage. Any time the ninja's target would be denied her Dexterity bonus to AC (whether she actually has a Dexterity bonus or not) or when the ninja flanks the target, the ninja's attack deals +1d6 points of damage. This extra damage increases by an +1d6 points every other level (+2d6 at 3rd level, +3d6 at 5th level, and so on). Should the ninja score a critical hit with a sneak attack, this extra damage is not multiplied. This class ability stacks with any other sneak attack the character possesses.

It takes precision and penetration to hit a vital spot, so ranged attacks only count as sneak attacks if the target is 30 feet away or less.

A ninja can only sneak attack living creatures with discernible anatomies—undead, constructs, oozes, plants, and incorporeal creatures lack vital areas to attack. Additionally, any creature immune to critical hits is similarly immune to sneak attacks. Also, the ninja must also be able to see the target well enough to pick out a vital spot and must be able to reach a vital spot. The ninja cannot sneak attack while striking at a creature with concealment or by striking the limbs of

a creature whose vitals are beyond reach. If a ninja gets a sneak attack bonus from another source (such as rogue levels), the bonuses to damage stack.

Improved Evasion: At 2nd level, a ninja's evasion ability improves. She still takes no damage on a successful Reflex saving throw against attacks such as a dragon's breath weapon or a *fireball*, but henceforth she only takes half damage on a failed save.

Kuji-kiri **(Sp):** By making mystical hand gestures as a standard action, the ninja can render opponents helpless as if he would cast *hypnotic pattern*. The ninja can affect 2d4 +1 per ninja level HD with kuji-kiri, and subjects must make Will saves against DC 12 + the ninja's Charisma bonus to avoid the effect. The hypnotic pattern lasts as long as the ninja continues to gesture, plus one additional round. The ninja can use this power once daily for each level of ninja.

Poison Use: Ninjas are trained in the use of poison and never risk accidentally poisoning themselves when applying poison to a blade.

Fast Climb: The ninja can scurry up a wall at unbelievable speed. With each successful Climb check, the ninja can move half his speed as a move-equivalent action or his speed as a full-round action. Furthermore, he retains his Dex bonus to AC while climbing.

Silencing Attack (Su): If the ninja successfully hits a flat-footed opponent with a melee attack, the opponent is unable to speak for one round. This prevents casting spells with a verbal component and shouting warnings or alarms.

Fast Sneak: When using Move Silently and Hide, the ninja can move at his normal speed without suffering a penalty to those skills.

Invisibility **(Sp):** The ninja can turn invisible (as the spell *invisibility*, but targeting himself only) once daily for each level of ninja.

Opportunist: Once per round, the ninja can make an attack of opportunity against an opponent who has just been struck for damage in melee by another character. This attack counts as the ninja's attacks of opportunity

TABLE 2–14: THE ORDER OF THE BOW INITIATE

Class Level	Base Attack Bonus	Fort Save	Ref Save	Will Save	Special
1st	+1	+0	+2	+2	Ranged sneak attack +1d6
2nd	+2	+0	+3	+3	Close combat shot
3rd	+3	+1	+3	+3	Ranged sneak attack +2d6
4th	+4	+1	+4	+4	Superior Weapon Focus
5th	+5	+1	+4	+4	Ranged sneak attack +3d6
6th	+6	+2	+5	+5	Free attack, Zen Archery
7th	+7	+2	+5	+5	Superior Weapon Specialization
8th	+8	+2	+6	+6	Ranged sneak attack +4d6
9th	+9	+3	+6	+6	Banked shot
10th	+10	+3	+7	+7	Ranged sneak attack +5d6

for that round. Even a ninja with the Combat Reflexes feat cannot use the opportunist ability more than once per round.

Gaseous Form (**Sp**): You can assume *gaseous form*, as the spell (see the *Player's Handbook*), once per day for 1 round per class level. Using this ability requires a full-round action.

Improved Kuji-kiri (**Sp**): The ninja's swirling hand gestures are harder to resist. Kuji-kiri now affects 3d6 +1 per ninja level HD of creatures, and the Will save DC is 15 + the ninja's Charisma bonus.

Blindsight (**Ex**): Using nonvisual senses, such as sensitivity to vibrations, scent, acute hearing, or echolocation, the ninja maneuvers and fights just as well in darkness as in light. Invisibility and darkness are irrelevant, though the ninja still cannot discern ethereal beings. The ninja's blindsight extends for 60 feet.

Always Sneaky: The ninja is always taking 10 on Move Silently and Hide. Unless the ninja wants to be seen or heard, make opposed Spot and Listen checks to detect the ninja's presence.

Ethereal Jaunt (**Sp**): By focusing his *ki*, the ninja can become ethereal for a moment or two. Three times a day as a free action, the ninja can make an ethereal jaunt (as the spell of the same name, except the duration is only 1 round).

ORDER OF THE BOW INITIATE

The Way of the Bow is used by some for spiritual self-improvement, by others a philosophical art. Others practice it as a way of life, and yet others employ it as a religious ceremony. Of course, many find the art of killing with the bow to be an important skill in a dangerous world. The Way of the Bow is always what you make of it. The Way of the Bow embraces the following concepts:

Through one's archery, one's true character can be determined.

The Way of the Bow is a spiritual art. By learning it, the archer learns about himself. By improving in the Way of the Bow, the archer improves himself.

The Way of the Bow is a highly meditative martial art whose ultimate goals are Truth, Goodness, and Beauty.

When asked, "What is Truth?", a Master Archer picks up his bow, fires an arrow and, without saying a word, lets his mastery of the bow serve as the gauge of the archer's progress along the "way," thereby showing the archer's knowledge of reality, or "truth" itself.

The Way of the Bow is a matter of precision and discipline: the relationship you have with your bow, the arrow, your body, and your mind. The Way of the Bow is standing meditation. When you shoot, you can see the reflection of your mind, as in a mirror. The target is the mirror. When you release, you also let go of your ego. You can see your own mind.

Fighters are the most common initiates of the Order of the Bow. Powerful rangers, paladins, and even barbarians utilize these skills and philosophies as well.

Hit Die: d10.

Requirements

To qualify as an initiate, a character must fulfill all the following criteria:

Base Attack Bonus: +5.

Knowledge (religion): 2 ranks.

Proficiency: Longbow or shortbow or composite longbow or composite shortbow.

Feats: Point Blank Shot, Precise Shot, Rapid Shot, Weapon Focus (longbow or shortbow or the composite version of either, Weapon Specialization (longbow or shortbow or the composite version of either).

Class Skills

The Order of the Bow's class skills (and the key ability for each skill) are: Knowledge (religion) (Int), Craft (bowmaking) (Int), Spot (Wis), Swim (Str), and Ride (Dex). See Chapter 4: Skills in the *Player's Handbook* for skill descriptions.

Skill Points at Each Level: 2 + Int modifier.

Class Features

Weapon and Armor Proficiency: None.

Ranged Sneak Attack: Any time the initiate's target would be denied his Dexterity bonus to AC (regardless of whether he has a Dexterity bonus), the initiate's ranged sneak attack deals extra damage. The extra damage is +1d6 at 1st level, and +1d6 every two levels after that. Ranged attacks only count as sneak attacks if the target is within 30 feet. The initiate cannot strike with such deadly accuracy beyond that range. In every other way, treat this ability as a rogue's sneak attack. If the character has the sneak attack ability as a rogue, the bonuses stack.

Close Combat Shot: At 2nd level, the initiate can attack with a ranged weapon in a threatened area and not provoke an attack or opportunity.

Superior Weapon Focus: Stacking with any existing Weapon Focus bonus, this adds an additional +1 to all attack rolls with the initiate's bow.

Free Attack: Once per round, whenever an ally within line of sight gains an attack of opportunity upon a foe, the initiate can make one ranged attack against the same foe, at his highest attack bonus as a free action.

Zen Archery: You gain this feat for free (see page 9). If the character already has this feat, then the Wisdom modifier stacks with the Dexterity modifier for ranged attacks.

Superior Weapon Specialization: This stacks with any existing weapon specialization bonus, and adds an additional +2 to all damage rolls made with a longbow or shortbow.

Banked Shot (Ex): This extraordinary ability allows the initiate to fire an arrow at a target within 20 feet of a wall (but not adjacent to the wall) and treat the target as if flat-footed for purposes of AC and damage inflicted. This is a full-round action, since it is extremely difficult.

RAVAGER

Feared by many, understood by few, the infamous Ravager is an individual who has dedicated himself to the service of Erythnul, Deity of Slaughter. Living a life of violence and savagery, the Ravager seeks to spread this deity's malignant influence wherever he goes, never resting long in one place lest the forces of good and law pursue him.

Ravagers who come from the ranks of fighters and monks find that the Ravager's offensive capabilities enhance their combat skills, while wizard, sorcerer, cleric and druid Ravagers find that their ability to cause terror in their foes is a very useful defensive measure. Ravagers spend much of their time with others of their kind, roaming the land in small, close-knit warbands, striking unsuspecting communities without warning, and retiring back into the wilderness to plan their next terrible raid. Sometimes the clergy of Erythnul commands a lone Ravager to undertake some mission or project that obliges the Ravager to join up with other, non-Ravager individuals, but such alliances are usually temporary and must be managed carefully, lest they lead to quarrels or worse.

NPC Ravagers are usually encountered in small warbands of from two to six individuals, but sometimes a lone Ravager may be met when undertaking a special mission.

All Ravagers are readily identified by the bizarre and fearsome facial tattoos they wear to mark themselves as Erythnul's instruments.

Hit Die: d10.

Requirements

To qualify to become a Ravager, a character must fulfill all the following criteria.

Alignment: Chaotic evil, chaotic neutral, neutral evil.
Base Attack Bonus: +5.
Feats: Dirty Fighting, Power Attack, Sunder.
Intimidate: 3 ranks.
Knowledge (religion): 3 ranks.
Wilderness Lore 4 ranks.
Other: Must survive the Ravager initiation rites. (See the Ravager organization description on page 50 of this book.)

Class Skills

The Ravager's class skills (and the key ability for ech skill) are Intimidate (Cha), Knowledge (religion) (Int), Move Silently (Dex), Profession (Int), and Ride (Dex).

TABLE 2–15: THE RAVAGER

Class Level	Base Attack Bonus	Fort Save	Ref Save	Will Save	Special
1st	+1	+2	+0	+0	Pain touch 1/day
2nd	+2	+3	+0	+0	Aura of fear 10' 1/day
3rd	+3	+3	+1	+1	Cruelest cut 1/day
4th	+4	+4	+1	+1	Pain touch 2/day
5th	+5	+4	+1	+1	Aura of fear 20' 2/day
6th	+6	+5	+2	+2	Cruelest cut 2/day
7th	+7	+5	+2	+2	Pain touch 3/day
8th	+8	+6	+2	+2	Aura of fear 30' 3/day
9th	+9	+6	+3	+3	Cruelest cut 3/day
10th	+10	+7	+3	+3	*Visage of terror*

See Chapter 4: Skills in the *Player's Handbook* for skill descriptions.

Skill Points at Each Level: 2 + Int modifier.

Class Features

Weapon and Armor Proficiency: All Ravagers are proficient with all simple and martial weapons, with all types of armor, and with shields.

Pain Touch (Su): Erythnul teaches that life is pain, and so is the touch of a Ravager. A Ravager can make an unarmed touch attack that causes 1d8 hit points of damage, plus one point per the Ravager's level. Weapon attacks also transmit the pain of Erythnul, but only at the rate of 1d4 extra points of damage, plus 1 point per the Ravager's level. The Ravager may make one additional pain touch attack for every three levels above 1st.

Aura of Fear (Su): Enemies within the stated distance of the Ravager suffer a –2 morale penalty on all saving throws for as long as they remain within range. This is a supernatural ability, usable a number of times per day as given on the table.

Cruelest Cut (Su): Your familiarity with pain and fear grants you a cruel precision with your melee attacks. You must declare you are using cruelest cut before making any attack rolls. If you miss all your attack in that round, you lose one use of the cruelest cut. If you strike successfully, you deal 1d4 points of temporary Constitution damage to your target, in addition to normal damage on one attack. You may use cruelest cut once per day for every three levels you have attained.

Visage of Terror **(Sp):** You have plumbed the true depths of horror and hopelessness. Once per day, you can trigger a spell-like ability similar to the arcane spell *phantasmal killer* (save DC 14 + the Ravager's class level) as a standard action. To the foe you select, you seem to take on the visage of what the target fears most. To others including yourself, no effect is discernible. In order for the phantasm to touch the target, the Ravager must make a successful touch attack. In all other respects, this ability functions as the spell in the *Player's Handbook*.

RED AVENGERS

The Red Avenger is the master of *ki*, an ancient and formidable discipline that allows the user to accomplish the extraordinary. Through study and training, the Red Avenger learns to channel the *ki* energy and thereby achieve a variety of effects, up to and including the ability to damage an opponent by releasing the *ki* energy in her own body. Though their primary concerns revolve around settling an age-old score (see the Red Avenger class organization for details), the Red Avengers sometimes accept employment with those who can afford their services, becoming agents of injury and destruction.

Most Red Avengers are monks: The mastery of *ki* is a natural extension of the monk's own class abilities. Fighters, rangers and paladins sometimes become Red Avengers and find that their *ki* abilities make them more formidable in combat. Rogues enjoy the versatility of the Red Avenger's *ki* mastery, while druids find that the study of *ki* energy can offer new insights on the natural world.

NPC Red Avengers are normally monks who are engaged in carrying out activities that support the clan's primary goals.

Hit Die: d8.

Requirements

To qualify to become a Red Avenger, a character must fulfill all the following criteria.

Base Attack Bonus: +5.
Feats: Improved Unarmed Strike, Stunning Fist.
Listen: 8 ranks.
Tumble: 8 ranks.

TABLE 2–16: THE RED AVENGER

Class Level	Base Attack Bonus	Fort Save	Ref Save	Will Save	Special
1st	+1	+2	+2	+2	*Stunning shout* 1/day
2nd	+2	+3	+3	+3	*Ki save* 1/day
3rd	+3	+3	+3	+3	*Ki skill* 1/day
4th	+3	+4	+4	+4	*Ki healing*
5th	+4	+4	+4	+4	*Deadly shout* 1/day, *stunning shout* 2/day
6th	+5	+5	+5	+5	*Ki save* 2/day
7th	+6	+5	+5	+5	*Ki skill* 2/day
8th	+6	+6	+6	+6	*Greater ki healing*
9th	+7	+6	+6	+6	*Deadly shout* 2/day, *stunning shout* 3/day
10th	+8	+7	+7	+7	*Free ki*

Base Attack Bonus: Note that, like a monk, this class makes unarmed iterative attacks at a –3 penalty, not the usual –5 penalty.

WAI. 2000

Class Skills

The Red Avenger's class skills (and the key ability for each skill) are Balance (Dex), Gather Information (Cha), Hide (Dex), Listen (Wis), Move Silently (Dex), Spot (Wis), Tumble (Dex).

Skill Points at Each Level: 4 + Int modifier.

Class Features

Weapon and Armor Proficiency: The Red Avenger is proficient with all simple weapons, light armor, medium armor, and shields. (Note: Armor heavier than leather carries a penalty on the Red Avenger skills Hide and Move Silently.)

Ki: At 1st level, the Red Avenger gains a greater understanding of the supernatural ability to control and utilize *ki*. *Ki* is an energy source created by and flowing through all living creatures. Much of the Red Avenger's training is devoted to understanding and learning to focus *ki*, and the effects she can produce at each level reflect the increasing complexity of their education.

Stunning Shout (Sp): The Red Avenger releases her *ki* energy in a sonic attack. You can blast *ki* energy in a cone 30 feet long. The attack stuns all targets in the cone for one round unless they make a successful Fortitude save (DC 15 + Red Avenger's Wisdom modifier). The attack is a standard action, and requires the Red Avenger to be able to vocalize in order to use the ability.

Ki Save (Ex): At 2nd level, the Red Avenger gains the ability to channel her *ki* into protecting herself from adverse effects. She gains a bonus equal to her Wisdom bonus on *any* one saving throw of her choice.

Ki Skill (Ex): At 3rd level, the Red Avenger gains a bonus to any skill check when using any Red Avenger class skill, equal to her Wisdom bonus.

Ki Healing (Sp): At 4th level, the Red Avenger gains the ability to channel *ki* into healing energy. When she lays her hands on a living creature, she conducts the *ki* in such a way that it heals a number of hit points each day equal to her class level multiplied by her Wisdom bonus. She may choose to divide her *ki healing* energy among multiple recipients, and she need not use it all at once. *Ki healing* is a supernatural ability whose use is a standard action.

Starting at 8th level, a red avenger can heal a number of hit points each day equal to twice her class level multiplied by her Wisdom bonus.

Deadly Shout (Sp): The Red Avenger releases her *ki* energy in a sonic attack. You can blast *ki* energy in a cone 30 feet long. The attack deals 3d6 + your Wisdom modifier in damage to all within the cone. A successful Fortitude save (DC 15 + the Avenger's Wisdom bonus) halves the damage. The attack is a standard action, and requires the Red Avenger to be able to vocalize in order to use the ability.

Free Ki: The Red Avenger has mastered the use of *ki* energy and channels it with ease. Whenever using any class ability that is imbued with *ki*, you may add double your Wisdom bonus.

Multiclass Note: Monk characters can freely multiclass with this class. In other words, you can give your monk PC a Red Avenger level, then return to the monk class for your next level, take a Red Avenger level after that, and so on.

TRIBAL PROTECTOR

The tribal protector is the battlefield champion of a savage humanoid race. While a tribe's warriors make up the bulk of its military forces, and barbarians may be its fiercest soldiers, tribal protectors are disciplined and deadly fighters who lead any martial endeavor.

TABLE 2–17: THE TRIBAL PROTECTOR

Class Level	Base Attack Bonus	Fort Save	Ref Save	Will Save	Special
1st	+1	+2	+2	+0	Bonus feat, tribal enemy, homeland
2nd	+2	+3	+3	+0	Wild fighting
3rd	+3	+3	+3	+1	Terrain AC bonus +2
4th	+4	+4	+4	+1	Smite 1/day
5th	+5	+4	+4	+1	Bonus feat
6th	+6	+5	+5	+2	Terrain AC bonus +3
7th	+7	+5	+5	+2	Smite 2/day
8th	+8	+6	+6	+2	Terrain AC bonus +4
9th	+9	+6	+6	+3	Bonus feat
10th	+10	+7	+7	+3	Smite 3/day

Most tribal protectors are fighters, warriors, or barbarians who adopt this prestige class to gain (or continue) a fighter's specialized training in combat maneuvers, fierce and destructive attack abilities, and a home field advantage in their tribal lands and fighting their traditional foes. Sometimes tribal adepts, clerics, or sorcerers take on this role, depending on the tribe.

NPC tribal protectors are often found in the vanguard of a humanoid army. If honor demands a battle between champions, the tribal protector steps forward. Otherwise, the protector seeks out the leading warriors of the enemy army and engages them in single combat, or—as a last resort—cuts swaths through the rank and file of the opposing troops.

Hit Die: d10.

Requirements

To qualify to become a tribal protector, a character must fulfill all the following criteria.

Alignment: The same alignment as the majority of the character's tribe.

Race: Any humanoid or monstrous humanoid *except* dwarf, elf, gnome, halfling, half-elf, or human.

Base Attack Bonus: +5.

Feats: Power Attack, Cleave, Great Cleave.

Wilderness Lore: 4 ranks.

Class Skills

The tribal protector's class skills (and the key ability for each skill) are Bluff (Cha), Climb (Str), Craft (Int), Hide (Dex), Intimidate (Cha), Intuit Direction (Wis), Jump (Str), Move Silently (Dex), Sense Motive (Wis), and Wilderness Lore (Wis). See Chapter 4: Skills in the *Player's Handbook* for skill descriptions.

Skill Points at Each Level: 2 + Int modifier.

Class Features

Weapon and Armor Proficiency: The tribal protector is proficient with all simple and martial weapons, all types of armor, and shields.

Bonus Feats: The tribal protector gains a bonus feat at 1st, 5th, and 9th level. These bonus feats must be chosen from the list of bonus feats available to a fighter.

Tribal Enemy: At first level, a tribal protector declares a specific group of people or monsters as his tribal enemy. This is a much narrower category than a ranger's favored enemy. Tribal enemies might include the neighboring human nation, members of a specific religion, a rival humanoid tribe, or the drow beneath the mountains. Tribal protectors gain a +3 bonus to Bluff and Sense Motive checks when using these skills against their enemies. They gain the same +3 bonus to weapon damage rolls against these creatures. This damage bonus does not apply to damage against creatures that are immune to critical hits, and the tribal defender does not gain this bonus when using a ranged weapon against a target more than 30 feet distant. A tribal defender who is also a ranger chooses a tribal enemy that is a subset of his favored enemy. The bonuses stack.

Homeland: Tribal protectors gain a +2 bonus to Hide, Intuit Direction, Move Silently, and Wilderness Lore checks when they are within the terrain type and geographical area of their tribal homeland. Examples of homelands include the County of Urnst, the Adri Forest, or the Vale of the Mage. This bonus reflects the protector's intimate familiarity with his home terrain.

Wild Fighting (Ex): Similar to a monk attacking with a flurry of blows, a tribal defender of 2nd level or higher can enter a state of wild fighting, attacking in a storm of ferocious assaults. The character gains one extra attack per round, at his highest base attack bonus, but all the character's attacks in that round suffer a −2 penalty. This penalty lasts for an entire round, so it also affects any attacks of opportunity the protector might make in that round.

Terrain AC Bonus: You take great advantage of your homeland's features and gain the listed deflection bonus to your AC when in your homeland (see above).

Smite (Su): Beginning at 4th level, a tribal protector gains the supernatural ability to make a single melee attack with a +4 attack bonus and a damage bonus equal to his class level (if he hits) against a member of his tribal enemy. The protector must declare the smite before

36

attacking. At 7h level, the protector can smite twice per day. At 10th level, this increases to three times per day.

WARMASTER

On a green hill outside the Furyondan capital of Chendl sprawls a vast, white mansion surrounded by stables and fortifications. Most civilian passersby deem it the home of some wealthy lord, but a practiced military eye notes that many of the walls and catapults face each other, not any outward threat. Also, military officers across the world recognize the mansion as a hallowed training grounds: The Furyondan College of War.

Graduates of the College of War—called warmasters—have served Furyondy's military for generations, providing most of the army's high-ranking generals. Receiving an assignment to train at the College of War is the best assignment a young officer can hope for, and those who excel in the harsh training there become a formidable presence on the battlefield.

Warmasters are generally drawn from the ranks of standing armies, so fighters predominate at the College of War. But the appointment process has a political aspect (as does everything else in Furyondy), so civilian "heroes of the realm" sometimes find themselves training to become warmasters. Clerics and paladins of Heironeous and St. Cuthbert are common, but other classes are rare (every class at the College of War has at least a few wizards and rangers, however). Would-be warmasters are most often human, although every race is represented at the College of War.

NPC warmasters are usually found at the head of an army, either on the march or defending a castle at a strategically important site. Most are eager to lend a hand to fellow warmasters; the college's alumni form a loose "old soldier's network." Sometimes the bonds of comradeship even stretch across battle lines, although warmasters stress loyalty as a primary virtue.

This prestige class may not be suitable for all campaigns, due to the responsibilities that warmasters have thrust on them and the complexities involved in maintaining a keep or castle. As in all things, your DM decides on the viability of this class in your game.

Hit Die: d10.

Requirements

To qualify to become a warmaster, a character must fulfill all the following criteria.

Base Attack Bonus: +7.
Diplomacy: 5 ranks.
Alignment: Any nonchaotic, nonevil.
Feats: Leadership (found in the DUNGEON MASTER's Guide), Martial Weapon Proficiency, Weapon Specialization.

Class Skills

The warmaster's class skills are Bluff (Cha), Craft (Int), Diplomacy (Cha), Intimidate (Cha), Knowledge (Int), Profession (Wis), Ride (Dex), Sense Motive (Cha). See the Player's Handbook, Chapter 4, for skill descriptions.

Skill Points at Each Level: 4 + Int modifier.

Class Features

Brotherhood: Warmasters are a fraternal organization, and members are generally willing to lend a hand to their fellows. You gain a +4 competence bonus to Diplomacy checks made to influence other warmasters. This is a two-way street: You are expected to treat other warmasters honorably and charitably.

Leadership Bonus: Warmasters earn bonuses to their leadership level (character level + Cha bonus), enabling them to attract more powerful cohorts and followers when they use the Leadership feat upon earning a new level.

Battle Cry (Su): When your shout rings across the battlefield, it lifts the spirits of your allies. This ability functions as the bard's inspire courage ability, found on page 28 of the Player's Handbook. This bonus lasts a number of rounds equal to your Charisma bonus, and

TABLE 2–18: THE WARMASTER

Class Level	Base Attack Bonus	Fort Save	Ref Save	Will Save	Special
1st	+1	+2	+0	+0	Brotherhood, Leadership bonus +1
2nd	+2	+3	+0	+0	Battle cry
3rd	+3	+3	+1	+1	Direct troops, Leadership bonus +2
4th	+4	+4	+1	+1	Tower, rally troops
5th	+5	+4	+1	+1	Hard march, Leadership bonus +3
6th	+6	+5	+2	+2	Keep
7th	+7	+5	+2	+2	Battle standard, Leadership bonus +4
8th	+8	+6	+2	+2	Castle
9th	+9	+6	+3	+3	Die for your country, Leadership bonus +5
10th	+10	+7	+3	+3	Huge castle

you can shout a battle cry once per day for every level of warmaster you have attained.

Direct Troops (Su): As a full-round action, you can give compelling directions. You can bestow a +2 competence bonus on either attacks or skill checks to all allies within 30 feet. This bonus lasts a number of rounds equal to your Charisma bonus.

Tower: An organization affiliated with you (the army or an important lord, for example) has offered to build you a tower in a mutually agreeable location. As long as you uphold the ideals of the organization involved, you can manage the affairs of the tower as you wish, although you are responsible for upkeep costs. A tower is a round or square, three-level building made of stone.

Rally Troops (Su): Your presence is enough to grant any allies within 30 feet a second saving throw against *fear* and charm effects that they have already succumbed to. Even if they fail the second saving throw, any *fear* effects are less severe: panicked characters are only frightened, frightened characters are only shaken, and shaken characters are unaffected.

Hard March: You can exhort your troops to march faster. Anyone traveling with you gains a +4 morale bonus to Constitution checks required for making a forced march or any other task requiring extended exertion. Animals are not affected.

Keep: As "Tower" above. A keep is a fortified stone building with fifteen to twenty-five rooms.

Battle Standard (Su): The mere sight of your coat of arms or other heraldic display is enough to turn the tide of battle. Allies within 30 feet of your standard gain the effects of both Battle Cry and Rally Troops (above) as long as the standard is within range and held by you. If your standard is captured in battle, all allies within range aware of its loss suffer a –1 morale penalty to attacks and damage until it is recovered in addition to losing the benefits described above.

Castle: As "Tower" above. A castle is a keep (also above) surrounded by a 15-foot-high stone wall with four towers. The wall is 10′ thick.

Die for Your Country (Su): Your presence inspires your troops to make the ultimate sacrifice for your cause. Any allies within 30 feet of you can continue to fight while disabled or dying without penalty. They continue until they reach –10 hit points.

Huge Castle: As "Tower" above. This large complex has numerous associated buildings (stables, a forge, granaries, etc.), and an elaborate 20-foot-high, 10-foot-thick wall creating bailey and courtyard areas. The wall has six towers.

WEAPON MASTER

The monk, the red avenger, the drunken master, and the master samurai all harness *ki* energy as part of their martial disciplines; they are not, however, the only such persons to do so. Some pursue the study of *ki* by mastering a single melee weapon. To unite this weapon of choice with the body, to make them one, to use the weapon as naturally and without thought as any other limb, is the goal of weapon master.

Monks who follow this path may choose unarmed attacks or the kama, nunchaku, siangham (see the *Player's*

TABLE 2–19: THE WEAPON MASTER

Class Level	Base Attack Bonus	Fort Save	Ref Save	Will Save	Special
1st	+1	+0	+2	+0	*Ki* damage 1/day/level
2nd	+2	+0	+3	+0	Increased multiplier 1/day
3rd	+3	+1	+3	+1	Superior Weapon Focus
4th	+4	+1	+4	+1	Increased multiplier 2/day
5th	+5	+1	+4	+1	Superior Combat Reflexes
6th	+6	+2	+5	+2	Increased multiplier 3/day
7th	+7	+2	+5	+2	*Ki* critical
8th	+8	+2	+6	+2	Increased multiplier 4/day
9th	+9	+3	+6	+3	*Ki* Whirlwind Attack
10th	+10	+3	+7	+3	Increased multiplier 5/day

Base Attack Bonus: Note that, like a monk, this class makes unarmed iterative attacks at a –3 penalty, not the usual –5 penalty.

Handbook, Chapter 7) or the three-section staff (see Chapter 5 of this book) as their weapon of choice. In order to gain any of the special abilities of the weapon master class, you must use your weapon of choice. Once chosen, the weapon of choice cannot be later changed.

This does not mean that, if your weapon of choice is the longsword, you can only use the longsword you owned when you first became a weapon master. The only material requirement for the class is a masterwork version of your weapon. It means you can use any masterwork longsword and gain the benefits of the weapon master.

If you use any other weapon, you can use none of the special abilities of the prestige class.

Hit Die: d10.

Requirements

To qualify to become a weapon master, a character must fulfill all the following criteria:

Base Attack Bonus: +5.
Intimidate: 4 ranks.
Proficiency: With your weapon of choice.
Weapon: Masterwork weapon (unless unarmed).
Feats: Dodge, Mobility, Combat Reflexes, Expertise, Spring Attack, Weapon Focus, Whirlwind Attack, Dex 13+.

Class Skills

The weapon master's class skills (and the key ability for each skill) are: Intimidate (Cha), Knowledge (weaponry) (Int), Listen (Wis), Sense Motive (Wis), and Spot (Wis). See Chapter 4: Skills in the *Player's Handbook* for skill descriptions.

Skill Points at Each Level: 2 + Int modifier.

Class Features

Ki Damage: After you score a hit with your weapon of choice, you do not roll dice to determine the damage. Instead, you figure the normal maximum damage (not a

critical hit) you can inflict with that weapon and do that much damage to the target. Assume you use a longsword, have a base attack bonus of +7, and possess a 17 Strength. A longsword does 1d8 damage, so its maximum damage is 8 points. Your Strength modifier is +3, so add that for a total of 11. Additional damage, such as from using the Power Attack feat (following all the rules for it normally) and the sneak attack ability are determined normally; they are not maximized. This ability cannot be used when you roll a successful critical hit.

Increased Multiplier: Determine the standard critical multiplier for your weapon of choice. With this ability, you can increase that multiplier by +1. For example, the longsword has a critical multiplier of ×2. Using this ability, you can increase that multiplier to ×3 (2+1=3) once per day at 2nd level. You must declare the use of this ability before you roll any damage dice.

Superior Weapon Focus: Stacking with any existing Weapon Focus bonus, this adds an additional +1 to all attack rolls with the weapon master's weapon of choice.

Superior Combat Reflexes: This ability lets you make a total number of attacks of opportunity in a round equal to your Dexterity modifier plus your Wisdom modifier.

Ki Critical: Gain the Improved Critical feat for free. If you already possess this feat, add an additional +2 to your weapon of choice's threat range for critical hits. This +2 bonus is applied last, after any multipliers, such as those given by the Improved Critical feat or by keen weapons.

Ki Whirlwind: You can make a Whirlwind Attack as a standard action rather than a full attack action. Only one Whirlwind Attack can be made per round.

Multiclass Note: Monk characters can freely multiclass with this class. In other words, you can give your monk PC a weapon master level, then return to the monk class for your next level, take a weapon master level after that, and so on.

CHAPTER 3: WORLDLY MATTERS

Thus far, this book has provided you with new feats and prestige classes to add to your campaign. Both new feats and classes represent new rules and new options for your PCs. We would be amiss, however, if we did not provide some context in which you take full advantage of these rules: hence, this chapter. Here we examine the roles of fighters and monks in the campaign world, how both players and DMs can adjust those roles, and several groups to which fighters and monks, be they PC or NPC, can join and which DMs can add to their campaigns.

FIGHTERS AND MONKS AND THE WORLD THEY LIVE IN

"Everybody's got an agenda: everybody."

—Tordek

No character exists in a vacuum. One cannot help but be affected by, and take account of, the world around oneself. This becomes doubly true for player characters, since their stock-in-trade requires that they interact with their surroundings with more care and concern than normal folks. Peasants, fishermen, and even nobles do not seek out the varied and dangerous situations in which PCs constantly find themselves. Whether the adventurer finds herself in town or dungeon, forest or desert, the world and its various elements—people, monsters, buildings, geography, climate, religion, and customs—informs her choices and options, and affects her adventuring career, and those of her companions.

The Fighter and the World

Whether you play a fighter who plays the role of honorable knight-errant or callous mercenary, gallant cavalier or king of the highwaymen, the world in which you adventure and live has an impact on your choices and alternatives. A common stereotype dogs many fighter characters: The ordinary person whose only contribution to the party involves the ability to swing a sword. While a sword (or an axe, mace, or halberd) is unarguably a fighter's most obvious role during a game session, consider how the fighter's relations to the world around him might affect this stereotype.

Fighters who exist in campaign worlds in which wizards and sorcerers are the dominant power may find themselves relegated to roles of a more supporting nature, protecting the arcane spellcasters from harm so that they can rain destruction down on the enemy from a distance. In other campaigns, religion comprises the dominant factor in the world, and clerics are the primary movers and shakers. Fighters are often members of the church or even the clergy when this condition prevails, acting as templars and religious guardians.

Most fighters do not have any structural organizations built into their class; unlike paladins and clerics, they belong to no hierarchy, no group larger than the party itself. Although they may worship a particular deity, follow a certain noble leader, or devote themselves to a personal cause, they are generally left to make their own way in the world without benefit of any such hierarchies on which they rely for support and resources. More often than not, fighters are ex-soldiers or ex-mercenaries, selling their martial prowess for money.

Sometimes, however, fighters are in fact able to found or become members of organizations, fraternities, or societies expressly for warriors. Perhaps your fighter joins a knightly order, such as the

Knights of the Watch (see page 47), or purchases entry into a large mercenary company. He might even demonstrate his worth to an individual of high station, such as a noble or a high priestess, and so be invited to join a retinue as a privileged bodyguard or special agent. Such circumstances often alter the fighter's role within the adventuring party, because the fighter no longer exists solely for kicking in doors and bashing monsters. He now possesses responsibilities and commitments beyond those to his adventuring comrades, and this leads both to new adventuring opportunities and internal disputes for the party at large.

Adventuring Roles

Nearly every fighter who elects to pursue adventuring as a regular enterprise has the same role to play in their respective parties: They are the first to fight, whether eliminating opposing creatures or defending their comrades from attack. This should come as no surprise, for no other character class has better general fighting capabilities than the fighter. Below are a few brief ideas for fighters' roles beyond just door-smasher and orc-basher. (For even more on PC backgrounds, see the *Hero Builder's Guidebook*.)

Professional Soldier: This fighter serves in the standing army or constabulary of some higher authority, often a member of the nobility or even a community. He generally accompanies adventuring parties at the request of his employer, often to ensure that the (untrustworthy?) hired adventurers accomplish the goals for which they were contracted, or to provide additional martial support to achieve their missions.

Mercenary: Like the soldier, this sort of fighter trades his skills for pay, but usually on a much more temporary basis. He normally contracts to provide his services for a specified amount of time, although occasionally the period of service can be indefinite. Mercenaries often join up with adventuring parties when they are between contracts, and usually for a predetermined share in the loot.

Knight: This is a special type of fighter. He belongs to a knightly order, and swears to uphold a set of ideals or an ethos that the organization prizes. Knights frequently join adventuring parties that are engaged in missions which support the order's goals, or that espouse ideals that reflect (or at least do not conflict with) those of the order.

Racial Issues

No discussion of any class is complete without also discussing the template for all player characters: race. Racial issues play a part both when designing a PC and when playing one during the game.

Dwarf: The dwarf is the quintessential choice for the fighter class. If you play a dwarf fighter, realize that you have a considerable advantage due to the very nature of the dwarf. Although you do not gain the extra feat allotted to humans, you enjoy the significant benefits of darkvision, a bonus to your Constitution ability score, and the not-inconsiderable advantage of an improved attack bonus and Armor Class against certain types of creatures (such as giants). Feats such as Weapon Focus, Power Attack, Cleave, and Improved Bull Rush are all excellent choices that complement the dwarf's racial assets.

Elf: The elf's Dexterity score bonus often means that elf fighters often take Weapon Finesse as a feat early in their careers. Likewise, elf fighters often concentrate on ranged weapons, such as the longbow, rather than on melee weapons. Thus, feats such as Point Blank Shot, Precise Shot, Far Shot, and others also qualify as sound choices.

Gnome: The Gnome's Strength penalty often means that the gnome fighter's Strength may be less than optimal. However, the racial bonus to Constitution score offsets this. This can be further enhanced with the Toughness feat and its stackable effect.

Half-Elf: It seems at first glance that only the bravest player would play a half-elf fighter. The race suffers from a complete lack of ability score bonuses and it boasts no racial bonuses to attack rolls, saving

throws, or Armor Class. However, a half-elf fighter remains a viable choice, provided you note the factors mentioned above. The half-elf suffers from no ability score penalties, which means if you rolled a pair of 16s as your highest ability scores, your half-elf fighter keeps them both, rather than ending up with one likely reduced to a 14. But perhaps the half-elf's greatest advantage is that she can multiclass without suffering an XP penalty for her highest-level class, because all classes are her favored class. This benefit, shared only with humans, sets the half-elf apart from all the other races, including that of the elf parent.

Halfling: Like the elf, the halfling fighter often makes great use of the improved Dexterity score by taking Weapon Finesse as an early feat. Their small size gives them a benefit to Armor Class, and this trait combined with a high Dexterity score sometimes allows the halfling fighter to start out with less expensive and lighter armor, thus keeping the halfling from suffering movement penalties due to heavy armor. The halfling's bonus to attack rolls with thrown weapons makes a dagger, a hand axe, or a sling good choices for a short-range weapon.

Half-Orc: The half-orc's Strength score bonus makes him an ideal candidate for the fighter class. The darkvision racial ability can be invaluable when adventuring underground. Unfortunately, the half-orc suffers a penalty to his Intelligence ability score, which means fewer skill points and lower skill totals; although, when you have a 20 Strength score, few may care about your skill totals.

Human: With the extra feat at 1st level, and the additional feats granted to the fighter class, human fighters are obvious, excellent characters. The number of feats granted to such characters allows their creator, player or DM, to customize the human fighter into a number of configurations.

Pursuing the feat paths that begin with Dodge, Expertise, Point Blank Shot, Mounted Combat, and Power Attack all evolve the character in different directions.

The Monk and the World

Monks also too often fit neatly into a stereotypical mold: The introspective ascetic who, when not adventuring, pursues a life of inward contemplation in search of spiritual fulfillment. The typical adventurer monk tends to be reserved, spiritual, and capable of delivering an unarmed attack or a snippet of Zen with equal ease. However, the monk exists for more than merely the quest for physical and spiritual perfection. Like the fighter, the monk is a master of combat, striking swiftly with her bare hands and feet, or sometimes with specialized weapons. While generally incapable of absorbing the same punishing amount of damage a fighter can bear, monks eventually need not be concerned about this since they develop several class abilities that help them avoid being hit at all.

Monks usually participate in some sort of structured life, whether as a member of a monastery, a temple, or some other organization. Sometimes this structure exists primarily to instill in its members certain beliefs or values, enabling the monk to interact with the outside world in a relatively normally fashion, provided she follows the prescribed code of behavior or other system of ethics. In some instances, the structure resembles a more formal hierarchy, obliging the monk to accept orders and tasks from those individuals who occupy the ranks above her. In both cases the monk relies on this organization for some amount of support and resources, the exact details of which varies according to the nature of the structure itself.

Adventuring Roles

Sometimes it requires a stretch of the imagination to rationalize why a monk, who ostensibly desires nothing more than to attain a near-mythical perfect union of mind, body, and spirit, would ever leave her temple to undertake an enterprise as distracting and perilous as adventuring. Every day spent helping her comrades raid a dungeon of its treasures, or defending a village from marauding humanoids, is a day that she does not immerse herself in the studies and practices that are *de rigueur* for an individual with such goals.

Or is it? Some monkish traditions teach that the world is an exemplary classroom, and that each person, place, and event has a lesson to teach, the learning of which can be an invaluable aid in helping the monk perceive her true place in the cosmos. Other traditions encourage monks to leave their monasteries for a period of time in order to give a frame of reference to their studies, to see what other people deem important enough to strive toward. Below are few roles monks in your game can exemplify.

Penitent: This type of monk undertakes, voluntarily or otherwise, a quest or other activity outside her monastery to compensate for some fault or flaw. This shortcoming can be real or imagined, and its significance varies with the nature of the teachings the monk pursues. Sometimes the penitent joins an adventuring company in order to learn a particular lesson about herself or the world at large.

Zen Master: This variety of monk joins adventuring companies primarily because she believes that a vital part of her attempts to achieve her ultimate goals of physical and spiritual perfection lie on the challenges faced by such groups. She sees adventuring as an opportunity to hone and perfect her martial skills under duress.

Spiritual Advisor: Spiritual advisors usually join adventuring companies because they believe strongly that one or more of its members benefit significantly from her presence. Perhaps the monk is charged with mentoring a member of the party who herself may be a prospective candidate for becoming a monk, or perhaps the monk has decided to take an individual with a promising but unstructured mind under her wing and teach her the benefits of the monk's chosen spiritual doctrine and discipline.

Spiritual Enforcer: This type of monk joins an adventuring party only on a temporary basis. She has been charged, either by her monastery or by her own conscience, to share in the party's mission because it supports the goals of her organization or ethos. Monks of this sort are often single-minded in the pursuit of their goal, but they lend invaluable resources and skills to the party.

Racial Issues

Even more so than with fighters, a monk character's race often impacts not only the combat capabilities of the character, but the PC's role in the group as well. Rules for Small and Medium-size monks are in the *Player's Handbook*, and rules for larger monks are found on page 61 of this book.

Elf: The elven mind is well suited to the extended pursuit of goals, even if the agenda remains somewhat esoteric (as in the case of many monastic teachings). The elf's Dexterity bonus is an obvious advantage to the monk, who must rely on speed for both attack and defense, particularly at lower levels. Weapon Finesse and Improved Initiative are good feat choices.

Dwarf: The dwarven mindset usually does not include the outlook and traits that make for a successful monk. Dwarf monks seldom succeed.

However, if this appeals to you, work with your DM to establish a suitable rationale for your character to explore this alternative. Keep in mind that your dwarf character may suffer some roleplaying repercussions for choosing to devote himself to the monastic life. In particular, his family, clan, or community may take issue with his decision, and ostracize him (or worse). For such a role, a defensive feat such as Expertise may apply.

Gnome: Few gnomes have the disposition to undertake long periods of training within a monastery, and even fewer care to suffer from the diminished damage and speed scores that the monk class inflicts on them due to their size. Hence, very few gnomes are found among the ranks of monks. However, it is possible for a gnome to be a monk, and even to excel at it, provided he finds a means (perhaps magical) to compensate for the lower traits. One such means involves choosing to fight with the monkish weapons that allow him to attack as if he were unarmed, thus using the better attack rate and bonus of his class.

Half-Elf: Half-elves raised among human communities have no difficulties in accepting the constraints and lifestyle of the monastery. Half-elves who grow up in elven communities are usually no more or less likely to become monks than the elves with whom they are raised.

Halfling: Like the gnome, the halfling suffers a reduction to his damage and speed scores, making the monk class less attractive than others. More importantly, halfling culture rarely produces individuals who are suited to the rigid and often stationery nature of monastic life. Halflings do not normally thrive when confined to a single location, or when obliged to devote themselves to long-term, single-minded contemplation of a single interest or regimen.

Half-Orc: Those half-orcs who are raised within human society, or at least in such a manner that their outlook is more human than orc, have as little trouble accepting the monastic rigors as humans do. Half-orcs who are raised outside human communities, however, seldom develop the patience or self-awareness necessary to become a successful monk.

Human: The nature of humans makes them much more suited to the monastic life than most other races, and it is for this reason that most monks are humans.

ORGANIZATIONS: A LITTLE HELP FROM MY FRIENDS

It never hurts to have a little help when facing down the dangers of the big, bad world. Your character need not go into peril alone: The organizations listed below provide your character with resources, support, and

information that may just give him the edge he needs when the chips are down.

Using Organizations in the Campaign

Each organization has its own structure, membership requirements, goals, and features. They are designed to fit easily into any campaign world or setting. However, not every organization may work equally well with your campaign and playing style. Players and the DM should work together to identify any potential problems with any organization that appeals to you, and then revise the details of the organization so that it meshes more smoothly with your setting.

You might decide that the Knight Protectors of the Great Kingdom fits exactly the kind of organization that your 5th-level fighter would attempt to join, but maybe a decaying remnant of a once-powerful nation does not in your campaign world. No problem: If everyone agrees, you can establish an alternate origin for the organization, drawing on the history of your setting to provide an alternate explanation for the Protector's background, and giving the organization new goals to pursue.

Note that several organizations presented here also have prestige classes defined in Chapter Two. Players and DMs are encouraged to use both when both appear here, or to create a class or an organization in the instances where only one or the other is defined in this book.

Also, entrance into these groups is not solely the province of fighters and monks, but such characters do comprise a significant portion of these groups' membership.

The Fists of Hextor
"Might makes right. It also makes a pretty good living."

The time often comes when even the most tyrannical despot may face military challenges that cannot be overcome by the strength of his own army. Humanoid invasions, organized insurrection, and even well-supported peasant uprisings have toppled more than one evil but civilized monarch who lacked the might to restore order in his own demesne. Fortunately, support can be found for the discriminating tyrant, provided he can pay the price. If he can afford them, he just might be able to hire some of the most infamously brutal mercenaries ever known: The Fists of Hextor.

Created and supported by the Church of Hextor, the Fists of Hextor are considered part of its clergy. They serve the Scourge of Battle by fighting only in those causes approved and sanctioned by Hextor's priests. Well-known both for their efficient brutality and their strict adherence to any bargain struck, those who would hire the Fists of Hextor must take care to stipulate the terms of their employment most carefully, lest they find themselves the victim of an unfortunate misunderstanding. (An infamous disagreement between the Fists of Hextor and a past employer resulted in the mercenaries' sudden withdrawal from the field of battle at a crucial moment, leaving their *former* employer to the tender mercies of his opponents.)

Those who would hire any number of Fists of Hextor must first approach the Church of Hextor and establish the nature of their cause to the satisfaction of its Discordians (priesthood). Generally, a prospective employer must demonstrate that the fighting to be undertaken by the Fists of Hextor serves, or at least does not conflict with, Hextor's dogma. Those who seek to crush unlawful rebellions, thwart the random savagery of humanoid invasion, or restore the rule of law to uncivilized lands are typical of the sort of employers the Discordians accept on behalf of the Fists of Hextor. The more ruthlessly tyrannical the supplicant, the more likely his request is to be granted.

An explicit agreement is then drawn up by the Church, and signed by the highest-ranking priest in the vicinity and the Fists' of Hextor employer, who are warned to honor the exact terms of the contract in order to avoid conflict with both the Fists of Hextor and the Church. (Unsurprisingly, not every employer who prevails with the help of the Fists of Hextor has been happy in his victory.)

Employers who violate a contract suffer not only the obvious consequences, but are never permitted to hire the Fists of Hextor again. Finally, the Church requires a substantial tithe in return for providing its most skilled warriors for the cause in question.

The exact price depends on a variety of circumstances, including the immediate needs of the Church, the number of Fists of Hextor required, the nature of the fight ahead (battles for causes deemed pleasing to Hextor often require a smaller tithe), and the hazards to be faced. Any agreement that brings the Fists of Hextor into conflict with the Church of Heironeous is almost certain to be approved with alacrity. If an employer possesses both good fortune and a deep purse, he hopes that a Patriarch-General, a battle-scourge of truly formidable power, leads the Fists of Hextor he hires.

Once engaged, the Fists of Hextor fight with cold, merciless efficiency. They pursue they their goal with single-mindedness and an unbridled ferocity that has earned them a reputation for cruelty. Fists of Hextor continue to fight until the opponent is defeated, the terms of their agreement are fulfilled, or the contract is terminated. In no event do the Fists of Hextor quit the battlefield for any other eventuality. They are quite prepared to die in the service of the Champion of Evil. A martial faith, the Church expects the Fists of Hextor to prevail even against considerable hardship, and to employ any methods necessary to ensure victory. Failure is not tolerated, which is undoubtedly the chief reason the Fists of Hextor are so zealous in their pursuit of success in warfare: Should they fail to achieve their designated objective, a fate far worse than an honorable death in battle awaits them upon their return to their church fathers.

Becoming a member of this infamous fraternity of lethal mercenaries is no less difficult task than attempting to hire them. Those who would join must first seek out a temple dedicated to Hextor and present themselves to the clergy in charge of recruitment. Obtaining an audience with these clerics requires little, but what follows is always arduous and sometimes fatal. Hextor's clergy have no need of run-of-the-mill cutthroats or brigands: They desire only the most callous and brutal soldiers. Candidates must prove themselves by undergoing a series of rigorous and sometimes sadistic tests, known collectively as the Trials of Hextor. The Trials are designed to weed out the faint-hearted and weak-willed from the suitable applicants. The Trials require the applicant to inflict what can only be termed casual brutality and suffering, and sometimes even death, on targets chosen by the recruiting clergy. The Church of Hextor believes firmly that the Trials allow applicants to demonstrate the proper attitude and resolve necessary for inclusion in the ranks of the Fists of Hextor. The Trials also have the incidental benefit of exposing any infiltrators who might think to gain admission into the organization and spy or wreak havoc from within. More than one brave paladin or cavalier has revealed himself for what he was by refusing to participate in the slaughters and indignities required of potential Fists of Hextor, so consigning themselves to death rather than a violation of their principles or moral codes. The horrific details are left to each campaign to determine.

After an applicant has satisfied the recruiting clergy of her worthiness, she enters the same temple of Hextor where she first sought the honor of becoming a Fist of Hextor, to await the time of the induction ceremony. The Church of Hextor inducts new Fists of Hextor only at certain times of the year that conform to the deity's holy days, and the accepted applicants must await these appointed times confined within the temple structure. They are unable to exit, even as far as the immediate exterior grounds, on pain of death.

While awaiting induction, they pass their days receiving tutelage in the religious dogma of Hextor from the recruiting clergy, and performing whatever menial or degrading tasks the clerics set before them (as further proof of their devotion to Hextor, of course).

When the time of induction arrives, the clergy collect the current candidates and take them to the place of ceremony, often a remote and isolated location some distance from the temple, though some of the larger and more prosperous temples of Hextor boast ceremonial sites within their very walls. (These are usually located far below the main floors, to deaden the sounds that the ceremony produces.) The induction ceremony is rumored to be so cruel and inhuman that it forever changes the outlook of the survivors. Those who survive become Fists of Hextor. Folk speak in hushed tones, with many a paranoid glance over their shoulders, of human sacrifice, ritualistic murders, and orgies of bloodshed so vile as to make what the Fists of Hextor perpetrate on the field of battle seem a stroll in a summer meadow by comparison. However, since the Fists of Hextor and the clergy of Hextor are forbidden to speak of the ceremony to anyone outside the Church structure, no concrete details are known. What facts reveal are merely the visible evidence: the candidates who survive the ceremony to become full-fledged Fists of Hextor invariably emerge from the induction ceremony bearing hideous scars on their faces, necks, and arms. These, too, remain unexplained by those who bear them, though it is not unknown for the expression of a Fist of Hextor who is questioned about them to linger somewhere between pride and fear.

The Knight Protectors of the Great Kingdom

"Good sir, you bar me from my sworn duty: Either stand aside, or draw your sword."

Moral decay. Corrupted ethics. Tainted honor. These are the enemies of the Knight Protectors, and to eradicating such foes, the order devotes its days and knights with fanatical zeal. The Protectors believe that only they stand between the world and its ruination at the hands of these foul opponents, and that they can succeed only by restoring the glory of that which has been lost.

Of all the orders of knighthood in the long history of the world, none has been acknowledged as greater than the fabled Knight Protectors of the Great Kingdom. Once many hundreds in number, their membership has since dwindled to a paltry few, with perhaps no more than two dozen surviving to the present day. Throughout their long history, they have been formidable warriors with a matchless reputation for courage and honor. They have become the model for innumerable orders of knighthood that have since sprung up in their wake to imitate their example. Their legends still permeate the cultures of all the former provinces of the Great Kingdom. From its inception, the order was unique in the Great Kingdom in that the Knight Protectors chose their own membership through contests of skill and courage. Positions were not appointed, nor could they be bought. They numbered both Heironeans and Hextorians in their ranks, and while this produced strong rivalries, deadly conflicts were few.

The goal of the order in former days was always a united and protected the Great Kingdom under an honorable monarch. Alas, the order's high ideals did not last and the order declined, speeding the Great Kingdom's fall from its lofty position until it became a

mere shadow of its former self, and then fell into dissolution. Today, the Protectors cling desperately to the hope that the return of the Great Kingdom will save the world from its current state of moral collapse, and bring order, peace, and prosperity to its subjects.

The first element in the Protectors' attempt to achieve their goal involves modeling their behavior after what is still known about their predecessors' code of honor, expecting others to heed their example and emulate their conduct. The second, and far more dangerous, part of their plan includes challenging those creatures, individuals, and even institutions that the order considers to be contributing factors to the decline of civilization. The final aspect of their plan is locating a true descendant of the Great Kingdom's last monarch and restoring that individual to the throne of the bygone nation.

Exactly how this final element of the plan may be achieved is less than certain. The Protectors do not know, exactly, where such a person might be found! Rumors circulate among the Knights that the chief of their order has obtained a crucial clue that may enable him to identify an heir to the Kingdom, and that he is directing the order's current missions toward that end.

Knight Protectors of the Great Kingdom are known to be in Ratik, mostly refugees from the Bone March, where Clement was a powerful member of the order. The Knight Protectors once resided in Chathold but now wander the Kingdom of Ahlissa. Some knights purportedly are hiding in the Grandwood and Adri Forests, and a few joined the Iron League or found refuge among the lands of the Cranden. With the apparent passing of Ivid Vin Rauzes following the wars, some expect the Knight Protectors to emerge from their dormancy and take a more active role in the recovery of the Great Kingdom.

Today, the Knight Protectors practice what they believe to be an accurate representation of the chivalric code once espoused by their predecessors. Their ethos, while relatively simple in theory, but like any moral code, can be difficult to apply consistently under the pressures and rigors of life's experiences.

- Uphold the honor and good name of the Great Kingdom unto your last breath. Tolerate no disrespect or mockery of neither the Kingdom nor your station. Demonstrate through force of arms the error of those who would ridicule the most noble and honorable of all nations and knightly orders. It is better to die in service to the Kingdom and the order than to suffer such indignities.
- Defend those who cannot defend themselves. Take the part of the weak and the helpless, and give succor and support to those in need. Do not allow the stronger to take advantage of the weaker, nor allow

yourself to be tempted down this path of dishonorable accord.

- Display honor and truth in all your dealings and behaviors. Let it never be said that you told a lie, for lies corrupt the very foundation of our land. Make your word your bond, so that all may know that your oath, deed, and intent are the same. Give none cause to doubt neither your vow nor your honor.
- Smite evil wherever it may be found, and stem the tide of chaos with your sword and body. Mete out justice to those who perpetrate evil acts.
- Bestow your loyalty to the head of the order, and follow his commands in all things. Unite in the face of adversity, and cleave to your fellow knights that you may overcome any obstacle and defeat any challenge. Only through unity and strength of purpose shall the future of the Kingdom prevail.

Aspiring to such high-minded ideals is easy, but making them part of one's everyday life is not. Nonetheless, this very challenge the Knights Protector must meet daily (and sometimes more frequently than that when the forces of adversity threaten his convictions).

To join the Knight Protectors, a candidate must first prove himself through feats of arms. Once each year, the Protectors hold a great melee at a location that they conceal, lest their enemies discover them. This makes it rather difficult for prospective candidates to present themselves, but discovering and reaching the location of the melee safely and without being followed is the very first sign that a candidate may be worthy to join. The melee itself involves all manner of martial feats, lasting several days. Contestants take part in jousts, wrestling, challenges to single combat, weight lifting, archery, and horsemanship. Wounds and injuries are quite common as a result, but fatalities are rare indeed. The object of these trials is not to kill, but to demonstrate capability.

But the ideal Knight Protector must be more than a mere soldier: His very existence should be a beacon of hope for those who also desire to see a restored and strong Great Kingdom, as well as to those who prize goodness and order. To this end, candidates for knighthood must demonstrate more than simple martial prowess. Any thug, after all, can swing a sword or hurl an axe. The applicants for membership are also required to display the less tangible qualities of honor, obedience, mercy, and wisdom. It is for this reason that how a candidate comports himself during the tests of skill, and indeed throughout the duration of the event, is at least as important as how well he performs in those tests. In the past, the Protectors have selected a candidate whose feats of arms show more promise than mastery, but who also demonstrates behavior that reflects the order's cherished ideals. "One can be taught swordsmanship, but honor cannot be learned" is some Knights' motto during this event.

Only a handful of candidates, if any, are selected from each annual melee. Those who accept this invitation are assigned immediately to a Protector who acts as the probationary member's constant tutor, guide, and companion for a year and a day. During this time, the two are inseparable: Where the elder knight goes, so goes the new member. Together they undertake the duties and meet the challenges assigned to them by the order. Following the end of the prescribed training period, the elder knight must recommend to the order whether it should accept his pupil as a full-fledged Knight Protector. Only the most unusual circumstances warrant this recommendation being refused: The only documented instance was when the order suspected (rightly, as it turned out) that the elder knight was forced under magical duress to speak in favor of the candidate. New Knights undergo a brief ceremony during which they receive the accolade that makes them a full member of the order.

The Knights of the Watch
"The code is all!"

The Knights of the Watch formed several centuries ago to defend the lands of their people against the incursions of the savage tribes who struck from the dry steppes to the extreme west. Built upon the foundation of an earlier organization that was based in Gran March, the Watchers, as they came to be known, were tasked with protecting the lands and folk of Keoland, Gran March, Bissel, and Geoff from the marauding Paynim nomads and westerlings. The organization maintains several castles, fortresses, and strongholds along the border with Ket, as well as in the western mountains, from which they launch their constant patrols of the border areas. The order's strongest bases of power can be found in Gran March (Hookhill), Geoff (Hochoch), and Bissel (Pellak), though members of the knighthood are drawn from the best and wisest of the lands throughout the Sheldomar Valley.

The peoples of the lands they guard recognize the Knights of the Watch as stalwart defenders of safety and security, and some might even call them heroes. Most folk presume that the Watchers accomplish their goals solely through strength of arms, since the order's public image is little different from knightly orders that do just that. When the citizenry stands aside to allow a coterie of mounted Watchers to pass by, they see only the trappings of their outward warlike appearance: the well-polished and well-used arms and armor; the magnificent war horses, the

The Twelve

Address each Knight always with his proper title, that we may be reminded of the respect and honor due one another.

Obey the Knight of higher station in all things.

Let the magnificence of our arms and armor proclaim our worthiness and readiness to the world.

Value the honor of our order above our personal honor; value our order above our lives.

Render such aid to those in need as to a fellow Knight; indulge the ignorant or witless even unto a fault, but suffer no slur or insult to our honor from those who lack such excuse.

Assemble each day upon rising to partake of our fellowship, and to rededicate ourselves to the Twelve and the Seven, which we pledge to defend even at the cost of our lives.

Never violate an oath you have sworn. Never swear an oath you know you cannot keep.

Engage the enemy forthrightly that he may know the origin of his doom; set no ambush nor indulge in any base trickery to overcome the foe.

Give quarter to those who yield and render up prisoners in honorable exchange.

Let no patrol or command be tainted with the stain of cowardice; once the enemy has been engaged, let him fall under our sword or let us fall under his.

Refuse no honorable truce or parley.

Suffer not to shelter among us any who would violate, ignore, or dishonor this code.

---

shields emblazoned with the silver owl (the Watcher's coat of arms), and the alert expressions on the faces of these courageous and resolute defenders of the land. They do not see what hides beneath this carefully contrived and maintained public image.

The Knights of the Watch are, in truth, devotees of a near-monastic school of philosophical teachings based on the ancient writings of the philosopher-sage Azmarender, who first chronicled a code of duty and belief known as the Twelve and Seven Precepts. The Twelve Precepts govern how a knight of the order carries out his day-to-day activities, with a particular eye toward traditions of battle: these are the customs and rules by which the Watchers conduct their martial endeavors, and more besides. The Watchers strive to imbue the essence of the Twelve into every aspect of their lives, from the manner in which they interact with one another to the proper means of addressing their protectorate, from the methods by which they conduct their patrols and enter into armed conflict with the enemy. If one observes the Watchers carefully over time, the patterns inherent their behaviors become evident, allowing one to guess at the sort of counsel that some parts of the Twelve must offer.

The Seven precepts, on the other hand, are said to guide "life beyond the self," giving meaning to existence and the universe beyond the concerns of warfare and battle. While the Watchers' outward behaviors might hint at the contents of the Twelve, they guard the nature of the Seven with jealous zeal. Indeed, so fanatical are the Watchers regarding the contents of these latter teachings that they reveal them only in order, one by one, to the knights who advance in station through the ranks of the organization by dint of proven merit and demonstrated worth. The Seventh Precept itself is known only the knight who occupies the very highest level of knighthood that can be attained in the order: The Grandiose Imperial Wyvern (currently the ailing Hugo of Geoff). A handful of sages have speculated, based on the rare few scraps of writing from Azmarender's pen that exist outside the walls of the Watcher's strongholds, that the Seventh reveals ancient secrets concerning the establishment of Oerth itself. The only known

attempt to steal the secret of the Seventh Precept occurred a decade ago and met with spectacular failure when the would-be thieves, who somehow managed to gain entry into the chambers of the Grand Imperial Wyvern himself, were unable to disarm the powerful magic protections that guarded their objective. The Watchers hung what remained of their bodies from the ramparts of the stronghold, a grim reminder to all that the acquisition of knowledge often comes only through payment of a hideously steep price.

As befits the mysticism that dwells at the heart of their organization, the Watchers are known internally by a selection of fanciful titles. Common Knights, the lowest in rank, are called Vigils, with minor ranks adding to the base title (Stalwart Vigil, Resilient Vigil, Radiant Vigil, etc.). As Knights ascend in rank, a number of adjectives are added to their titles, with "vigil" replaced by the names of fantastic beasts (manticore, hippogriff, griffon, etc.), such that a mid-level commander is known as the Magnificent Elder Gorgon. Few outside the order understand the ranking system of the Watchers, a fact that gave rise to the peasant saying, "frightful as a Watcher's title" to denote someone who wishes to appear grander than he truly is.

The Schism

Recent wars and their grim aftermath brought new and unwelcome developments to the knighthood: a fractionalization of the order into two distinct branches, the traditional Knights of the Watch and the new Knights of Dispatch. The Watchers continue much as they always have, patrolling the borders of civilization and guarding its inhabitants against the assaults and incursions of the steppe raiders.

The Dispatchers, however, have apparently eschewed the order's traditional rites of battle, often forming themselves into small scouting bands to range within conquered Geoff (and, until recently, Sterich). The Knights of Dispatch have traded their hatred of the west for a deep loathing of the marauding humanoids who have caused their homelands so much trouble in the last decade, and have vowed to completely exterminate these foul creatures wherever they might be found, and by whatever means necessary, including such tactics as ambushes, forbidden by the Twelve. The Dispatchers have also been known to retreat from the field of battle if fortune goes against them, a direct contradiction of the Twelve's commands.

No small number of Watchers despise what they perceive to be the cowardly tactics of the Dispatchers, and accuse the members of this offshoot order of turning their back on the Twelve and the Seven. Meanwhile, some Dispatchers disparage the members

of the Watch as "hidebound has-beens" who have failed to realize that the teachings of Azmarender can survive and flourish only by adapting to the realities of the current times. The resentment between some members of both branches runs so deep that, when they meet open hostilities sometimes follow, to the dismay of the people whom both orders are sworn to protect.

For reasons that are not clear to anyone, including the Knights, the leaders of both branches have pledged support for one another, and ordered their members to cooperate. To make matters even more bewildering to protector and protected alike, both branches of the order continue to share the same confusing hierarchy, and the same coat of arms. Individual members can be distinguished, however, by their behavior: Only a few moments of observation or conversation is necessary to determine whether one addresses a Watcher or a Dispatcher. The former acts and fights in a manner largely defined by his formal code of conduct, while the latter behaves in a much more casual fashion.

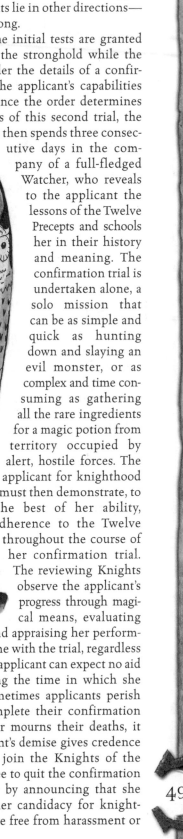

In order to join the Knights of the Watch, a candidate must apply in person at the stronghold of the Grandiose Imperial Wyvern. The ideal candidate hails from the Sheldomar Valley, but exceptions have been made, particularly in the wake of the wars that so sharply reduced the populations of many nations. An elite squad of Knights, hand-picked by the Grandiose Imperial Wyvern himself, examines and chooses candidates for admission into the order. The preliminary tests are exactly what one might expect from a martial order: feats of arms and tests of combat skill that pit the applicant against a variety of opponents. In former days, the Watchers tended to favor trials that focused solely on physical fighting skills, but today, they have relaxed slightly to allow for the fact that the best candidates for knighthood might bring other, non-martial, skills to the order that may prove equally useful. Thus, the order has concocted some preliminary trials that allow applicants whose primary talents lie in other directions—stealth, magic, and even song.

Applicants who pass the initial tests are granted permission to remain at the stronghold while the reviewing knights consider the details of a confirmation trial that befits the applicant's capabilities and promise. Once the order determines the details of this second trial, the applicant then spends three consecutive days in the company of a full-fledged Watcher, who reveals to the applicant the lessons of the Twelve Precepts and schools her in their history and meaning. The confirmation trial is undertaken alone, a solo mission that can be as simple and quick as hunting down and slaying an evil monster, or as complex and time consuming as gathering all the rare ingredients for a magic potion from territory occupied by alert, hostile forces. The applicant for knighthood must then demonstrate, to the best of her ability, adherence to the Twelve throughout the course of her confirmation trial. The reviewing Knights observe the applicant's progress through magical means, evaluating and appraising her performance. They do not intervene with the trial, regardless of the circumstances. The applicant can expect no aid from the Watchers during the time in which she undertakes this test. Sometimes applicants perish while attempting to complete their confirmation trial, and while the order mourns their deaths, it maintains that an applicant's demise gives credence to her unworthiness to join the Knights of the Watch. An applicant is free to quit the confirmation trial at any time, simply by announcing that she relents and withdraws her candidacy for knighthood. Those who do so are free from harassment or scorn from the Watchers—not everyone is destined for knighthood, after all—but they are never permitted to apply a second time.

The Ravagers

"Your pleas for mercy only make me more angry."

Fortunately for the more civilized areas of the world, the total number of individual Ravagers, a tight-knit group of deadly marauders, remains relatively small, numbering perhaps one hundred at most. However, these unrepentant slayers make up in sheer ferocity what they lack in numbers. Gathering in warbands from as few as three to as many as two dozen, they strike without warning, descending on unsuspecting towns, villages, and hamlets, and sometimes even upon isolated farmsteads or traveling caravans. Their violent depredations are made all the more horrible by the fact that their principle motives seem to be maiming and killing, rather than theft or kidnapping or some other more understandable (if detestable) reason.

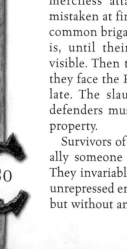

The Ravagers visit upon their unfortunate targets a whirlwind of death and destruction that apparently lacks any identifiable rationale. Their merciless attacks are often mistaken at first for the work of common brigands or bandits—that is, until their distinctive facial tattoos are visible. Then their disheartened victims know that they face the Ravagers, but by then, it is already too late. The slaughter has already started, and the defenders must look to their lives as well as their property.

Survivors of Ravager attacks are few, but occasionally someone escapes, usually through sheer luck. They invariably report that the slayers attacked with unrepressed enthusiasm that borders on sadistic glee, but without any other sign of what prompts them to undertake such wholesale slaughter. A few survivors claimed that their communities attempted to surrender to the marauders, only to have their overtures completely ignored. The Ravagers are said by survivors to depart from the scene of their crimes as rapidly as they arrived, leaving death, despair, and devastation in their wake. Indeed, some speculate that the spread of terror itself might be the Ravagers' chief objective, for as like as not their warbands leave behind any treasures or valuables that might have been theirs for the taking.

Who are the Ravagers? That question always passes the lips of their surviving victims, and lies uppermost in the minds of many a noble or monarch whose lands have suffered their depredations. If any have the answer to this pressing question, or indeed any detailed knowledge of these killers, they are not talking. (And if they did, the very slayers whose secrets they revealed might well silence them quickly.)

The Ravagers make a point of trusting no one outside their own warbands, and it is thought that, given the nature of their deeds, trust between individual Ravagers exists but rarely. What little is known of the Ravagers has yet to save a single community from their murderous intentions. Some good folk and rulers have considered attempting to infiltrate their ranks, but they admit that such a plan remains unlikely to succeed until something more is known about the group's motives and whereabouts. Certainly any attempt to spy on the Ravagers from within their number would be hazardous in the extreme to the agents who try it, but some might consider the risk worth the danger if the loss of life this group inflicts could somehow be reduced or eliminated. Certainly, the reward for doing so would be nothing less than spectacular.

Some say that the men and women who join the Ravagers do so because they no longer revere life, and this speculation is true, as far as it goes. Hatred, malice, and bitterness toward all other folk indeed seem to be the core of the Ravager's beliefs and behaviors, but underlying reasons for this truth are even more dire. The Ravagers are nothing less than an instrument of Erythnul, Deity of Slaughter, sometimes called "The Many." Some of the most thoroughly evil and foul acts the world has ever known can be laid squarely at the feet of the Ravagers, all perpetrated to further Erythnul's despicable ethos. Among their number are found some of the most irredeemable and vile persons ever to walk free under the sun. Soldiers who betrayed their country and oaths for profit, kidnappers who murdered their victims though the ransom was paid in full, mass murderers whose crimes are too heinous to mention; these the Ravagers accept into their warbands eagerly, for they are the ideal candidates to carry Erythnul's message of chaos and destruction into the world. The Ravagers serve their master by fostering panic, malice, and ugliness wherever they go. They attack random targets, killing, maiming, looting, and destroying at random, leaving behind as much chaos and horror as they can. Only the Ravagers know of any purpose behind their terrible acts of malignant aggression.

Since they would be hunted down and attacked at once if they exposed themselves freely, the Ravagers do not maintain a central base of operations. Indeed, most places of worship dedicated to Erythnul are hidden for the same reason. Communities of larger size sometimes have a small cult of his followers hidden somewhere in the rougher parts of town, and occasionally these places function as safe havens for a Ravager warband, but such permanent locales are rare.

The warbands usually lead a semi-nomadic existence, establishing more or less permanent encampments hidden away in the wilderness and other remote areas, from which they plan their savage raids. They occasionally enter towns and cities in which they know a secret temple dedicated to Erythnul can be found, but they do so clandestinely, lest they be recognized and attacked for the murderous rogues that they are. On these occasions, the Ravagers often receive supplies and equipment from the local clergy, and sometimes the clerics give them special assignments that single out persons or places that The Many would grant his very personal attention. Those who are unfortunate enough to come across a Ravager encampment usually meet the same fate as the Ravagers' intended victims: The Deity of Slaughter plays no favorites, and neither do his instruments.

This life of secrecy, skulking in the backcountry and maintaining a low profile, makes locating the Ravagers difficult not only for their would-be opponents, but also for those who might seek to join them. Finding the Ravagers and living long enough to make one's intention to join them clear are two very different enterprises, and the small total number of the organization serves as testimony to the difficulty of both tasks. Though some folk whisper of Ravager warbands that function as press gangs, kidnapping new recruits from remote villages or stealing young children from their beds to raise as new members, these rumors are unfounded. The Ravagers have no need of resorting to such extreme measures in order to secure new recruits. The sad fact is that the Ravagers know that the infamy of their deeds inevitably attract those like-minded individuals for whom the deeds of the Ravagers seem an appealing way of life.

When a prospective member approaches a warband and makes his intention known, the Ravagers' standard tactic involves attacking him *en masse*. If the newcomer holds his own for a predetermined period of time (usually between 3 and 10 rounds, depending on the size of the warband and the relative ruthlessness of the leader), he earns a shot at becoming a Ravager; otherwise, he earns only a shallow grave. The warband then chooses one of its own at random to meet the applicant in single combat, no holds barred with the exception of spell casting, for they firmly believe that any Ravager should be able to win a place through force of arms alone. If the newcomer wins—the fight is always to the death— he is accepted as a potential Ravager and subjected to the final segment of his initiation: The Fire Sacrifice. (Members

Red Avengers in Your Game

At first glance, it may seem like the DM who wishes to include the Red or White clan in the campaign has no choice but to include the other as well. Either clan *can* be incorporated into your game without the other. In the case of the Red Avengers, simply exchange the clan's rivalry with the White clan for an organization, person, or creature that meshes more comfortably with your plans. For example, you could choose to make a particular city, nation, or race the focus of the Red Avenger's hatred. Maybe the organization lives to destroy every last descendent of a dwarf king who double-crossed them centuries ago. Perhaps the Red Avengers' secrets were stolen recently by a particular thieves' guild or cabal of sorcerers, and the clan will not rest until it recovers their lost property and punishes the thieves in an appropriately gruesome and final fashion. The Red Avenger clan could even have a rivalry with another prestige class that you prefer over the White clan, such as the arcane archers, the loremasters, the Ravagers, or the Fists of Hextor. Simply determine the exact nature of the enmity between the two groups, make the appropriate changes, and have fun.

Vendettas in the Game

The thirst for revenge can be a strong component of an exciting story and an interesting character. Vendettas also create problems in your game if allowed to run free, without adequate supervision. An eternal thirst for vengeance can, for example, make it difficult to find adequate and believable reasons for the vengeful character to join or cooperate with the rest of the adventurers. Consider the questions raised by integrating a Red Avenger character into an existing party of adventurers, none of whom are engaged in anything even remotely connected to the object of the Red Avenger's hatred. Why should the Red Avenger join this group of adventurers? What does she gain by accompanying them? Why does she not do something that supports her clan's ultimate goal?

Fortunately, the Red Avenger's presence in a party of adventurers can be easily rationalized. Perhaps the party engages in activities (such as fighting monsters in the depths of the earth) that make the Red Avenger stronger and more skilled if she participates and survives, and thus better able to contribute to her clan's chief goal. Maybe the party plans to go after a particular treasure that would be very useful to the Red Avengers in their quest to wipe out their rivals: The Red Avenger character could participate in the adventure in order to try to acquire the item, or to convince the party to help the Red Avengers in their cause.

losing the combat to an initiate who fought according the ravagers' code are resurrected by Erthynul.)

While the candidate waits on his knees, praying to Erythnul to fill his heart with hate and malice, other members of the warband acquire a suitable sacrificial victim (preferably human, but in a pinch an elf, dwarf, halfling or gnome will do). The would-be Ravager must sacrifice the victim in accordance with the unholy rites of Erythnul, which involve blood-letting followed by burning the sacrifice alive. Following this cruel and horrific act, the warband applies a distinctively repulsive set of tattoos to the applicant's face, which forever marks him as a Ravager. Once the ceremony is complete, the only escape is in death.

Note: To join the Ravagers means leaving behind all that is good and decent. No redeeming features of this organization or its members exist. Those who seek to join their number should be prepared to participate fully in their divine mission of wanton malice, or face destruction at the hands of their fellows. The Ravagers work best in a campaign not adversely affected by an atmosphere that is more grim, perhaps even oppressive, than the norm, as the inclusion and presence of the Ravagers may lead to just such conditions.

DMs should feel free to make the Ravager initiation ceremony as morally and ethically repulsive and physically arduous as her imagination (and her playing group's shared sense of good taste) allows.

The Red Avengers
"We live only for vengeance."

The Red Avengers exist for one reason only: vengeance. Clan lore tells of a grievous wrong suffered long ago at the hands of its archrivals, the White clan. The dishonor and outrage engendered by this wrong has festered deep in the soul of the Red Avenger clan ever since the White clan stole the secret knowledge of *ki* powers from the Red. Each member of the clan should take up this burden and shoulder it for as long as she lives, directing her best efforts and energies toward undermining and eradicating the White clan.

The Red Avengers' history claims that the clan discovered the existence of *ki* centuries ago, and has been working to perfect its understanding of the power ever since. The Red Avengers believe that *ki* is energy possessed by all living creatures. Much of the Red Avenger's training revolves around understanding and learning to focus *ki*, and the effects she produces as she improves her mastery of this discipline are increasingly impressive. Red Avengers receive most of their training and indoctrination in small, well-hidden temples located both in populated and desolate areas. The main temple is located in the depths of a dense forest.

The details, history, and (perhaps different) *ki* powers of the White clan are left to each campaign.

Most Red Avengers are born rather than made: Almost all the Red Avengers are related by blood and claim the ties of kinship with one another. Some family members are exposed to the study of *ki* energies at an early age, especially if they demonstrate some natural affinity for the power. Others are not introduced to this discipline until they come of age. Some are never brought into this circle of education at all, but are expected to fulfill other roles and duties the clan requires in order to support itself.

There have been rare instances of the clan accepting outsiders into its *ki* training, but this normally occurs only when the individual renders some great service to the Red Avengers. The fortunate few who are granted this honor are expected to use their newfound abilities to aid the Red Avengers in exacting their revenge on their enemies, in essence becoming a member of the clan. Those who abuse their training or use it for purposes not in accordance with the clan's designs find themselves the target of a very personalized vendetta.

CHAPTER 4: THE GAME WITHIN THE GAME

In this chapter, we present several ways in which both players and DMs can take advantage of the rules of the game during play. The advice and additional rules herein expand and clarify many aspects of choices and their ramifications during the game.

BEING ALL YOU CAN BE

"Most battles are won before a single blow lands. Your wits are your greatest weapon."

—Ember

One of the great things about the DUNGEONS & DRAGONS game remains its versatility. Have you ever wished that there were more character classes, so that you can play exactly the type of fighter or monk you want? Maybe you want to play a fighter who earns his gold through piracy rather than dungeon looting, or a monk who raids desert caravans rather than hangs about the monastery. You can customize your character, without the necessity of creating a new character class, through ability-score prioritization, and the careful selection of skills and feats. Some of the roles discussed below share names or concepts with some of the prestige classes presented in Chapter 2. The information and choices below offer another avenue of advancement, for those who just cannot wait for their character to qualify for the class in question.

Duelist

Perhaps seeking your fortune in lightless dungeons and battling dragons with your battleaxe just is not your cup of tea. Maybe you would rather swing from chandeliers, fight Florentine-style, and trade witty banter with your comrades in a more sophisticated setting. How to create such a hero? Read on.

Adventuring Role

The duelist's wit is as ready as his blade, particularly when he adventures on his home ground. Duelists often find themselves at the forefront of the party's activities, and sometimes even as the party's spokesperson. His devil-may-care style can be both an asset and hindrance to his companions, depending on the situation, but little doubt exists that his charm and skill with a blade makes him a valuable ally when the party leaves the dungeon for the big city.

Ability Scores

Your best friend is your Dexterity score. Duelists usually prefer to sacrifice some protection for more speed, so you need to be fast on the attack and quick on the defensive. When you cannot avoid the enemy's blows, a good Constitution score keeps you alive longer. Since your charm and wit may make the difference between getting into the king's court and being tossed into the castle dungeon, a good Charisma score is the hallmark of any self-respecting duelist.

Skills and Feats

The duelist is most at home in the big city, but that does not mean his comrades do not require his aid when they venture off into a wilderness or dungeon setting. So a duelist needs a good mix of skills he can call on whether he flatters the ladies-in-waiting or fights off an owlbear.

Skills

Balance (Dex), Bluff (Cha), Climb (Str), Diplomacy (Cha), Innuendo (Cha), Jump (Str), Knowledge (Int), Ride (Wis), Tumble (Dex).

Feats

Ambidexterity, Blind-Fight, Combat Reflexes, Dodge, Mobility, Spring Attack, Expertise, Improved Disarm, Improved Trip, Improved Initiative, Lightning Reflexes, Off-Hand Parry, Quick Draw, Weapon Finesse.

Warrior Monks of Shao Lin

The legendary fighting monks of antiquity were famous both for their martial prowess and dedication to the search for inner peace and cosmic awareness. Though they dwelled in secluded monasteries, these monks did not disdain the outside world, as did many other ecclesiastical orders: They followed political and social developments with interest, and involved themselves when and where it suited their best interests.

Adventuring Role

Warrior monks do not generally leave the safety of their monasteries unless some great need demands their presence in the world, nor do they customarily travel alone. When circumstances demand that a warrior monk travels singly, she frequently dons a disguise and conceals her identity and profession. Hence, a warrior monk found among an adventuring party may be present under false pretenses, and helps or hinders the party according to her temple's instructions.

Ability Scores

Like the standard representative of this class, a warrior monk relies heavily on her Wisdom and Dexterity scores. A good Charisma score is also useful, since the warrior monk often relies on deception to achieve her goals.

Skills and Feats

A warrior monk should possess skills that enable her to carry out her temple's instructions while avoiding unwanted attention.

Skills

Balance (Dex), Bluff (Cha), Craft (any) (Int), Decipher Script (Int), Diplomacy (Cha), Disguise (Cha), Gather Information (Cha), Heal (Wis), Jump (Str), Knowledge (any), Listen (Wis), Move Silently (Dex), Search (Int), Sense Motive (Wis), Spot (Wis), Tumble (Dex), Wilderness Lore (Wis).

Feats

Alertness, Ambidexterity, Blind-Fight, Circle Kick, Dodge, Extra Stunning Attacks, Lightning Fists, Mantis Leap, Mobility, Pain Touch, Spring Attack, Endurance, Expertise, Improved Disarm, Improved Trip, Whirlwind Attack, Improved Unarmed Strike, Deflect Arrows, Snatch Arrows, Skill Focus, Two-Weapon Fighting.

Gladiator

You live to fight, and fight to live. Maybe you love the roar of the crowd and the public acclaim, or maybe you do it for the money. Maybe you relish testing your strength and courage in a continual life-or-death struggle . . . or perhaps you are a slave, forced to fight for the amusement of others until you can find a way to win your freedom. Whatever the reason, you are a professional warrior who pits his body and his skills against a host of foes while others look on, cheering for your victory or your demise.

Adventuring Role

The gladiator exists in a society that places some value on public combat, whether purely for sport or as a means of disposing of unwanted individuals. The gladiator who joins an adventuring party often does so for one of two reasons. He is a free man who fights in the arena for money and fame, and who is thus able to do as he pleases in his free time. Otherwise, he could be an escaped gladiatorial slave. Regardless of his motivation, the gladiator's role in the adventuring party always remains fighting: He is usually in the forefront of any melee, and uses the skills and tricks he learned in the arena to contribute to his companions' victory.

Ability Scores

As is true for most combatants who spend most of their time in melee, face-to-face and hand-to-hand with the enemy, good Dexterity and Constitution scores help ensure survival. Gladiatorial combat often relies on dealing out punishment, even the battles are not to the death. As a result, a high Strength score helps the warrior put down his oppo-nent more quickly by adding to both his melee attack and damage rolls.

Skills and Feats

Choose skills that will enhance your fighting prowess and help keep you alive, especially when you face multiple foes in the arena.

Skills

Animal Empathy (Cha), Balance (Dex), Escape Artist (Dex), Intimidate (Cha), Open Lock (Dex), Tumble (Dex).

Feats

Ambidexterity, Blind-Fight, Blindsight 5-foot Radius, Cleave, Dodge, Endurance, Improved Critical, Improved Unarmed Strike, Pin Shield, Power Attack, Shield Expert, Toughness, Two-Weapon Fighting, Improved Two-Weapon Fighting, Weapon Focus.

Pirate

Not all adventurers make their way in the world by sacking dungeons. Some sack ships and island fortresses instead! Pirates are the scourge of trade routes on the high seas, lakes, and even large rivers of the campaign world.

Adventuring Role

Pirates are outlaws. They live by means that almost all civilized nations consider illegal, and they are motivated by a strong desire for personal freedom as often as they are motivated by greed. Hence, the pirate is a wanted and villainous criminal to some, and a freedom-loving hero to others.

Ability Scores

You need to be strong and tough to survive the life of the seafaring buccaneer, so give priority to Strength and Constitution scores. Your Dexterity score also deserves attention, as wearing any heavy armor in this line of work tends to lead only to drowning.

Skills and Feats

Pirates are most at home aboard ship, so you want to select skills that give you the advantage when at sea.

Skills

Balance (Dex), Climb (Str), Craft (shipbuilding) (Int), Intimidate (Cha), Intuit Direction (Wis), Knowledge (boating, cartography, geography, navigation, sea lore) (Int), Profession (carpenter, fisherman, shipwright) (Int), Spot (Wis), Swim (Str), Use Rope (Dex).

Feats

Ambidexterity, Cleave, Combat Reflexes, Dodge, Endurance, Improved Two-Weapon Fighting, Improved Unarmed Fighting, Mobility, Off-Hand Parry, Power Attack, Spring Attack, Toughness, Weapon Focus, Two-Weapon Fighting.

Desert Raider

A semi-nomadic warrior, you survive in a dangerous environment: the desert wastes. Your first duty is to defend your people against the many dangers that infest this unforgiving place, including rival tribes and horrific monsters. You do what you must in order to survive, and that includes raiding the encampments of other tribes that inhabit the desert, as well as those oasis towns that offer the richest prize of all: water.

Adventuring Role

In your home environment, you sometimes act as guide and guardian for those individuals or groups who have earned your favor, whether through coin or friendship. When outside of your element, you present an exotic and sometimes menacing figure as you cope with the strange customs of other cultures. In either situation, you remain a deadly opponent.

Ability Scores

Wisdom should be your first priority, since the foolish perish quickly in the harsh desert wastes. As heavy

WAT. 2000

armor kills in the desert far more readily than it saves, a high Dexterity score benefits the raider.

Skills and Feats

In such a harsh environment, skills are paramount to your continued survival. Choose wisely, as your life may well depend upon your choices.

Skills

Animal Empathy (Cha), Climb (Str), Craft (Int), Handle Animal (Cha), Hide (Dex), Intuit Direction (Wis), Knowledge (Int), Listen (Wis), Ride (Dex), Spot (Wis), Wilderness Lore (Wis).

Feats

Alertness, Blind-Fight, Cleave, Endurance, Mounted Combat, Mounted Archery, Trample, Ride-By Attack, Spirited Charge, Power Attack, Track, Weapon Focus.

ADVANCEMENT: WISE CHOICES

You just gained enough experience points to make the transition from 2nd to 3rd level, and so you prepare to choose a new feat! Which one should you choose? Ask yourself these questions before you make your decision:

What do I want to do in the future?
What have I already done?

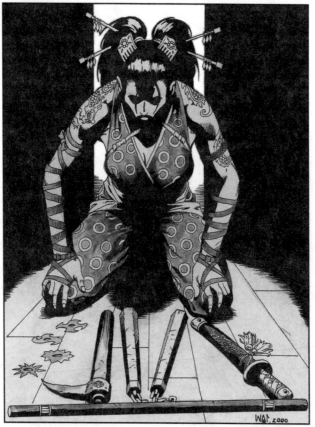

Are you on the road to qualifying for a prestige class? If so, that should be your guiding philosophy as you acquire new feats. Consider this example:

Character: 2nd-level half-elf fighter.
Goal: Blackguard prestige class.
Current feats: Improved Initiative, Power Attack, Cleave.

The logical choice for the character's next feat is Sunder, as taking it fulfills all the feat requirements to qualify for the prestige class.

Now assume you instead wish to one day qualify for the cavalier prestige class from this very book (see page 12). Let us see what represents the wisest choice here.

Character: 2nd-level half-elf fighter.
Goal: Cavalier prestige class.
Current feats: Blind-fight, Dodge, Mounted Combat.

One of the prerequisites for the cavalier class is the Spirited Charge feat. You note that in addition to the Mounted Combat feat, you also need the Ride-by Attack feat. Foresight pays off for you as you take the Ride-by Attack feat now, so you can get the Spirited Charge feat when you reach 4th level.

HOW TO FIGHT NEARLY EVERYTHING (AND SURVIVE)

"Discretion is the better part of valor—except when the lives of your comrades are on the line."

—Ember

Opponents with Reach

The very best advice for fighting opponents with reach bears repeating: Stay out of reach! However, employing other strategies also works.

- Attack with ranged weapons. Hit these opponents with arrows, bolts, spears, and spells from a distance.
- Make use of feats such as Mobility, which grant you a bonus to your Armor Class when you are exposed to attacks of opportunity. You have a better chance of standing up to an opponent with reach if you minimize his advantage in this way.
- Send in a character with Mobility and a good Armor Class, and while he is taking the heat from the enemy with reach, send another character around to flank (or better yet, sneak attack) the enemy with reach.
- Take to the air any way you can and rain down attacks from overhead, remaining safely out of reach.

Undead Opponents

When dealing with undead creatures, forewarned truly is forearmed. If you know you face undead opponents ahead of time, do not stray too far from your cleric, otherwise you may wish you had taken a few levels in that class yourself. When journeying through undead-infested areas, make sure that the cleric is ready to make a turning attempt at the appropriate time. This means protecting him when battling other enemies, so that he does not incur injuries that might affect his combat ability when you meet up with the undead. Do not begrudge the cleric who uses some of her precious healing on herself before battle with undead. If the cleric falls in combat, the entire party faces their doom.

Once you have entered combat against these foes, remember that they do not share many of the weaknesses of living creatures. You cannot soften them up with sword and fist in preparation for the wizard's *sleep* spell—the undead are not susceptible to that spell. Worse, in addiction to inflicting normal damage, the touch of the undead often carries some unpleasant side effects—such as the ghoul's paralysis or the wight's energy drain. Touch attacks ignore most Armor Class bonuses, so do not think that suit of chainmail will protect you against a wraith!

Try employing ranged attacks against the undead whenever possible, in favor of closing for melee. You can buy yourself some time in this manner, and if you can take out any of these opponents at a distance before they get close enough to threaten you with their touch attacks, so much the better.

Flying Opponents

Your ability to combat opponents on the wing depends almost entirely on whether you, too, can fly. If not, you have your work cut out for you, and your best bet may be to find some cover and hit the airborne foe with ranged attacks and spells until it flees or dies.

If you do have the capability to become airborne yourself, you want to get aloft quickly and fight the opponent in the air. Remember, the fact that you are flying negates none of your customary attack forms: You can still charge and flank, even while flying. In fact, your flanking possibilities now involve all three dimensions.

Unbeatable Opponents

Sometimes you confront enemies that, try as you might, you just cannot beat. Unless you are playing in a campaign that was designed intentionally to permit some very strange circumstances, four 1st-level monks simply do not triumph over a trio of dire bears. Learning to identify fights you cannot win is a skill you should acquire early in your adventuring career, particularly if you want to enjoy a career that is both lengthy and successful.

This may seem like odd advice considering that heroism often necessitates refusing to surrender, even when faced with overwhelming odds. However, if you live by the sword without any compromise, you can expect to have a short and perhaps unimpressive stint as an adventurer. You are also going to irk your comrades when they acknowledge that a strategic withdrawal is sometimes more appropriate than slugging it out toe-to-toe with an enemy they cannot defeat. Particularly when you have a specific mission to accomplish, insisting on fighting every opponent to the death along the way does not help you achieve your goal.

If you think that a given encounter may be too difficult to overcome, weigh the potential risk of fighting against the potential gain of a victory. For example, let us say that your party is infiltrating the forest lair of a green dragon with the intent to slay it (and claim its treasure hoard). You know that the wyrm is somewhere in the forest, though you are uncertain about its exact location. Suddenly, a pair of hill giants emerges from the canopy of trees and stop to talk, blocking your route. Should you fight them?

The answer depends on what you stand to gain from the fight versus the risk involved.

Think about your party's condition and resources: Do you have the weapons, skills, feats, and equipment necessary to defeat these opponents? If the answer is "No," not only should you avoid the giants, but also you should not be out in the forest hunting for dragons in the first place.

Are you in good fighting trim, with plenty of hit points and healing magic at your disposal? The answer must be "Yes," if you hope to find and kill that dragon.

Is a fight against the giants likely to leave you with sufficient resources to still tackle the dragon? If not, you need to decide whether your original goal is more important than dealing with these new foes. Should you triumph over the giants at the expense of a significant portion of your hit points and magic, you must consider going after the dragon another day, after you have rested.

Do the hill giants appear to be carrying anything of value, and in particular, anything that might help you find or fight the dragon you know to be lurking hereabouts? If they do (maybe one of the giants is carrying a big club that you recognize as a +3 *club of dragon subdual*), determine whether the advantage of possessing that item is worth the damage the giants might inflict on you when you try to take it.

Do you have any reason to believe that, if defeated but not slain, the hill giants can offer you any useful information about your quarry? If so, it might be a good idea to attack them, but also to attempt to subdue or capture, rather than kill, at least one of them.

TACTICS

The *Player's Handbook* and DUNGEON MASTER's *Guide* both do a great job of explaining the facts of combat, but both books are so full of information that numerous examples of the rules just did not fit. So, we are taking this opportunity to include some combat-related examples.

Using Cleave

Before deciding whether to take the standard attack action or the full attack action, make sure that you place your character in the position that is most favorable for any heroic feats or skills that you might want to use. Example:

Tordek, a 15th-level fighter with both the Power Attack and Cleave feats, is fighting a pair of fire giants. Tordek begins his action this round in the following position (each square=5 feet):

		G1
G2		
		T

During his action Tordek, relishing the thought of using the full attack action against Giant #1, moves in and attacks. If he wants to take the full attack action, he can only move 5 feet on his action (before, during or after attacking) so he moves in front of Giant #1 like so:

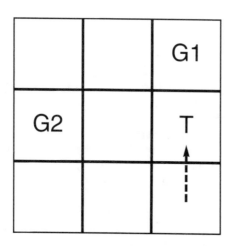

What is wrong with this picture? Tordek made a mistake: He moved in such a way that he cannot take advantage of all the benefits that the full attack action and the Cleave feat offer him. He threatens only Giant #1 from this position, and if he manages to drop his target, he cannot use Cleave against Giant #2. (Cleave prohibits you from making a 5-foot adjustment before using it to attack!)

Instead, Tordek should move so that he ends his action in this position:

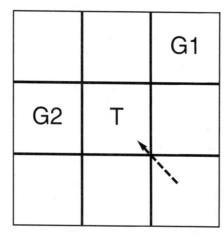

From this position, Tordek threatens both Giant #1 and Giant #2, and he can take total advantage of the full attack action and Cleave. Look at the advantages gained this situation against only the threat of being hit one additional time.

- Tordek does not need to specify the targets before he makes his attacks.

- He can delay the decision about whether to take the full attack action until he makes his first attack of the round.
- If he does not drop giant #1 with his first attack, he can take the full attack action and gain two more iterative attacks.
- If he drops Giant #1, he can use Cleave to attack Giant #2 as noted earlier.

The Benefit of Reach: The ogre (with a 10-foot reach) can strike at Mialee, but she cannot strike back because she only has a reach of 5 feet. And if she uses her bow, she provokes an attack of opportunity. So Mialee is in big trouble . . .

. . . and the ogre makes it worse by making a 5-foot adjustment to be closer to Mialee. Now Mialee cannot withdraw without provoking an attack of opportunity; withdrawing only gives you a "free pass" out of the first square along your withdrawal path and the ogre still has that 10-foot reach. Whether Mialee goes north or southwest, she has to leave a square threatened by the ogre. This ogre is pretty clever—if it had made its 5-foot adjustment northwest rather than due west, Mialee could have escaped to the north because the ogre cannot make attacks of opportunity against opponents with one-half or better cover (which the corner provides).

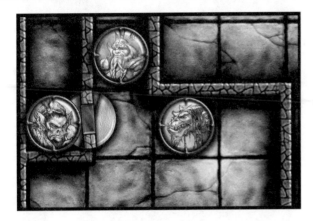

Fighting around corners: Corners provide one-half cover if you are fighting around them, and three-quarters cover if you are just peeking. Tordek gains a +4 cover bonus to AC against the ogre, and the ogre gets the same bonus against attacks from Tordek. If the goblin behind the door just opens it to see what the commotion is, it gets a +7 AC bonus against attacks from Tordek. If it opens the door and throws a javelin, though, it only gets a +4 AC bonus, and Tordek gets a +4 AC bonus against the javelin attack. Tordek does not get an attack of opportunity against the goblin, because the cover makes the goblin immune to attacks of opportunity.

Flanking: Tordek and Lidda both get +2 flanking bonuses to their attacks against the ogre because they are exactly opposite each other. Furthermore, Lidda gets to make a sneak attack against the ogre every round. If the ogre takes a move action to get out of the way, he provokes an attack of opportunity from at least one of the adventurers (and maybe both of them). But the ogre can make a 5-foot adjustment without provoking attacks of opportunity—and it can make all its iterative attacks if it does so. If it moves due north, Tordek and Lidda can keep up the flanking attacks by shifting one square north themselves. If the ogre moves northwest, south, or southeast, it temporarily prevents the flanking attacks, because it takes Tordek at least 2 rounds to reestablish the flanking with their own 5-foot adjustments. But if the ogre adjusts northeast, it

becomes immune to further flanking effects as long as it stays put. Sometimes it is good to have your back against the wall.

DOING THE MATH

Just when is it a good idea for a monk to unleash her flurry of blows? When is a *+2 weapon* better than *a +1 keen weapon*? Well, have no fear; we have done the math for you here.

To Flurry or Not

When a monk uses her flurry of blows, she gains an extra attack at the cost of accepting a −2 penalty on each attack. Generally, the flurry is a good idea against enemies that are easy to hit and a bad idea against those that are hard to hit. The following table summarizes how many hits you can expect in a round if you use the flurry and if you do not, depending on what you need to roll on the d20 to score a hit (with your first, best attack) and on the number of attacks you'd get without the flurry.

For example, at 6th level Ember gets two unarmed attacks per round at +7 and +4. If she flurries, she gets three attacks at +5, +5, and +2. If she is attacking a bugbear with AC 17, then the player needs to roll a 10 on the d20 to hit with her first attack. If Ember does not use the flurry of blows, her player should expect to get .95 hits per round. He first attack has a 55% chance to hit and her second attack has a 40% chance to hit. If

TABLE 4–1: EXPECTED HITS PER ROUND WITH FLURRY

Number of Normal Attacks	Natural Roll Needed to Hit			
	5+ (80%)	10+ (55%)	15+ (30%)	18+ (15%)
One attack	.8	55	.3	.15
One attack + flurry	1.4 (.7+.7)	.9 (.45+.45)	.4 (.2+.2)	.1 (.05+.05)
Two attacks	1.45 (.8+.65)	.95 (.55+.4)	.45 (.3+.15)	.2 (.15+.05)
Two attacks + flurry	1.95 (.7+.7+.55)	1.2 (.45+.45+.3)	.45 (.2+.2+.05)	.15 (.05+.05+.05)
Three attacks	1.95 (.8+.65+.5)	1.2 (.55+.4+.25)	.5 (.3+.15+.05)	.25 (.15+.05+.05)
Three attacks + flurry	2.35 (.7+.7+.55+.4)	1.35 (.45+.45+.3+.15)	.5 (.2+.2+.05+.05)	.2 (.05+.05+.05+.05)
Four attacks	2.3 (.8+.65+.5+.35)	1.3 (.55+.4+.25+.1)	.55 (.3+.15+.05+.o5)	.3 (.15+.05+.05+.05)
Four attacks + flurry	2.6 (.7+.7+.55+.4+.25)	1.4 (.45+.45+.3+.15+.05)	.55 (.2+.2+.05+.05+.05)	.25 (.05+.05+.05+.05+.05)
Five attacks	2.5 (.8+.65+.5+.35+.2)	1.35 (.55+.4+.25+.1+.05)	.6 (.3+.15+.05+.o5+.05)	.35 (.15+.05+.05+.05+.05)
Five attacks + flurry	2.7 (.7+.7+.55+.4+.25+.1)	1.45 (.45+.45+.3+.15+.05+.05)	.6 (.2+.2+.05+.05+.05+.05)	.3 (.05+.05+.05+.05+.05+.05)

she uses the flurry of blows, each hit has a smaller chance to succeed, but the player can expect, on average to get more than one hit per round (1.2 hits, actually). When fighting a ravid (AC 25), it does not pay for Ember to use the flurry of blows. If she did, each of her attacks would succeed only on a 20.

TABLE 4–2: MAGIC WEAPON ABILITIES

Weapon	Armor Class of Target		
	20	26	32
+2 axe			
# of hits	.95 + .70	.65 + .40	.35 + .10
Damage	15.95	15.95	15.95
Mean	26.3	16.7	7.2
+1 keen axe			
# of hits	.90 + .65	.60 + .35	.30 + .05
Damage	16.2	16.2	16.2
Mean	25.1	15.4	5.7
+1 energized axe*			
# of hits	.90 + .65	.60 + .35	.30 + .05
Damage	18.35	18.35	18.35
Mean	28.4	17.4	6.4

*Flaming, frost, or shock.

# of hits: On average, how many hits the Tordek scores per full round of combat, represented as the chance that the first attack hits plus the chance that the second attack hits.

Damage: On average, the amount of damage that Tordek deals per hit. Extra damage from critical hits is figured into this number.

Mean: The mean damage that Tordek deals per full round of combat.

Magic Weapon Abilities

The magic weapon abilities of flaming (+1d6 points of fire damage), frost (+1d6 points of frost damage), keen (double threat range), and shock (+1d6 points of electricity damage) are all rated in cost as if they were an additional +1 on the weapon's enhancement bonus (see the DUNGEON MASTER's *Guide*). Depending on a character's chance to hit the target and the damage that character deals, each of these abilities can be better or worse than an additional +1 on a weapon's enhancement bonus.

The following table shows how these abilities affect mean (average) damage per attack for a particular character. In this case, assume that the weapon is a dwarven waraxe wielded by Tordek at 10th level. He has a Strength of 21 (including his +4 enhancement bonus from a *belt of giant strength*), and he has both Weapon Focus and Weapon Specialization with the dwarven waraxe. His attack bonus is +16/+11 + the weapon's enhancement bonus. His damage is 1d10+7 + bonus damage from the weapon.

In terms of mean damage, the keen axe is inferior to the others, but different weapons in the hands of different characters benefit more or less from being keen. In general, the more damage a weapon deals, the larger its original threat range, and the larger its critical damage multiplier, the more it benefits from being keen. Just because it does not pay off for Tordek does not mean it works for no one. In addition, the keen ability increases a combatant's chance to deal lots of damage with a single blow.

MONSTROUS FIGHTERS AND MONKS

A bugbear stands guard at the entrance to an evil monastery. Dismissing the creature as a minimal threat, the experienced adventurers rush the gate. Before they are fully aware of what transpires, the bugbear erupts into a flurry of unarmed attacks, striking with the deadly accuracy of a high-level monk. "WHAT?", shout the players.

Why not? Bugbears have above-average Strength and Dexterity scores, and their Wisdom is no worse than human average. If their culture were more ordered and stable, bugbears would make excellent monks. Nevertheless, a savage society does not prevent an occasional bugbear—or a gnoll, minotaur, or even an ogre mage—from being trained in the path of the monk. Some of these monsters excel at this discipline.

Fighters are even more common among monstrous kinds, though Warriors (an NPC detailed in the DUNGEON MASTER's *Guide*) and Barbarians are the likely choices for the military-minded among them. Still, an orc who puts aside his savage nature to study the maneuvers and tactics of the expert fighter is not to be discounted. His brute strength, combined with a fighter's access to feats, makes him a deadly foe.

The ability and feats of a fighter or the unarmed attacks and special abilities of a monk can transform a monster—particularly one with high natural Strength and Constitution scores—into a combat nightmare. An exceptional minotaur can have a Strength score as high as 26, making the Power Attack feat particularly effective. An ogre mage monk, adding spell-like abilities such as *levitation* and *gaseous form* to the monk's already impressive repertoire of abilities, becomes a fearsome opponent with devastating unarmed attacks. Some of the characteristics that make monsters exceptional fighters or monks include large size, extra limbs, flight, and natural weapons.

Large Monsters

Large creatures enjoy several advantages over smaller opponents, including reach, increased damage potential, and bonuses to special maneuvers.

Reach is the wonderful ability possessed by creatures that are larger than Medium-size (and Medium-size creatures wielding

---

Large and in Charge
[General]

You can prevent opponents from closing inside your reach.

Prerequisites: Reach (Large size or larger), Str 17+.

Benefit: When you make a successful attack of opportunity against an opponent who is moving inside your threatened area, you can force the opponent back to the square he was in before he provoked the attack. After you hit with your attack of opportunity, make an opposed Strength check against your opponent. You gain a +4 bonus for each size category larger than your opponent you are, and an additional +1 bonus for every 5 points of damage you dealt with your attack of opportunity. If you win the opposed check, your opponent is pushed back 5 feet into the square he just left.

certain Large-size weapons) to threaten opponents who do not threaten you. A monster with a reach of ten feet threatens everybody within 10 feet. This means that when Medium-size fighters charge that monster, they suffer attacks of opportunity when trying to close in, unless they do it carefully. (A 5-foot adjustment never provokes an attack of opportunity, so a Medium-size creature can move into the monster's threatened area, then adjust and attack in the next round—unless the monster moves away first.) No matter what, having reach means you get to bash your enemies before they get close enough to bash you.

Skilled fighters of Large-size or greater learn ways to take advantage of their natural reach. One such way is the Large and In Charge feat (described below). With this feat, an oversized fighter can present a nasty surprise to opponents who decide to risk an attack of opportunity in order to close. If the oversized fighter's Large and In Charge attack is successful, the opponent remains within the fighter's reach, but cannot reach the fighter to attack.

An ogre's longsword is not the same as a human's longsword. A weapon's damage increases with its size, in the same way a monster's damage from its natural attacks does. To calculate the damage a larger-than-normal weapon deals, first determine how many size categories it is increasing. A longsword (normally Medium size, commonly used by Medium-size beings) in the hand of a Huge cloud giant increases two size categories. For each category increase, consult the following table (reproduced from the *Monster Manual*), finding the weapon's original damage in the left column and reading the new damage from the right column.

TABLE 4-3: WEAPON DAMAGE BY SIZE

Old Damage (each)	New Damage
1d2	1d3
1d3	1d4
1d4	1d6
1d6	1d8
1d8 or 1d10	2d6
1d12	2d8

For example: An ordinary Medium-size bastard sword deals 1d10 damage. The first size increase (a Large bastard sword) brings the damage to 2d6. The second increase (making it Huge) transforms *each* 1d6 into 1d8, for a damage of 2d8. After the cloud giant's +12 Strength adjustment, adding a +2 bonus for Weapon Specialization from the fighter class is just adding insult to injury.

A monk's unarmed attack damage also increases with greater creature size. Unarmed damage for

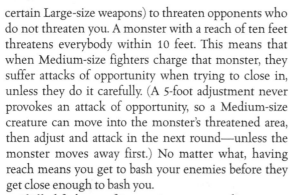

Multitasking [General]

You can perform different tasks with different limbs.

Prerequisite: Multiattack feat, Dex 15+, Int 13+, Improved Two-Weapon Fighting, Two-Weapon Fighting.

Benefit: If you have four or more arms, you can use each pair of arms to perform a distinct partial action. Thus, you could attack with one or two arms while using a magic item, reloading a crossbow, or even casting a spell with two other arms.

monks of unusual size is summarized on the table below. Small monks deal damage as shown on table 3–11 in the *Player's Handbook*.

TABLE 4-4: MONK DAMAGE BY SIZE

Level	Tiny	Large	Huge	Gargantuan	Colossal
1–3	1d3	1d8	1d10	1d12	2d8
4–7	1d4	1d10	1d12	2d8	2d10
8–11	1d6	1d12	2d8	2d10	2d12
12–15	1d8	2d8	2d10	2d12	4d8
16–20	1d10	2d10	2d12	4d8	4d10

Large, Huge, Gargantuan, and Colossal creatures enjoy special benefits when using maneuvers such as bull rush, disarm, grapple, and trip. Bull rushes and trips call for opposed Strength checks between the two combatants. Not only are large creatures usually quite strong, they get an additional bonus to this check based on their size. Disarming an opponent requires an opposed attack roll, with a bonus to the larger weapon. Since large creatures tend to use large weapons, they have an advantage here as well. Grappling requires an opposed grapple check, which includes bonuses for both high Strength and great size. These advantages make feats such as Improved Bull Rush, Improved Disarm, Improved Overrun (described in Chapter One), and Improved Trip excellent choices for oversized fighters.

Extra Limbs

Athachs, marilith demons, mutant sahuagin, xills, and other creatures have more than two arms with which to use weapons, shields, or other items. Some of these monsters have access to the feat called Multidexterity that allows them to attack with all of their arms with no penalty, while others have a feat called Multiattack that reduces the penalty for additional natural attacks. The feat Multiweapon Fighting reduces the penalties for fighting with multiple weapons. All three of these feats are fully defined in the *Monster Manual*.

At the Dungeon Master's option, creatures with more than two arms can get a bonus to grappling checks when they wrestle an opponent with their arms. (The bonus would not apply, for example, to a marilith's constrict attack.) This bonus is +4 per extra pair of arms—so a marilith would get +8 (in addition to its size modifier), while a xill or a mutant sahuagin would gain a +4 bonus.

A creature with four or more arms can wield multiple two-handed weapons, such as greatswords or longbows, using two hands on the same side of its body for each weapon. However, no creature can use more than one double weapon simultaneously, since these weapons must be wielded across the body (one left hand and one right hand) for proper use. A creature can use a double weapon and carry a shield or other weapons in its other hands, however.

A creature can receive the armor bonus for only one shield at a time. A character who chooses to carry two or more shields gains no additional armor bonus, but does suffer an additional armor check penalty.

A creature with more than two arms that holds a weapon in at least one arm can perform certain actions that require the use of two hands (loading a crossbow, lighting a torch, or even drinking a potion) without provoking attacks of opportunity, since it can use its other arms in defense. By learning an additional feat presented below, Multitasking, such a creature can perform partial actions with each pair of its arms.

Flying Monsters

A human who drinks a *potion of fly* is fairly limited in aerial tactics, though he certainly has an advantage over an earthbound character. A creature born to flight, however, such as a gargoyle, an ogre mage, or a half-dragon, has the opportunity to learn feats that improve its ability to fight on the wing. The Flyby Attack feat (in the *Monster Manual*) is better than a simple Spring Attack, because it allows the creature to take any partial action during its move, not just an attack action. Therefore, a half-dragon could use Flyby Attack to pick up a dropped weapon (a move-equivalent action) in the middle of its move. Dragons and half-dragons can learn two additional flying feats, which at the Dungeon Master's option can be extended to other flying fighters as well: Hover and Wingover, both of which are described in the dragon entry in the *Monster Manual*.

Although it is not a prerequisite for Flyby Attack, the Mobility feat is a good choice for flying creatures, since they may be subject to attacks of opportunity when flying in for an attack. Note that flying creatures can make dive attacks—effectively a flying charge that deals double damage with claw attacks.

Flying monks do not increase their flying speed as they advance in level. (See Speed, below.)

Natural Weapons

A fighter or monk whose kind has natural attacks, such as claws, slams, or a bite, use natural attacks just like weapons. This means, among other things, that the character effectively has the Improved Unarmed Strike feat. Any feat that applies to a specific weapon, such as Improved Critical, Weapon Finesse, Weapon Focus, and Weapon Specialization in the case of fighters, apply to natural weapons as well. Of course, it is impossible to disarm an opponent who is attacking with natural weapons.

Speed

Some monsters are faster or slower than the basic character races described in the *Player's Handbook*. Use the

following table to calculate the increase in a monster's speed as it increases in monk levels, based on its kind's natural speed. Monstrous monks with a base speed of 20 feet use Table 3–11 in the *Player's Handbook* to calculate their speed as they advance in level.

TABLE 4-5: MONK SPEED BY BASE SPEED

Level	15 ft.	40 ft.	50 ft.	60 ft.
1–2	15 ft.	40 ft.	50 ft.	60 ft.
3–5	20 ft.	50 ft.	65 ft.	80 ft.
6-8	25 ft.	60 ft.	80 ft.	100 ft.
9–11	30 ft.	70 ft.	95 ft.	120 ft.
12–14	35 ft.	80 ft.	110 ft.	140 ft.
15–17	40 ft.	90 ft.	125 ft.	160 ft.
18–20	45 ft.	100 ft.	140 ft.	180 ft.

If a monk's race has a natural climb speed, that speed increases with the monk's level as well. Burrow, fly, and swim speeds do not increase.

Sample Creatures

➤**Gresk:** Male minotaur Ftr4; CR 8; Large monstrous humanoid; HD 6d8+24 plus 4d10+16; hp 89; Init +1; Spd 30 ft.; AC 21 (touch 10, flat-footed 20); Atk +17/+12 melee (2d8+9/×3, *Huge +1 greataxe*), +10 melee (1d8+3, gore); SA Charge 4d6+9; SQ Darkvision 60 ft., natural cunning, scent; AL CE; SV Fort +12, Ref +7, Will +6; Str 22, Dex 13, Con 19, Int 7, Wis 10, Cha 7.

Skills and Feats: Hide −6, Intimidate +4, Jump +11, Listen +8, Search +6, Spot +8; Cleave, Great Cleave, Great Fortitude, Improved Bull Rush, Power Attack, Sunder, Weapon Focus (greataxe), Weapon Specialization (greataxe).

Possessions: +1 light fortification breastplate, Huge +1 greataxe, ring of climbing, potion of alter self, potion of bull's strength.

Keiri: Female ogre mage Mnk6; CR 13; Large giant; HD 11d8+55; hp 102; Init +8; Spd 50 ft., fly 40 ft. (good); AC 29 (touch 21, flat-footed 25); Atk +14/+9 melee (1d10+12, unarmed strike) or +12/+7 melee (1d10+8, unarmed strike) and +12 melee (1d10+4, unarmed strike), or +7/+2 ranged (2d6+5/×3, Huge +1 mighty composite longbow [+4 Str bonus]); SA Flurry of blows, spell-like abilities, stunning attack (7/day); SQ Darkvision 60 ft., evasion, fast movement, purity of body, regeneration 2, slow fall (30 ft.), spell resistance 18, still mind; AL LE; SV Fort +14, Ref +10, Will +11; Str 26, Dex 19, Con 20, Int 12, Wis 20, Cha 14.

Skills and Feats: Balance +10, Concentration +8, Hide +0, Jump +10, Listen +13, Move Silently +8, Spellcraft +3, Spot +13, Tumble +10; Blind-Fight, Deflect Arrows, Dodge, Improved Initiative, Improved Trip, Power Attack.

Special Attacks: Spell-like Abilities (Sp): At will—*darkness* and *invisibility*; 1/day—*charm person, cone of cold, gaseous form, polymorph self,* and *sleep.* These abilities are as the spells cast by a Sor9 (save DC 13 + spell level). Stunning Attack (Su): Once per round (but not more than 7/day), Keiri can stun a creature damaged by her unarmed attacks.

Possessions: Huge +1 mighty composite longbow (+4 Str bonus), ring of protection +2, bracers of armor +3, monk's belt, gloves of Dexterity +2.

Mounted Opponents

While a mounted opponent does not have to be a terrifying encounter for a character on foot, a skilled combatant on a trained steed should strike fear into those unequipped to deal with the situation. Not only does a mounted foe probably move much faster than you, he gains a +1 bonus to melee attacks against you, and he probably has feats that dramatically improve his ability to deal damage against you. Even the mount itself is a formidable combatant—the average warhorse can deal out 10 or 15 points of damage per round without breaking a sweat.

Even worse, eventually your mounted opponent will charge you, either to skewer you with a lance or trample you with an overrun attack. If you know this attack is coming, ready a melee attack against the mount (do not bother readying an attack against the rider unless you have reach). Assuming this does not disable or kill the mount, by all means get out of the way of the overrun attack (unless your opponent has the Trample feat, in which case you do not have the option to avoid it).

Thus, when faced with a mounted opponent, the character on foot must seek to equalize the situation as quickly as possible. Assuming you do not have access to your own trained mount (and an untrained mount really is not a viable option in combat), your best option is to neutralize your opponent's mount.

You can accomplish this goal in a variety of ways, some of which are similar to those tactics used against opponents with reach. Ranged combat works well, though the mount's superior speed ensures that it and its rider eventually catches up to you. Airborne attacks work well unless your opponent rides a griffon or similar flying steed.

The most effective way to balance the playing field is to eliminate the mount entirely. This is not easy, since any rider with the Mounted Combat feat can replace his mount's AC with the result of a Ride skill check. However, unless your opponent is of low level, the mount probably has fewer hit points than the rider does.

Alternatively, you can try to pull the rider from the mount. This is the equivalent of a trip attack, except that the rider can use his Ride skill in place of his Dexterity or Strength check to oppose your Strength check. If you can, use a reach weapon with tripping ability for this attack, such as a guisarme, spiked chain, or whip.

An Opponent on Foot While You Are Mounted

The flip side of the situation comes when you are mounted, facing one or more groundling opponents. In this case, stay mobile—you do not want to let your opponents try to pull you off your steed—and charge a lot, preferably with a lance. The Ride-By Attack and Spirited Charge feats give you the capability of dealing immense amounts of damage while maintaining your distance. The Mounted Archery feat lets your mount make a double move while you fire at only a −2 penalty. If you do find yourself in melee, a Ride skill check (DC 10) lets your mount attack along with you, and a warhorse can deal out significant damage!

Do not forget to make Ride skill checks to use your mount as cover (DC 15)—particularly useful if your mount has a) more hit points than you or b) damage reduction—or to negate hits against your mount. (You cannot double this up, though—if you use your mount as cover, you cannot then make a Ride skill check to negate a hit against it, since the attack was not targeting your mount.)

COMBAT EXAMPLES #1: MOUNTED COMBAT

This example demonstrates a one-on-one battle between two mounted combatants of equal character level but very different abilities. Both combatants use a variety of feats and skills to maximize the advantages of mounted combat.

The evil ranger Druga has tracked his foe, the paladin Alarion, for many days. Suddenly, he spots him on a low rise about 400 feet away. *Druga and Alarion roll initiative. Druga rolls a 14 and adds +3 for 17. Alarion rolls a 12. Druga wins initiative.* They lock gazes for a moment, then Druga fires a pair of arrows, one of which strikes Alarion's trusty warhorse. *Druga draws his short bow (a free action due to his Quick Draw feat) and uses the full attack option to fire two arrows at Alarion's mount. He also declares that he will be using his Dodge feat against Alarion. The distance between the two characters is 400 feet. Since Druga has the Far Shot feat, his range increment with his short bow is 90 feet (1.5 × 60 feet), so this is only four range increments (a –8 penalty). Alarion's mount is flat-footed, so it loses its Dexterity bonus to AC. Druga rolls a 16, adds his attack modifier of +12 and subtracts the range penalty of –8 for a total of 20, which hits. (If Alarion were not flat-footed, he could attempt to negate the hit by using his Ride skill.) He rolls 1d6+3 and inflicts 7 points of damage to the mount, reducing its hit points to 38. His second attack roll is a 7, which after adding his +7 attack modifier and subtracting the –8 range penalty is a 6, which misses.*

Alarion spurs his mount forward in a slow canter, drawing forth a javelin and calling upon the strength and wisdom of Heironeous. *Alarion's mount takes a move-equivalent action to move forward 50 feet. Along the way Alarion casts divine favor on himself. This will add +1 to his attack and weapon damage rolls for one minute. Since his horse is taking only a normal move, this does not require a Concentration skill check. Alarion uses his move-equivalent action to draw a javelin.*

Druga's abyssal warhorse now moves forward as well, and the huntsman fires another pair of arrows at the paladin's steed, scoring a second hit. *Druga's warhorse takes a move action. After his mount has moved 25 feet, Druga uses a full attack action to fire another two arrows at Alarion's warhorse. The distance between them has dropped to only 275 feet, which is just over three range increments (a –6 penalty). This time he rolls a 17, adds his attack modifier of +12 and subtracts –6 for the range for a total of 23—a hit.*

Alarion uses his Mounted Combat feat to try to negate the hit. *He must make a Ride skill check whose result is higher than the attack roll. He rolls a 6 and adds his +10 Ride skill modifier for a 16, which is not enough to negate the hit. Druga rolls 1d6+3 damage and inflicts 7 points of damage to Alarion's warhorse, bringing its hit point total to 31.*

On Druga's second arrow attack, he rolls a 3 and misses.

Alarion's warhorse now accelerates into a trot. *Alarion decides that his warhorse makes a double move. The paladin*

attempts to heal his mount's wounds with a spell but the horse's movement ruins his concentration and the spell fails. *After his mount moves 50 feet, the paladin casts cure light wounds on his warhorse to remove the damage inflicted by Druga's arrow. This requires a Concentration check (DC 11). He rolls a 3 and adds his +6 skill modifier for a total of 9, which is insufficient to succeed so the spell is lost.* Shaking his head, Alarion raises his shield and prepares for battle. *He then uses his move-equivalent action to ready his shield. After this his horse moves the remaining 50 feet of its double move. The distance between the two combatants is now only 200 feet.*

Druga grins evilly and spurs his abyssal mount into a light gallop. *Druga's mount takes a double move toward Alarion.* He fires an arrow into the flank of his enemy's horse, then puts away his bow and draws forth his black longsword. *After moving 50 feet, Druga fires a single arrow at Alarion's mount. He rolls an 18, adds his attack modifier of +12, subtracts –2 for the range increment of distance between them, and subtracts –2 because his mount is taking a double move. (If he did not have the Mounted Archery feat, this penalty would be –4.) The total is 26—a hit.*

Again *Alarion attempts to use his Mounted Combat feat and Ride skill to negate the hit, and again he rolls a 12, +10 for his Ride skill modifier is 22, which is not enough to negate the hit. Druga rolls 1d6+3 and inflicts 8 points of damage, bringing Alarion's steed's hit point total to 23.*

Alarion slows his mount to a walk and hurls his javelin at Druga, which deflects harmlessly off the magical hide of the fiendish beast. *Alarion's warhorse makes a normal move. After it moves 25 feet, he throws his javelin, but Druga reacts instantly to drop behind his mount and use it as cover. This requires a Ride skill check (DC 15), and Druga rolls a 9 and adds his +15 skill modifier for a total of 24, which easily succeeds.*

Alarion rolls a 14 on his attack, adds his +9 attack modifier and subtracts –2 (for the range increment of distance. The result of 21 would normally be sufficient to hit Druga's AC of 19 (including the Dodge feat bonus), but the half cover provided by Druga's mount increases his AC by +4 to 23. Thus, the javelin instead strikes the mount. Alarion rolls 1d6+3 for damage and inflicts 5 points of damage. Since the mount has damage reduction 5/+1, it suffers no damage from the attack.

The paladin then readies his heavy lance and prepares to charge his evil opponent. *Alarion uses his move-equivalent action to draw his heavy lance, and his horse completes its move, ending the move 50 feet away from Druga.*

Druga anticipates a charge from Alarion, so both he and his warhorse prepare to attack Alarion's mount when it approaches within range. *Druga and his horse ready attack actions (Druga with his longsword, the warhorse with a hoof).*

Alarion charges at Druga. *His mount covers the 50' of distance between the two enemies, bringing his steed into a square threatened by Druga's foul warhorse. The huntsman's mount lashes a hoof at the paladin's steed and scores a hit against its front flank. Druga's mount rolls a 14 and adds its attack modifier of +6 for a 20. Alarion's mount has an AC of 19 (normally 21, reduced by –2 because of the charge), so this*

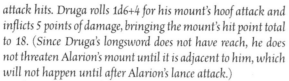

attack hits. Druga rolls 1d6+4 for his mount's hoof attack and inflicts 5 points of damage, bringing the mount's hit point total to 18. (Since Druga's longsword does not have reach, he does not threaten Alarion's mount until it is adjacent to him, which will not happen until after Alarion's lance attack.)

Then Alarion's lance impales the fiendish horse, channeling the holy power of Heironeous into a mortal blow. Alarion uses smite evil against the steed, which gives him a +2 bonus to attack and will add +7 damage. He rolls a 13 and adds his attack modifier of +13 and his charge bonus of +2 for a total of 28—a hit.

Druga attempts to use his Mounted Combat feat and Ride skill to negate the hit, but he rolls a 2, + his +15 skill modifier is 17, which is far less than the 29 he needed to negate the hit.

Since Alarion has the Spirited Charge feat, he inflicts triple damage with his lance when used as part of a mounted charge. He rolls 3d8+33 and inflicts 47 points of damage, which instantly kills the foul horse.

As his fiendish mount collapses, Druga rolls off and tumbles to the ground safely. The death of his mount forces Druga to make an immediate Ride check (DC 15) to make a soft fall. He rolls a 6 and adds his +15 Ride skill modifier for a total of 21. Druga takes no damage as he falls from his mount to the ground.

Alarion's warhorse does not break stride as it gallops past the fallen Druga. Since Alarion has the Ride-By Attack feat, he may continue moving after the charge attack (to a maximum of twice his mount's speed) without provoking attacks of opportunity from the opponent he attacks. However, as the horse passes Druga, he slashes at the horse with his sword. The DM allows Druga a Dexterity check against DC 15 to hold on to his weapon during the fall, and Druga rolls a total of 17. Thus, he can still make his readied attack, as well as an attack of opportunity against Alarion's mount as it moves past him (the Ride-By Attack feat only protects Alarion from attacks of opportunity against his target—in this case, Druga's steed). Since Druga is prone, he suffers a –4 penalty to each of these attacks. He rolls a 14 for the readied attack, which adjusts to a 20 (a hit for 6 points of damage) and a 7 for the attack of opportunity, which adjusts to a 17 (a miss). Alarion's mount now has only 12 hit points remaining.

Druga leaps to his feet and moves away from his opponent, ducking and weaving as he goes. Druga uses two move-equivalent actions to stand up and move away from Alarion. He also opts to use total defense, granting him a +4 dodge bonus to his AC (which raises it to 22, or 23 versus the opponent he chooses to Dodge, which remains Alarion). Alarion wheels his horse around and charges again, skewering the dark huntsman with his lance. His horse covers the 80 feet between the two combatants and Alarion makes a charge attack. Alarion rolls a natural 20—a threat! The critical roll is a 13, which adjusts to a 26. The attack inflicts five times normal damage (remember, ×3 from the Spirited Charge feat + ×3 from the critical hit equals ×5). Alarion rolls 5d8+20 and inflicts 43 points of damage, reducing Druga to 7 hit points. His warhorse adds a pair of kicks as it tramples

the huntsman into the dirt. The warhorse gets a charge attack against Druga (a single hoof), a trip attack as part of the overrun, and—if the trip attack is successful—a free hoof attack. Each attack receives the +2 bonus from the charge. Alarion rolls a 9 for the first hoof attack, which modifies to an 18: a miss. Next, the steed moves into Druga's square, which provokes an attack of opportunity. Druga rolls a 3, which misses despite the mount's reduced AC from the charge. Since Alarion has the Trample feat, Druga cannot choose to avoid the overrun. The horse makes its trip attack and rolls a total of 19, which hits (remember, this is a melee touch attack, so it disregards Druga's armor). The warhorse then makes a Strength check opposed by Druga's Strength or Dexterity check (Druga chooses Dexterity). The warhorse gets a +4 bonus for being one size category larger than Medium size. It rolls a 12 and adds this +4 bonus as well as its +4 Strength bonus for a total of 20. Druga rolls a 14 and adds his +3 Dexterity bonus for a total of 17. The warhorse wins the opposed check and trips Druga, who falls prone in his space. The horse may now make one free hoof attack against Druga (again thanks to the Trample feat). It rolls a 16 and adds its +6 attack modifier and a +4 modifier for Druga being prone for a total of 26. This inflicts 8 points of damage, which reduces him to less than zero. Druga is now dying, and Alarion has won the battle for good and law.

Druga: Male half-elf Ftr4/Rgr3; CR 7; Medium-size humanoid (elf); HD 7d10+7; hp 50; Init +3; Spd 30 ft.; AC 19 (touch 14, flat-footed 16); Atk +8/+3 melee (1d8+3/19–20, +1 longsword) and +8 melee (1d6+1/19–20, masterwork short sword) or +12/+7 ranged (1d6+3/×3, +1 mighty composite shortbow [+2 Str bonus] with masterwork arrows); SQ Favored enemy humans, half-elf traits; AL CE; SV Fort +8, Ref +5, Will +3; Str 14, Dex 16, Con 12, Int 8, Wis 13, Cha 10.

Skills and Feats: Handle Animal +6, Listen +2, Ride (horse) +12, Search +0, Spot +2, Wilderness Lore +4; Dodge, Far Shot, Mounted Archery, Mounted Combat, Point Blank Shot, Quick Draw , Track.

Possessions: +1 longsword, masterwork short sword, +1 mighty composite shortbow (+2 Str bonus), 20 masterwork arrows, +1 chain shirt, ring of protection +1.

Druga's Mount: Male abyssal heavy warhorse; CR 2; Large magical beast; HD 4d8+12; hp 30; Init +1; Spd 50 ft.; AC 17 (touch 10, flat-footed 16); Atk +6 melee (1d6+4, 2 hooves) and +1 melee (1d4+2, bite); SA Smite good; SQ Cold and fire resistance 10, damage reduction 5/+1, darkvision 60 ft., low-light vision, scent, spell resistance 8; AL CE; SV Fort +7, Ref +5, Will +2; Str 18, Dex 13, Con 17, Int 3, Wis 13, Cha 6.

Skills and Feats: Hide –3, Listen +7, Spot +7.

Special Attacks: Smite Good (Su): Once per day Druga's mount can make one normal melee attack to deal 4 extra points of damage against a good-aligned opponent.

Possessions: Masterwork studded leather barding.

CHAPTER 4: THE GAME WITHIN THE GAME

Alarion: Male human Pal7; CR 7; Medium-size humanoid; HD 7d10+7; hp 50; Init +0; Spd 20 ft.; AC 21 (touch 10, flat-footed 21); Atk +10/+5 melee (1d8+2/19–20, masterwork longsword or 1d8+3/×3, +1 *heavy lance*) or +8/+3 ranged (1d6+2, masterwork javelin); SA Smite evil, turn undead 5/day; SQ Aura of courage, detect evil, divine grace, divine health, empathic link with mount, heavy warhorse mount, lay on hands, remove disease 2/week, share spells with mount; AL LG; SV Fort +8, Ref +4, Will +6; Str 14, Dex 10, Con 12, Int 8, Wis 14, Cha 15.

Skills and Feats: Concentration +6, Knowledge (religion) +4, Ride (horse) +10; Mounted Combat, Ride-By Attack, Spirited Charge, Trample.

Special Attacks: Smite Evil (Su): Alarion may attempt to smite evil once per day with one normal melee attack. He gains a +2 bonus on his attack roll and a +7 bonus on damage.

Special Qualities: Lay on Hands (Sp): Alarion can cure 14 points of damage per day.

Spells Prepared: (2; base DC = 12 + spell level): 1st—cure light wounds, divine favor.

Possessions: +1 *full plate armor*, masterwork large steel shield, masterwork longsword, +1 *heavy lance*, 3 masterwork javelins.

Alarion's Mount: Male heavy warhorse; CR 6; Large magical beast; HD 6d8+18; hp 45; Init +1; Spd 50 ft.; AC 21 (touch 10, flat-footed 20); Atk +7 melee (1d6+4, 2 hooves) and +2 melee (1d4+2, bite); SQ Empathic link with paladin, improved evasion, low-light vision, scent, share saving throws with paladin, share spells with paladin; AL N; SV Fort +8, Ref +6, Will +3; Str 19, Dex 13, Con 17, Int 6, Wis 13, Cha 6.

Skills and Feats: Hide –3, Listen +7, Spot +7.

Possessions: Masterwork studded leather barding.

#2: THE DUEL

This example demonstrates a one-on-one battle between two skilled combatants of equal level and very similar ability. Both combatants use maneuvers such as bull rush, disarm, and trip in an attempt to gain a sliver of an advantage in what is otherwise a very even fight.

Shaez Mar-Yinan enters the common room of the Sleeping Dragon Inn, where her archrival, François is flirting with a young woman at the bar. Shouting a challenge, she draws her rapier, flames springing to life along its blade.

Shaez and François roll initiative. François rolls an 11 and adds +8 for 19. Shaez rolls a 15 and adds +4 for 19! François's Dexterity is 19, compared to Shaez's 18, so he wins initiative. His first "action" is to declare that he is using the Dodge feat against Shaez, bringing his effective AC to 22. He also uses Expertise, accepting a −2 penalty to his attacks in exchange for a +2 bonus to AC. His AC is 24, and his attacks this round (and until he declares otherwise) are at +15/+10/+5.

François springs up from his seat at the bar, then jumps up on the long table behind him, while the other patrons scatter for cover. *His Jump skill is +12, and he rolls a 7 and easily gets on top of the 3-foot-high table (a check result of 19, 9 above 10, clears just over 3 feet on a standing high jump). He then jumps to the next table to stand within reach of his foe. Rolling a 20, François's check result of 32 translates into a 14-foot standing broad jump, limited to 12 feet (twice his height) but still enough to clear the five feet between the tables.*

He thrusts with his rapier, dealing a cut to Shaez's shoulder. *François can make only a single attack after his 10-foot move. He rolls a 15, adds his attack modifier of +15, and an additional +1 for standing on higher ground, for a total of 31, easily enough to hit Shaez's flat-footed AC of 14. He deals 7 points of damage, bringing Shaez to 91.*

On her turn, Shaez also declares a Dodge against François, and uses Expertise to trade 2 points of attack bonus for an AC bonus. Her AC is 24, and her attacks are +15/+10/+5.

Stunned by François's ferocious attack, Shaez quickly finds her feet, tumbling past him and leaping on top of the table he just left. *Tumbling past an opponent without provoking an attack of opportunity requires a check against DC 15. Shaez rolls a 5, adds her skill modifier of +15, and easily gets by. Rolling a 5 on her Jump check gives her a result of 5 + 15 = 20, enough to get on top of the table.* While François is still turning around, her rapier point pierces his shoulder, and François cries out in pain. *Shaez rolls a natural 20, then rolls a 15 to determine if her hit was a critical; 15 + 15 = 30, so the hit is a critical. She rolls 2d6+4 for her base damage, and still adds 1d6 for Precise Strike and 1d6 for her flaming blade, dealing a total of 18 points of damage. François is at 69.*

Shaken by his serious wound, and having lost the advantage of higher ground on the tabletop, François tumbles away from Shaez to a clear spot near the fireplace. *Again, his Tumbling skill, even with a roll of 4, allows him to avoid any attack of opportunity from Shaez.* He pulls out a potion from his belt and drinks it in a quick gulp, soothing the pain and slowing the flow of blood in his shoulder. *His potion of cure serious wounds heals 11 points of damage, bringing him to 80.*

Shaez, too, leaps off the table and closes the distance to her enemy. *Since she must move 10 feet to threaten François, so she can only make one attack.* She lands another telling blow, cutting open a long gash in François's leg. *Shaez rolls a 17 + 15 = 32, hitting for 19 points even without a critical! François is at 61.*

At last, François focuses his energy on Shaez, moving his rapier in a blinding series of attacks. Focusing all his effort on attack, he knocks the tiefling's flaming blade from her hand, then cuts her arm wide open. *Dropping his Expertise (returning his AC to 22 and his attacks to their normal bonuses), François first makes a disarm attempt. Since he has the Improved Disarm feat, Shaez gets no attack of opportunity against him. The two combatants make opposed attack rolls. François rolls 14 + 17 = 31, while Shaez rolls 15 + 15 = 30. Shaez's rapier clatters to the floor. François's second attack roll is 15 + 12 =*

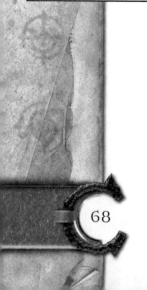

Rules Clarifications

For the sake of completeness, we are adding here a couple clarifications to the rules from the first printing of the *Player's Handbook*. These are official rules for the D&D game.

Shuriken Rules

When you throw three shuriken, make a separate attack roll for each, even though it counts as one attack. Sneak attack damage and a ranger's favored enemy bonus damage applies only to one of three shuriken that you throw. You do not have enough precision with the extra shuriken to get bonus sneak attack or favored enemy damage.

Striking with a Touch Spell

Normally when you use a touch spell, you merely try to touch the enemy to discharge the spell. Alternatively, you can try to strike the enemy with an unarmed attack. It is harder to connect with a solid blow than with a touch, but it is better if you succeed. Treat the attack as a normal unarmed attack (so most characters provoke attacks of opportunity when attacking this way). If the attack is a hit, you deal unarmed damage and discharge the spell. If the attack is a miss, you are still holding the charge.

27, hitting Shaez for 12 points of damage. Shaez is at 79. His third attack roll is 11 + 7 = 18, a miss.

Shaez crouches to pick up her weapon, dropping her guard enough for François to land another blow. *"Pick up an item" is a move-equivalent action that provokes an attack of opportunity. See Table 8–4 in the Player's Handbook. Neither Mobility nor Tumbling can help Shaez avoid this attack—one of the reasons why disarm can be a good option. François rolls 11 + 17 = 28, hitting Shaez for 9 points of damage and bringing her to 70.*

Her sword back in hand, Shaez attacks low and knocks François to the floor. *Repaying the humiliation of François's disarm, Shaez attempts a trip maneuver. She rolls 8 + 11 = 19, good enough to hit François as a touch attack. They make opposed ability checks—Shaez makes a Strength check, while François rolls a Dexterity check, since his Dexterity is higher than his Strength. Shaez rolls a 14 and adds her +1 Strength modifier for a total of 15. François rolls an unfortunate 6, adds his +4 Dexterity modifier, and falls to the floor with a 10. Shaez's Improved Trip feat allows her an immediate follow-up attack. No sooner does François hit the ground than Shaez's rapier punctures his shoulder again. Shaez rolls 17 + 15, + an additional +4 because François is prone, for a total of 36. She hits for 14 points of damage, bringing François to 47.*

François jumps quickly to his feet and works his rapier past the tiefling's guard again, poking her in the ribs. *"Stand up from prone" is a move-equivalent action that does not provoke an attack of opportunity—it is quite possible to remain on your guard while standing up. François decides to use his Expertise feat again, returning his AC to 24 and his attacks to +15/+10/+5. Since he used an action to stand up, he gets only one attack this round, rolling 12 + 15 = 27, hitting for 17 points of damage. Shaez is at 53.*

In response, Shaez adjusts her position slightly and charges toward her enemy, lowering her shoulder under his blade to push him backward, toward the fireplace. He brings his sword down hard on her back, but she manages to push him right up against the mantle. He barely avoids a burn from the fire, finding his feet just in time. *Without the Improved Bull Rush feat, Shaez provokes an attack of opportunity when attempting a bull rush maneuver. François rolls 11 + 15 = 26, hitting for 17 and bringing Shaez to 36. They make opposed Strength checks. Shaez rolls a 12 and adds her +1 Strength modifier, for 13. François rolls a 9 and has no Strength modifier. Shaez pushes him back 5 feet, and decides to continue moving back with him the additional 4 feet—1 foot for every point by which her Strength check result exceeded François's. One more foot, and François's derriere would have been in the fire!*

François returns with a series of blows, landing one good blow in the tiefling's chest. *François's first attack roll is 18 + 15 = 33, and he rolls a 14 + 15 = 29 to confirm the critical. His damage is 18 points, and Shaez is at 18. His remaining attacks are 12 + 10 = 22 and 11 + 5 = 16, both misses.*

Shaez takes a step back from François's whirling blades, and pulls out a potion of her own to heal her wounds. *Since Shaez's entire move is a 5-foot adjustment, she does not provoke an attack of opportunity while moving out of François's threatened area. She drinks a potion of cure moderate wounds and regains 14 hit points, leaving her with 32.*

François does not allow Shaez any respite, however, continuing his assault, but Shaez's rapier is already back into defensive position. François lands only one good blow, but Shaez's strength is failing. *François takes a 5-foot step forward and makes a full attack. He rolls 17 + 15 = 32, hitting for 12 points and reducing Shaez to 20. His remaining attacks (2 + 10 = 12 and 1 + 5 = 6) both miss.*

Beginning to fear for her life, Shaez makes another fierce jab at her foe, then tumbles backward along the bar to increase the distance between them. *She makes a single attack, rolling 11+15=26 and dealing 17 points of damage, bringing François to 30. She can use her Tumble skill to avoid an attack of opportunity as she withdraws. She rolls 7 + 15 = 22, and avoids any attack.*

Breathing heavily, François decides not to press the attack for a moment. Pulling out his second potion, he quaffs it to restore some of his health, then moves closer to Shaez without coming within reach of her blades. *François's potion of cure serious wounds restores 15 points, bringing him back up to 45. He moves only 10 feet forward, not wanting to enter her reach when he cannot make an attack.*

Springing toward François, Shaez pierces his left arm with her flaming blade, then springs back out of his reach before he can respond. *Shaez has the Spring Attack feat, which lets her do just that. She rolls 19 + 15 = 34 for her attack, but her roll to confirm the critical—8 + 15 = 23—is not good enough. Still, even without the critical damage, she deals 17 points of damage, and François falls to 28 hit points.*

Growing impatient with Shaez's bounding, François closes the distance and makes a wild jab, which Shaez easily deflects. *François rolls 5 + 15 = 20, a miss.* Shaez, tumbling around her foe's blade, leaps back onto the tabletop behind him, slashing a deep cut in his neck. *Shaez' Tumble and Jump skill scores make this footwork easy for her: she rolls 2 + 15 = 17 for her Tumble check, and 10 + 15 = 25 for the Jump. Her attack roll is 19 + 15 + 1 = 35 for standing on higher ground. She confirms the critical with a 17 + 15 = 32, then rolls a stunning 24 points of damage. François is at 4 hit points and getting desperate.*

Knowing victory is in his grasp despite the blood soaking his shirt, François presses the attack, focusing everything on scoring the final blows that will end the battle. A thrust to her chest, a feint to her legs, and a final cut to her neck all but finish the tiefling. *Dropping his Expertise, François rolls 7 + 17 = 24, hitting for 13 (Shaez is at 7), then 5 + 12 = 17, a miss, and finally 17 + 7 = 24, hitting for 7. Shaez is at 0, disabled but not yet dying.*

With her last gasp, Shaez steps off the table away from François and drinks her last potion, restoring a fragment of health to her sorely wounded body. *Her potion of cure moderate wounds heals 9 hit points, leaving her at 9. Undeterred, François continues his assault, driving his rapier through his opponent's heart. His first attack roll is 18 + 17 = 35, but he rolls a 1 he checks for the critical. Even so, his damage is 12, dropping Shaez to –3. She is dying, and he can quickly finish her off, ending a decade of intense rivalry.*

François: Male human Ftr7/Duelist4; CR 11; Medium-size humanoid; HD 11d10+11; hp 87; Init +8; Spd 30 ft.; AC 20 (touch 17, flat-footed 18); Atk +17/+12/+7 melee (1d6+3/18–20, +1 *rapier*); SA Precise strike (+1d6); SQ Canny defense, enhance mobility, grace; AL CG; SV Fort +7, Ref +12, Will +2; Str 10, Dex 19, Con 12, Int 14, Wis 8, Cha 13.

Skills and Feats: Balance +17, Bluff +14, Diplomacy +3, Intimidate +3, Jump +12, Perform +14, Tumble +17; Combat Reflexes, Dodge, Expertise, Improved Disarm, Improved Initiative, Mobility, Weapon Finesse (rapier), Weapon Focus (rapier), Weapon Specialization (rapier).

Possessions: +1 rapier, bracers of armor +3, gloves of Dexterity +2, ring of protection +1, amulet of natural armor +1, 2 potions of cure serious wounds.

Shaez Mar-Yinan: Female tiefling Ftr7/Duelist4; CR 11; Medium-size outsider; HD 11d10+22; hp 98; Init +4; Spd 30 ft.; AC 21 (touch 19, flat-footed 18); Atk +17/+12/+7 melee (1d6+2/18–20 plus 1d6 fire, +1 *flaming rapier*); SA *Darkness* 1/day, precise strike (+1d6); SQ Canny defense, cold, electricity, and fire resistance 5, enhanced mobility, grace, outsider traits; AL CE; SV Fort +8, Ref +12, Will +2; Str 12, Dex 18, Con 14, Int 16, Wis 8, Cha 8.

Skills and Feats: Balance +18, Bluff +15, Diplomacy +1, Hide +6, Intimidate +1, Jump +15, Perform +10, Tumble +15; Ambidexterity, Dodge, Expertise, Improved Trip, Mobility, Spring Attack, Weapon Finesse (rapier), Weapon Focus (rapier).

Special Attacks: Darkness (Sp): Casts *darkness* once per day as Sor11.

Possessions: +1 flaming rapier, ring of protection +2, bracers of armor +2, 2 potions of cure moderate wounds.

RULES VARIANTS

A DM might use these rules variants to address issues that sometimes come up with fighter and monk characters.

Counter Tumble

A character can make a Tumble check to get past or through an enemy. That check does not take into account the capability of the defender. With the Counter Tumble variant, the character that the Tumbler is trying to get past can make a Tumble check of his own. The Tumbler has to match the DC as normal but also has to beat the defender's Tumble check.

This variant hardly ever comes into play because most characters and monsters do not have any ranks in Tumble (and therefore cannot make Tumble checks). What the variant does, however, is make the experienced monk harder to Tumble past than an ogre.

For example, Ember needs to roll 15+ to Tumble past an enemy. When she tries to Tumble past an enemy monk, that monk makes a Tumble check with a result of 17. Now Ember needs to beat that result rather than matching 15. If the monk had gotten a result of 14 or lower, Ember would still have to get a result of 15+ to succeed.

Flexible Weapon Focus with Bows

A fighter who takes Weapon Focus (longbow) or (shortbow) at 1st level might be very sad once he can afford a mighty composite longbow or shortbow and starts using it. Rather than making a player live with a feat that does not work with a mighty bow, the DM can let the player swap Weapon Focus with one kind of bow for Weapon Focus with another kind. These weapons are similar enough that a character could conceivably use what he knows with one weapon to use another better. For the sake of realism, the character can swap the Weapon Focus only when his base attack bonus increases. That way, the character's capability with the first bow does not actually decrease.

For example, an elven fighter starts with Weapon Focus (longbow) at 1st level. Before reaching 2nd level, he has upgraded to a mighty composite longbow, to which his Weapon Focus feat does not apply. On reaching 2nd level, with the DM's permission, the player switches Weapon Focus to (composite longbow). The fighter's attack bonus with the longbow stays the same. (He loses the +1 bonus from the Weapon Focus, but his increase in base attack bonus makes up for the loss.)

Double-Handed Disarm

Attempting to disarm an opponent with both hands ought to be a lot easier than attempting to do so with a single hand. The two-weapon fighting rules are too stringent to represent the advantage of using both hands. As a variant, both hands used together count as a weapon that's the size of the attacker. (Used on its own, a character's hand counts as a weapon two size categories smaller than the character.)

For example, if Ember uses a bare hand to try to take an enemy's longsword away from him, the defender gets a +8 bonus on his opposed melee attack because the sword (Medium size) is two size categories larger than an unarmed attack (Tiny for a Medium-size character). If she uses both hands, however, the two hands count as a single Medium-size weapon. She still makes a single attack (not two for two hands), but the defender no longer gets the +8 bonus for having a bigger weapon.

69

CHAPTER 5: TOOLS OF THE TRADE

Money: You are going to need it, and unless a generous patron supports you, or you happen to belong to an organization with lots of resources, you are going to need a lot of it in order to pay for all that weaponry, armor, and adventuring gear you tote around. The advantages of money are obvious, manifesting usually around the time you return from your first successful adventure. Sometimes it might seem rather like a vicious cycle: Go adventuring, acquire money, spend money on gear, go adventuring with new gear, acquire more money, buy more gear, etc. It may even reach the point where you and your fellow adventurers feel like you are single-handedly contributing the primary source of income to your community, in effect becoming the mainstay of the local economy!

In an effort to help you find ways to spend your characters' hard-earned cash, we present you with a selection of new exotic weapons, a list of how some other unusual weapons translate into the game, magic items specifically designed for monks and fighters, and finally, a set of six different locales complete with maps, NPCs, and costs that players can explore, discover, build, and purchase.

NEW EXOTIC WEAPONS

"You can never have too many weapons."

—Tordek

Fighters and monks alike benefit from weapons with a "little something extra." In fact, an exotic weapon may become a character's signature weapon. However, before a character can pick up a war fan or a mercurial greatsword and use it proficiently, he is served best by taking an Exotic Weapon Proficiency feat. A character can use an exotic weapon without an associated Exotic Weapon Proficiency feat, but suffers a −4 penalty on all attack rolls with that weapon.

The "Ammunition" category below does not qualify as exotic weapons, and ammunition does not require the Exotic Weapon proficiency to use.

Alchemist's Arrow: Marvels of craftsmanship, each alchemist's arrow carries a deadly load of alchemist's fire in its hollow shaft. When a target is struck the arrow's shaft shatters, releasing the alchemist's fire directly onto the target. One round after impact, the alchemist's fire ignites on contact with air, dealing 1d4 points of damage. The target can take a full-round action to attempt to extinguish the flames before taking this additional damage. It takes a successful Reflex saving throw (DC 15) to extinguish the flames. Rolling on the ground allows the character a +2 bonus. Submerging (such as by leaping into a lake) or magically extin-

TABLE 5-1: EXOTIC WEAPONS
EXOTIC WEAPONS—MELEE

Weapon	Cost	Damage	Critical	Range Increment	Weight	Type
Unarmed Attacks						
Ward cestus	10 gp	*	*	—	4 lb.	—
Tiny						
Stump knife	8 gp	1d4	19–20/×2	—	2 lb.	Piercing
Triple dagger	10 gp	1d4	19–20/×2	—	1 lb.	Piercing
Small						
Battlepick, gnome	10 gp	1d6	×4	—	5 lb.	Piercing
Bladed gauntlet	30 gp	1d6	19–20/×2	—	4 lb.	Slashing
War fan	30 gp	1d6	×3	—	3 lb.	Slashing
Medium-size						
Chain-and-dagger	4 gp	1d4	19–20/×2	—	4 lb.	Piercing
Mercurial longsword	400 gp	1d8	×4	—	6 lb.	Slashing
Large						
Duom	20 gp	1d8	×3	—	8 lb.	Piercing
Gyrspike	90 gp	1d8/1d8	19–20/×2	—	20 lb.	S and B
Manti	15 gp	1d8	×3	—	9 lb.	Piercing
Mercurial greatsword	600 gp	2d6	×4	—	17 lb.	Slashing
Three-section staff	4 gp	1d8	×3	—	8 lb.	Bludgeoning
Huge						
Fullblade	100 gp	2d8	19–20/×2	—	23 lb.	Slashing

guishing the flames automatically kills the flames.

Battlepick, Gnome: A gnome battlepick is crafted and weighted to be used by creatures of Small size only. A Small-size character uses a gnome battlepick two-handed as a martial weapon.

Bladed Gauntlet: Unlike a standard gauntlet, an attack with a bladed gauntlet is not considered an unarmed attack. The bladed gauntlet possesses two cruelly sharpened blades that extend from the back of the wrist following the line of the forearm. The cost and weight are for a single gauntlet.

Bolas, 2-ball: A set of 2-ball bolas consists of two heavy wooden spheres connected by lengths of cord. It is a ranged weapon used to trip an opponent. When you throw a set of bolas, you make a ranged touch attack against your opponent. If you hit, your opponent is tripped. If the opponent fails a grapple check versus your original attack roll, the opponent is grappled. Bolas only grapple Medium-size or smaller targets. The opponent can extricate itself from the 2-ball bolas

with a full-round action. Your opponent cannot trip you when making a trip attack with the 2-ball bolas.

Chain-and-Dagger: You get a +2 bonus on your opposed attack when attempting to disarm an opponent (including the roll to keep from being disarmed yourself, if you fail to disarm your opponent). You can also use this weapon to make trip attacks, gaining a +2 bonus on your trip attempt. If you are tripped during your own trip attempt, you can opt to drop the chain-and-dagger instead of being tripped.

Crossbow, Great: A great crossbow requires two hands to use effectively, regardless of the user's size. You draw a great crossbow back by turning a winch. Loading a great crossbow is a full-round action that provokes an attack of opportunity.

A Medium-size character cannot shoot or load a great crossbow with one hand at all. With training, a Large-size creature can shoot, but not load, a great crossbow with one hand at a –4 penalty. If a Large-size creature attempts to fire a separate great crossbow in each hand simultaneously, the standard penalties for two-weapon fighting apply.

EXOTIC WEAPONS—RANGED

Weapon	Cost	Damage	Critical	Range Increment	Weight	Type
Tiny						
Fukimi-Bari (mouth darts)	1 gp	1	×2	10 ft.	1/10 lb.	Piercing
Skiprock, halfling	3 gp	1d3	×2	10 ft.	1/4 lb.	Bludgeoning
Small						
Bolas, 2-ball	5 gp	1d4*	×2	10 ft.	2 lb.	Bludgeoning
Medium-size						
Spinning javelin	2 gp	1d8	19–20/×2	50 ft.	2 lb.	Piercing
Spring-loaded gauntlet	200 gp	1d4	×2	20 ft.	4 lb.	Piercing
Large						
Crossbow, great	100 gp	1d12	19–20/×2	150 ft.	15 lb.	Piercing
Harpoon	15 gp	1d10	×2	30 ft.	10 lb.	Piercing
Shotput, orc	10 gp	2d6	19–20/×3	10 ft.	15 lb.	Bludgeoning
Special						
Whip, Mighty*						
+1 Str bonus	200 gp	1d2†	×2	15 ft.*	3 lb.	Slashing
+2 Str bonus	300 gp	1d2†	×2	15 ft.*	4 lb.	Slashing
+3 Str bonus	400 gp	1d2†	×2	15 ft.*	5 lb.	Slashing
+4 Str bonus	500 gp	1d2†	×2	15 ft.*	6 lb.	Slashing
Whip dagger*	25 gp	1d6	19–20/×2	15 ft.*	3 lb.	Slashing
Whip dagger, Mighty*						
+1 Str bonus	225 gp	1d6	19–20/×2	15 ft.*	4 lb.	Slashing
+2 Str bonus	325 gp	1d6	19–20/×2	15 ft.*	5 lb.	Slashing
+3 Str bonus	425 gp	1d6	19–20/×2	15 ft.*	6 lb.	Slashing
+4 Str bonus	525 gp	1d6	19–20/×2	15 ft.*	7 lb.	Slashing
Ammunition (not Exotic Weapons)						
Alchemist's arrow** (1)	75 gp	—	—	—	1/5 lb.	—
Tumbling bolt** (1)	50 gp	—	—	—	1/5 lb.	—

*See weapon entry for special rules. **See weapon entry for damage.
†Deals subdual damage.

Duom: The duom is a longspear with a standard spear-head, as well as two blades curved so that they point backward along the shaft. The weapon has reach, allowing you to strike opponents 10 feet away with it. Those proficient with the spear can also use it to attack adjacent foes with the reversed heads with a practiced "reverse thrust." Apply a +2 bonus to the attack roll for the first attack made by the duom against an adjacent opponent.

Fukimi-Bari (Mouth Darts): These slim, almost needle-like metal darts are concealed in the mouth and then spit at the target. Their effective range is extremely short, and they do little damage, but they are highly useful when taking an opponent by surprise. You can fire up to three mouth darts per attack (all at the same target).

Do not apply your Strength modifier to damage with mouth darts. They are too small to carry the extra force that a strong character usually imparts to a thrown weapon. The cost and weight are for a single mouth dart.

Fullblade: A fullblade is 18 inches longer than a greatsword, and is too large for a Medium-size creature to use at all. A Large creature could use the fullblade with one hand, but would suffer the standard −4 nonproficiency penalty to its attack rolls, or with two hands as a martial weapon. A Large creature with the Exotic Weapon proficiency could use the fullblade in one hand with no penalty. A fullblade is also called an ogre's greatsword.

Gyrspike: A gyrspike is a double weapon. A stout shaft holds a flail on one end and a longsword on the other. You can fight with it as if fighting with two weapons, but if you do, you incur all the normal attack penalties for two-weapon fighting, as if you were using a one-handed weapon and a light weapon.

You get a +2 bonus on your opposed attack roll when attempting to disarm an enemy when you wield a gyrspike (including the opposed attack roll to avoid being disarmed yourself if you fail to disarm your enemy).

You can also use this weapon to make trip attacks. If you are tripped during your own trip attempt, you can drop the gyrspike to avoid being tripped.

Harpoon: The harpoon is a broad-bladed spear forged with cruel barbs. The shaft of the harpoon has a trailing rope attached to control harpooned opponents. Though intended to be used in hunting whales and other large sea creatures, the harpoon can be used on dry land. Even if an Exotic Weapon Proficiency is taken for the Harpoon, creatures of less than Medium size suffer a −2 penalty to their attack rolls due to the weapon's weight.

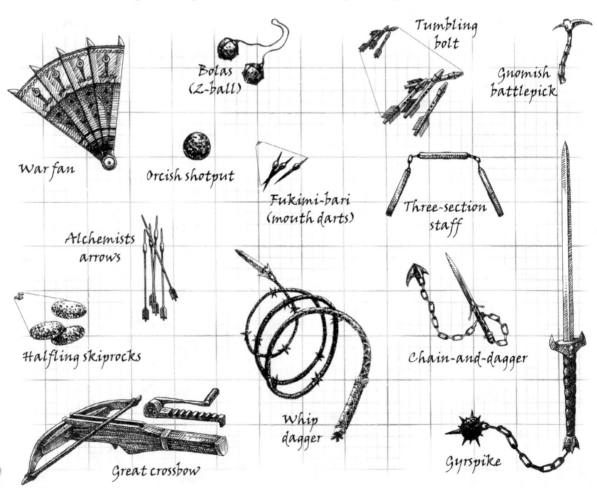

War fan

Bolas
(2-ball)

Orcish shotput

Tumbling
bolt

Gnomish
battlepick

Fukimi-bari
(mouth darts)

Three-section
staff

Alchemists
arrows

Halfling skiprocks

Chain-and-dagger

Great crossbow

Whip
dagger

Gyrspike

If you inflict damage on your opponent, the harpoon may lodge in the victim if the victim fails a Reflex saving throw against a DC equal to 10 plus the damage you inflicted. The harpooned creature moves at only half speed and cannot charge or run. If you control the trailing rope by succeeding at an opposed Strength check while holding it, the harpooned creature can only move within the limits that the rope allows (the trailing rope is 30 feet long). If the harpooned creature attempts to cast a spell, it must succeed at a Concentration check (DC 15) or fail, losing the spell.

The harpooned creature can pull the harpoon from its wound if it has two free hands and it takes a full-round action to do so, but in so doing it inflicts damage on itself equal to the initial damage the harpoon caused. If you hit with a harpoon and do 8 points of damage and the target removes the harpoon, it takes another 8 points of damage.

Manti: A manti is a shortspear with four additional spear heads that project vertically from the shaft, creating a star pattern of five blade heads instead of just a single forward-pointing blade. The advantage for someone trained to use the manti is that you make one additional attack of opportunity during the round.

Mercurial Greatsword: This huge blade hides a secret reservoir of quicksilver (also called mercury by alchemists) that runs along the interior of the blade in a slender channel. When the blade is vertical, the mercury swiftly fills an interior bulb in the haft, but when swung, the heavy liquid flows out into the blade, making it heavier. In nonproficient hands, this shifting mass penalizes the wielder by an additional −3 penalty to attack rolls, beyond the normal nonproficiency penalty for using an exotic weapon untrained.

Mercurial Longsword: As above, except that in nonproficient hands, the shifting mass and feel of the blade penalizes the wielder by an additional −2 penalty to attack rolls, beyond the normal nonproficiency penalty for using an exotic weapon untrained.

Shotput, Orc: Special training turns a grapefruit-sized sphere of crude iron into a deadly missile. Even with the Exotic Weapon feat, a wielder must be Medium-size or larger to use the weapon effectively (or suffer an additional −3 penalty to attack rolls in addition to the standard nonproficiency penalty).

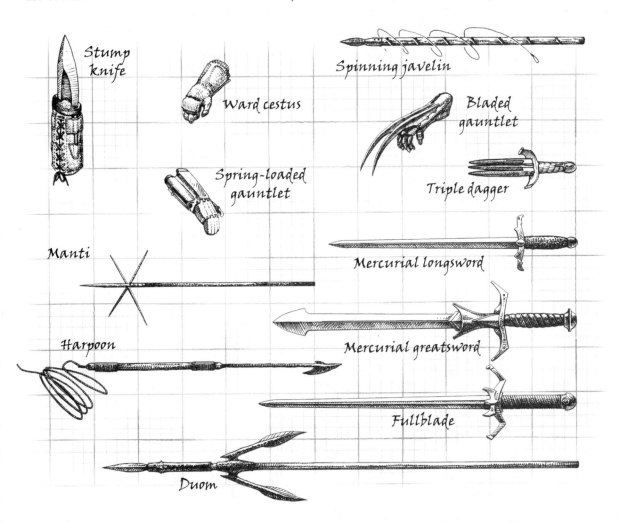

Stump knife

Ward cestus

Spring-loaded gauntlet

Manti

Harpoon

Spinning javelin

Bladed gauntlet

Triple dagger

Mercurial longsword

Mercurial greatsword

Fullblade

Duom

Skiprock, Halfling: These polished, perfectly weighted stones are prized by halflings, for if they throw them just so, they ricochet off one target to strike a second. If the skiprock hits its target, it ricochets toward another target (of the thrower's choice) adjacent to the original target (within 5 feet). The thrower immediately makes a second attack roll for the skiprock against the new target, with an attack bonus equal to the first roll –2.

Skiprocks could be used as sling bullets, but using a skiprock's ricochet ability in conjunction with a sling requires taking the Exotic Weapon proficiency specifically for that purpose.

Spinning Javelin: This light, flexible spear intended for ranged attacks resembles a standard javelin, except for the spiral grooves that run down its length. You can loop a throwing string around the shaft (the other end is tied to your finger). The string imparts spin to the javelin upon release, improving the weapon's accuracy, range, and penetrating power by permitting a harder cast. Looping a string around the javelin is a move-equivalent action that provokes an attack of opportunity. Tying a casting string around your finger is a full-round action that provokes an attack of opportunity, but the same string is reused for multiple javelins. The javelin can be thrown without spinning it, in which case its damage, range, and critical range is that of a standard javelin. If used in melee, treat the spinning javelin as a standard javelin.

Spring-Loaded Gauntlet: This gauntlet possesses a broad ridge of metal that extends along the bottom of the forearm to the edge of the wrist articulation, where a circular orifice is visible. This ridge of metal hides a wondrous spring-loaded mechanism whereby a crossbow bolt can be expelled with great force, akin to a very small crossbow. You load the gauntlet by inserting a bolt in the hole and pulling back a tiny lever. Loading the spring-loaded gauntlet is a move-equivalent action that provokes an attack of opportunity. You fire the spring-loaded gauntlet by sighting down your arm, then flip your hand back so that your palm faces your opponent—this motion fires the gauntlet. A character who attempts to fire two spring-loaded gauntlets at once suffers the standard penalty for two-weapon fighting. (The Two-Weapon Fighting feat does not reduce these penalties because it represents skill with melee weapons, not ranged weapons. The Ambidexterity feat lets someone avoid the –4 off-hand penalty.) The cost and weight are for a single gauntlet.

Stump Knife: A stump knife is akin to a punching dagger, except that it can be securely attached to the stump of a missing forelimb. For someone proficient in its use, the stump knife becomes an extension of his body. Against foes to whom you have dealt damage during the course of a continuous melee, the stump knife's critical range is doubled (17–20). Your opponent cannot disarm you of a stump knife.

Three-Section Staff: Originally a farm implement for threshing grain, this weapon is comprised of three sections of wood of equal lengths, joined at the ends by chain, leather, or rope.

A monk using a three-section staff (for which she must take an Exotic Weapon Proficiency feat due to the weapon's Large size) fights with her unarmed base attack bonus and her more favorable number of attacks per round, along with other applicable attack modifiers. The three-section staff requires two hands to use. A monk/weapon master may choose the three-section staff as her weapon of choice.

Triple Dagger: This weapon is used in the off-hand as a means to disarm an opponent—you hold it as you would a shield, not another weapon, and so do not suffer penalties for fighting with two weapons. When using a triple dagger, you get a +3 bonus on your opposed attack roll when attempting to disarm an opponent (including the roll to keep from being disarmed if you fail to disarm your opponent). The triple dagger could also be used as a normal dagger, if desired, but if used in the off-hand, all normal penalties for fighting with two weapons apply.

Tumbling Bolt: A tumbling bolt resembles a standard crossbow bolt save for a few tiny holes and vents along the shaft. In fact, a tiny channel allows air to pass through the bolt when it is fired which causes the bolt to tumble when fired. Opponents targeted by a tumbling bolt can apply only half their Dexterity modifier to their AC (round down) due to the unpredictable tumble of approaching missile.

War Fan: This weapon appears to the untrained eye as nothing more than a beautifully crafted lady's fan. In fact, the vanes of the fan are crafted from steel, and the tips are needle-sharp. When first brought into melee, the wielder may attempt a Bluff check against an opponent's Sense Motive check. If the wielder wins the contest, he adds a +4 bonus to the attack roll for his first round's attack(s).

Ward Cestus: This is a stout leather gauntlet with a well-forged metal weight sewn into it over the knuckles. A strike with a ward cestus is considered an unarmed attack. If you take an All-Out Defense action, you gain an additional +1 deflection bonus to your AC, representing blows you block with the back of your protected hand. Your opponent cannot disarm you of a ward cestus. The cost and weight are for a single ward cestus.

Whip Dagger: A character who takes an Exotic Weapon Proficiency in the whip is also proficient in the whip dagger. (You do not need to take a separate feat to use the whip dagger if you already have a feat for the whip.) The whip dagger is heavier than a standard whip and deals normal damage due to the barbs that run along its length and the dagger-like tip (which inflicts deep wounds when accelerated to strike by a proficient user). Unlike standard whips, armor bonuses and natural armor bonuses do not hinder its ability to deal damage.

Although you keep it in hand, treat it as a ranged weapon with a maximum range of 15 feet and no range penalties.

Because the whip dagger can wrap around an enemy's leg or other limb, you can make trip attacks with it. If you are tripped during your own trip attempt, you can drop the whip dagger to avoid being tripped.

You get a +2 bonus on your opposed attack roll when attempting to disarm an opponent (including the roll to keep from being disarmed yourself if you fail to disarm your opponent).

Whip or Whip Dagger, Mighty: A character who takes an Exotic Weapon Proficiency in the whip is also proficient in the mighty whip (or mighty whip dagger). A mighty whip or mighty whip dagger is made with especially heavy material that allows a strong character to take advantage of an above-average Strength score. The mighty whip allows you to add your Strength bonus to subdual damage for a whip (and normal damage if the lasher prestige class is chosen), and to standard damage for a mighty whip dagger, up to the maximum bonus listed on the chart above.

WEAPON EQUIVALENCY TABLE

Countless variations on familiar weapons exist, so many that simply listing and illustrating them all could fill another book! However, the functional differences between these variants and the weaponry presented in the *Player's Handbook* are small to nonexistent, making individual statistics for each variant unnecessary. Here is a sample list of weaponry and their *Player's Handbook* equivalents. Treat the variant weapon in the exact same fashion as its equivalent: A character wielding a flamberge, for example, is treated as if he were wielding a bastard sword when any adjudications based on the weapon must be made. Rather than attempting to define for the game an almost infinite number of minor variations on several common weapons, use the following table to translate such weapons into the game.

TABLE 5-2: WEAPON EQUIVALENTS

Katana	Masterwork bastard sword
Claymore	Greatsword
Wakizashi	Masterwork short sword
Gladius, scramasax (sax), ninja-to	Short sword
Flamberge	Greatsword
Broadsword	Longsword
Bow, Daikyu (strength bow)	Longbow
Bow, Hankyu	Shortbow
Nagimaki	Ranseur
Yari	Javelin
Bokken	Greatclub

No stick	Club
Jo stick	Quarterstaff
Saber, cutlass	Scimitar
Sai, tanto, jitte, main-gauche, dirk, bodkin, jambiya, stiletto	Dagger
Sickle	Kama
Cat-o'-Nine Tails	Whip dagger

MAGIC ITEMS

This section describes several new magic items of various types. These items are especially useful to fighters and monks.

TABLE 5-3: MAGIC ITEMS

Shield Special Ability		Market Price
Arrow Catching		+1 bonus
Dancing		+3 bonus

Magic Weapon Special Ability	Type	Market Price
Ki Focus	Melee	+1 bonus
Merciful	Melee, Ranged	+1 bonus
Seeking	Ranged	+1 bonus
Sure Striking	Melee, Ranged*	+1 bonus
Vicious	Melee	+1 bonus

*No bows, crossbows, or slings.

Specific Weapon	Market Price
Bow of true arrows	4,000 gp
Shatterspike	4,315 gp
Shuriken of tremendous shock	31,000 gp

Potion	Market Price
False life	300 gp
Flaming fists	300 gp

Ring	Market Price
Mage armor	12,000 gp
Shocking blows	13,000 gp

Wondrous Item	Market Price
Headband of ferocity	2,000 gp
Sandals of the tiger's leap	3,500 gp
Ki straps	5,000 gp
Amulet of mighty fists (+1)	6,000 gp
Vest of false life	12,000 gp
Gloves of fearsome grip	15,000 gp
Amulet of mighty fists (+2)	24,000 gp
Amulet of mighty fists (+3)	54,000 gp
Amulet of mighty fists (+4)	96,000 gp
Belt of mighty prowess	108,000 gp
Amulet of mighty fists (+5)	150,000 gp
Headband of perfect excellence	180,000 gp

Shield Descriptions

Arrow Catching: A shield with this ability attracts ranged weapons to it. It has a deflection bonus of +1 versus ranged weapons because projectiles and thrown weapons veer toward it. Additionally, any projectile or thrown weapon aimed at a target within 5 feet of the shield's wearer diverts from its original target and targets the shield's bearer instead. (If the wielder has total cover with respect to the attacker, the projectile or thrown weapon is not diverted.) Additionally, those attacking the wearer with ranged weapons ignore any miss chances that would normally apply. Projectiles and thrown weapons that have an enhancement bonus higher than the shield's base AC bonus are not diverted to the wearer (but the shield's increased AC bonus still applies against these weapons). The wielder activates this ability with a command word and can shut it off by repeating the command word.

Caster Level: 8th; *Prerequisites:* Craft Magic Arms and Armor, *entropic shield*; *Market Price:* +1 bonus.

Dancing: The wearer can loose a dancing shield as a standard action and command it to protect a single character (possibly the wearer himself). The dancing shield floats in the air in front of the protected character, darting in front of an opponent's weapons and providing cover against attacks from one opponent per round. (It provides cover against an attacker unless it has already done so since its wielder's last turn.) Use the shield's armor bonus (including its enhancement bonus) as the cover bonus to AC. At the end of 4 rounds, the dancing shield falls to the ground. The user must pick it up and command it for it to function again.

Only one dancing shield can protect a character. It is half as effective as normal (half the cover bonus to AC) when protecting a Large-size creature, and it cannot effectively provide cover for a Huge or bigger creature. The dancing shield only functions for a character that is proficient with using shields. It ceases dancing before 4 rounds have passed if so commanded.

Caster Level: 15th; *Prerequisites:* Craft Magic Arms and Armor, *animate objects*; *Market Price:* +3 bonus.

Magic Weapon Descriptions

Ki Focus: The magic weapon serves as a channel for the wielder's *ki*, allowing her to use her special *ki* attacks through the weapon as if it were an unarmed attack. These attacks include the monk's stunning attack, *ki strike*, and quivering palm, as well as the Stunning Fist feat. Only melee weapons can have *ki* focus.

Caster Level: 8th; *Prerequisites:* Craft Magic Arms and Armor, creator must be a monk; *Market Price:* +1 bonus.

Merciful: The weapon deals +1d6 points of damage, and all damage it deals is subdual damage. On command, the weapon suppresses this ability until commanded to resume it. Bows, crossbows, and slings so enchanted bestow the merciful effect upon their ammunition.

Caster Level: 5th; *Prerequisites:* Craft Magic Arms and Armor, *cure light wounds*; *Market Price:* +1 bonus.

Seeking: Only ranged weapons can have the seeking ability. The weapon veers toward the target, negating any miss chances that would otherwise apply, such as from concealment. (The wielder still has to aim the weapon at the right place. Arrows mistakenly shot into an empty space, for example, do not veer and hit invisible enemies, even if they are nearby.)

Caster Level: 12th; *Prerequisites:* Craft Magic Arms and Armor, *true seeing*; *Market Price:* +1 bonus.

Sure Striking: A sure striking weapon harms creatures with damage reduction as if it had a +5 enhancement bonus. Bows, crossbows, and slings cannot have the sure striking ability.

Caster Level: 6th; *Prerequisites:* Craft Magic Arms and Armor, *greater magic weapon*; *Market Price:* +1 bonus.

Vicious: When a vicious weapon strikes an opponent, it creates a flash of disruptive energy that resonates between the opponent and the wielder. This energy deals +2d6 points of damage to the opponent and 1d6 points of damage to the wielder. Only melee weapons can be vicious.

Caster Level: 9th; *Prerequisites:* Craft Magic Arms and Armor, *enervation*; *Market Price:* +1 bonus.

Specific Weapon Descriptions

Bow of True Arrows: This +1 mighty composite longbow (+1 Strength bonus required) stores the *true strike* spell, which the wielder can activate with a spell trigger (as with a wand). The wielder gains the benefits of the spell only when shooting an arrow from the bow. Unlike a wand, the bow casts the spell any number of times. Both arcane archers and initiates of the bow favor *bows of true arrows*.

Caster Level: 5th; *Prerequisites:* Craft Magic Arms and Armor, *true strike*; *Market Price:* 4,000 gp; *Cost to Create:* 2,250 gp + 140 XP.

Shatterspike: Wielders without the Sunder feat use *Shatterspike* as a +1 longsword only; wielders with the Sunder feat can use it as above, but also may use it to attack a foe's weapon without provoking an attack of opportunity. Furthermore, a wielder with the Sunder feat adds a +4 bonus (including the sword's +1 enchantment) to the opposed roll when attempting to strike a foe's weapon. If successful, *Shatterspike* deals 1d8+4 points of damage plus the wielder's Strength modifier to the target weapon (the target weapon's hardness must still be overcome with each hit). *Shatterspike* can damage enchanted weapons of up to +4.

Caster Level: 13th; *Prerequisites:* Str 13, Enchant Arms and Armor, Power Attack, Sunder, *shatter*;

Market Price: 4,315 gp; *Cost to Create:* 2,315 gp + 160 XP; *Weight:* 4 lb.

Shuriken of Tremendous Shock: The +1 *shuriken* come in sets of three. If a character hits an opponent with one shuriken, it deals +1d6 electrical damage. If she hits an opponent with two shuriken at the same time, the first deals +1d6 points of electrical damage and the second deals +2d6 points of electrical damage. If she hits an opponent with all three shuriken at the same time, the first deals +1d6 points of electrical damage, the second deals +2d6 points of electrical damage, and the third deals +3d6 points of electrical damage.

Caster Level: 12th; *Prerequisites:* Craft Magic Arms and Armor, *lightning bolt; Market Price:* 31,000 gp; *Cost to Create:* 16,000 gp + 1,200 XP.

Potion Descriptions

False Life: The drinker gains 1d10+3 temporary hit points. The effect lasts 3 hours.

Caster Level: 3rd; *Prerequisites:* Brew Potion, *endurance; Market Price:* 300 gp.

Flaming Fists: The drinker's hands burst into flame, adding +1d6 points of bonus fire damage to her unarmed attacks. The flames do not harm her. The effect lasts 3 minutes.

Caster Level: 3rd; *Prerequisites:* Brew Potion, *burning hands; Market Price:* 300 gp.

Ring Descriptions

Mage Armor: This ring protects the wearer as with the *mage armor* spell (+4 armor bonus to AC).

Caster Level: 1st; *Prerequisites:* Forge Ring, *mage armor;* Market Price: 12,000 gp.

Shocking Blows: On command, this ring imbues the wearer's hands with electrical energy. The wearer can make one touch attack each round that does 1d8+3 electrical damage. As with a regular touch spell, the wearer can also simply make unarmed attacks normally, the ring discharging whenever the wearer successfully hits.

Caster Level: 3rd; *Prerequisites:* Forge Ring, *shocking grasp; Market Price:* 13,000 gp.

Wondrous Item Descriptions

Amulet of Mighty Fists: This amulet grants an enhancement bonus of +1 to +5 to attack and damage rolls with unarmed attacks.

Caster Level: 5th; *Prerequisites:* Craft Wondrous Item, *magic fang,* caster must be of a level three times that of the bonus of the amulet; *Market Price:* 6,000 gp (amulet +1); 24,000 gp (amulet +2); 54,000 gp (amulet +3); 96,000 gp (amulet +4); or 150,000 gp (amulet +5).

Belt of Mighty Prowess: This wide, adamantine-studded leather belt grants the wearer a +6 enhancement bonus to Strength and Constitution.

Caster Level: 15th; *Prerequisites:* Craft Wondrous Item, *bull's strength, endurance; Market Price:* 108,000 gp.

Gloves of Fearsome Grip: These flexible leather gloves increase the strength of the wearer's grip. They grant the wearer a +5 enhancement bonus to Climb checks, grapple checks, and opposed attack rolls made during a disarm attempt (either offensively or defensively).

Caster Level: 10th; *Prerequisites:* Craft Wondrous Item, *bull's strength; Market Price:* 15,000 gp.

Headband of Ferocity: This headband made of wild boar leather lets the wearer keep going when she would normally collapse from her wounds. She can act normally at 0 hp (though taking strenuous actions still damages her). If she's at negative hp (as low as –9), she acts normally, although she still risks losing 1 hp each round, as normal. At –10 hp, she dies. Likewise, the wearer is harder to stop with subdual damage. Subdual damage does not stagger her, and she falls unconscious only when her subdual damage exceeds her hp by 10 or more.

Caster Level: 8th; *Prerequisites:* Craft Wondrous Item, *endurance; Market Price:* 2,000 gp.

Headband of Perfect Excellence: This pure silk cloth is worn as a headband. It grants the wearer a +6 enhancement bonus to Strength, Dexterity, and Wisdom.

Caster Level: 18th; *Prerequisites:* Craft Wondrous Item, *bull's strength, cat's grace,* and either *commune* or *legend lore; Market Price:* 180,000 gp.

Ki Straps: These leather straps, when wrapped around both hands, grant the wearer a +5 enhancement bonus to her DC with a monk's stunning attack or the Stunning Fist feat. Wearing the straps is like wearing gloves; they take up the "gloves" slot on the character's body.

Caster Level: 7th; *Prerequisites:* Craft Wondrous Item, monk level 3rd+; *Market Price:* 5,000 gp.

Sandals of the Tiger's Leap: These sandals allow the wearer to make devastating flying kicks. The wearer must have 5 ranks of Jump or Tumble to use them. On a charge, she can perform a flying kick. Treat this as an unarmed attack that deals double normal damage.

Caster Level: 9th; *Prerequisites:* Craft Wondrous Item, *jump; Market Price:* 3,500 gp.

Vest of False Life: While wearing the vest, a character gains +10 hp. When he takes it off, he loses 10 hp. (They are not temporary hp in the normal sense.)

Caster Level: 6th; *Prerequisites:* Craft Wondrous Item, *endurance; Market Price:* 12,000 gp.

VEHICLES

Sometimes walking or even riding a mount is not feasible. Whether it is because you are hauling more loot than you can carry or because you are moving large quantities of cumbersome items, the time comes when you need a vehicle. The *Player's Handbook* provides details on a few vehicles, but presented below are two options for those seeking more versatile means of transportation.

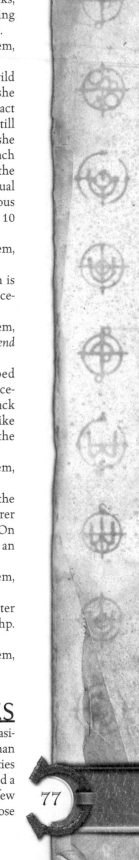

Two-Person Chariot

While most armies favor mounted knights in the cavalry role, some still favor the two-person chariot. Two heavy warhorses pull a small, two-wheeled platform on which two soldiers stand. The chariot is made of wood and iron and provides one-quarter cover to its occupants.

The chariot has a speed of 50 feet if being pulled by two horses, but a speed of only 40 feet if being pulled by only one. It cannot turn more than 90 degrees in a single round. If it takes a double move, it can only turn 45 degrees. If a chariot turns, it must travel at least 30 feet before it turns again, or 40 feet if it is turning in the opposite direction.

Driving the chariot uses most of the same rules as riding a horse and engaging in mounted combat, except Handle Animal is the relevant skill.

Handle Animal Task	DC
Fighting with one hand while driving with the other	5
Cutting a wounded/unconscious horse free of its harness	15
Avoiding a collision	Varies
Making a sideswipe attack	20

Collisions: Chariots are vulnerable to terrain obstacles such as fallen logs, deep mud, or the bodies of the fallen. If a chariot runs over such an obstacle, the driver must make a Handle Animal check to swerve away. (The DM sets the DC depending on the severity of the obstacle.) If the driver fails, the chariot upends and passengers and horses take 1d6 points of damage if the chariot was moving at a speed of 40 feet or less, 2d6 if it was moving faster.

Sideswipe Attack: Chariots often have scythelike blades attached to their wheels. If the driver maneuvers the chariot's side directly adjacent to an opponent's square, the blades make a free attack if the driver succeeds at a Handle Animal check (DC 20). Treat the sideswipe as a melee attack with a scythe that has +1 attack and damage bonus for every 10 feet the chariot moved that round before it reached the target square. For example, if the chariot moved 40 feet and made a sideswipe, the blade would attack at +4 and do 2d4+4 damage.

The passenger is generally equipped with a composite shortbow and a longspear, while the driver wields a halfspear (driving the chariot with one hand and fighting with the other).

Ranged attacks from a moving chariot suffer the same penalties as ranged attacks from horseback. It is possible to fire a longbow from a chariot, however.

If you are using a grid, the chariot is 5 feet wide and 10 feet long. A typical two-person chariot costs 300 gp +100 gp for scythes attached to the chariot's sides. It weighs 300 lb. and can carry a further 800 lb.,

including the riders and their equipment. It requires at least light warhorses to pull it.

If one of the mounts dies in combat, the chariot driver must immediately make a Handle Animal check (DC 15) to cut the animal free. If the chariot driver fails, the body of the horse is treated as an obstacle, requiring a Handle Animal check (DC 15) to avoid upending the chariot. This check must be made every round until the horse is cut free.

Chariot Collision DCs

Of course, a million things exist that you can drive your chariots over, into, and through. Here are some typical DCs for the Handle Animal checks required to avoid upending your chariot:

Item struck or run over	DC
Light underbrush	10
Log	10
Muddy ground	10
Small pedestrian	10
Medium-size pedestrian	15
Large pedestrian (including horse)	20
Wooden fence	20
Heavy underbrush	20
Hedgerow	25
Another chariot, side or rear	25
Another chariot, head-on	30

CHARIOT FEATS

The feats that charioteers use in combat parallel the mounted combat feats in Chapter 5 of the *Player's Handbook*.

Chariot Combat [General]

You are skilled in chariot combat.

Prerequisite: Handle Animal skill

Benefit: Once per round when either of your steeds is hit, you may make a Handle Animal check to negate the hit. The hit is negated if your Handle Animal check is greater than the attack roll (essentially, the Handle Animal check becomes the steed's Armor Class if it is higher than the steed's regular AC).

Chariot Archery [General]

You are skilled at using ranged weapons from a chariot.

Prerequisite: Chariot Combat, Handle animal skill.

Benefit: The penalty you suffer when using a ranged weapon from the chariot is halved: –2 rather than –4 if your chariot is taking a double move, and –4 instead of –8 if your mounts are running.

Chariot Trample [General]

You are trained in using your chariot to knock down opponents.

Prerequisite: Chariot Combat, Handle Animal skill.

Benefit: When you attempt to overrun an opponent with your chariot, the target may not choose to avoid you. If you knock down the target, your steeds each may make one hoof attack against the opponent, gaining the standard +4 bonus on attack rolls against prone targets. The wheels of the chariot do a further 2d6 points of damage automatically, but you must succeed in Handle Animal check (DC varies depending on the size of the opponent) or upend the chariot. See the chart below for sample DCs.

Chariot Sideswipe [General]

You are skilled at using your chariot's scythe blades against foes.

Prerequisite: Chariot Combat, Handle Animal skill.

Benefit: With a charge action, you may maneuver your chariot close to a foe, attack, sideswipe with the chariot's scythes (assuming it has any), and move away again. You must continue the straight line of the charge with your movement, and your total movement in the round cannot exceed double the chariot's speed. Neither you nor your steeds provoke an attack of opportunity from the opponent you are sideswiping.

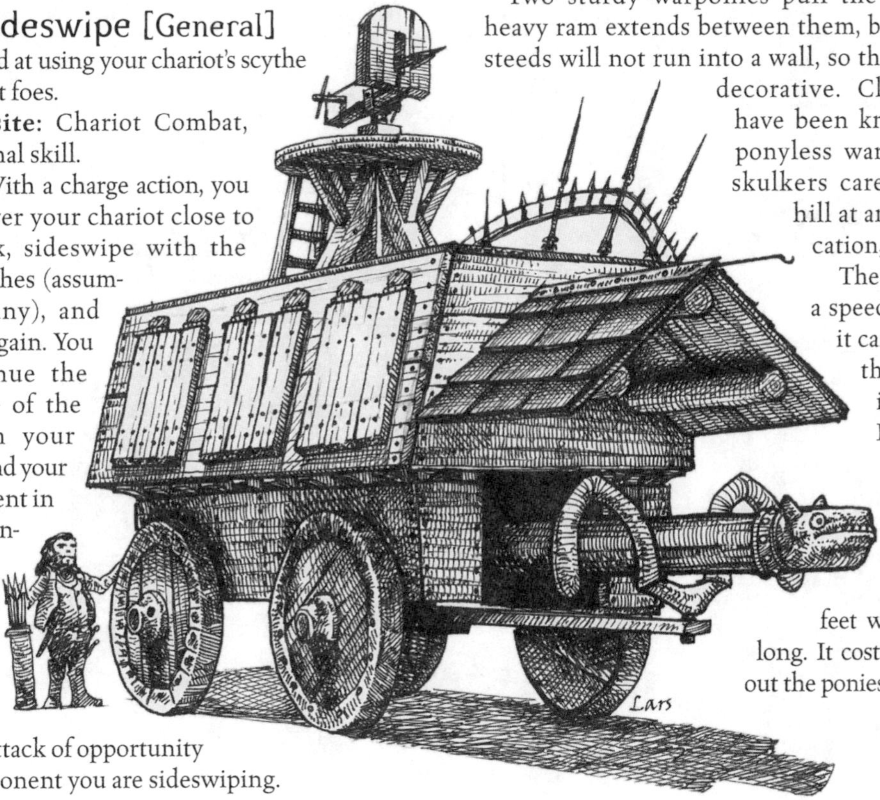

Chariot Charge [General]

You are skilled at charging with you chariot.

Prerequisite: Chariot Combat, Chariot Sideswipe, Handle Animal skill.

Benefit: When aboard a chariot and using the charge action, you deal double damage with a melee weapon (or triple damage with a lance or longspear).

Halfling War-Wagon

Many halflings clans wander from town to town in long wagon caravans. Therefore, it is no surprise that when halflings go to war, they adapt their wagons to martial use.

The halfling war-wagon is as large as a human-size wagon, but the interior is scaled to fit the brave halflings who fight from within it. The wagon has walls, floors, and ceilings of solid oak (5 hardness, 60 hp) and wide wheels that are less likely to sink into the mud of the battlefield.

The inside of the wagon is divided into two levels. The upper level holds six archers, who fire from the numerous arrow slits in the sides of the wagon. On the lower level crouch six halfling "skulkers"—scouts adept at dropping through a trap door in the wagon's floor, then quickly seizing an outside objective while the wagon rolls along.

Another halfling steers the wagon from an enclosed compartment at the front. Some wagons even mount ballistas on top, with a swiveling cupola (one-half cover) protecting the ballista operator.

Two sturdy warponies pull the war-wagon. A heavy ram extends between them, but even trained steeds will not run into a wall, so the ram is mostly decorative. Clever halflings have been known to send a ponyless war-wagon full of skulkers careening down a hill at an enemy fortification, however.

The war-wagon has a speed of 30 feet, but it cannot turn more than 90 degrees in any one turn. If it takes a double move, it can only turn 45 degrees.

The war-wagon is 10 feet wide and 15 feet long. It costs 5,000 gp without the ponies.

Lars

TOWERS, KEEPS, AND CASTLES

A fighter's home is his castle, where he gazes out at an army arrayed below him, secure behind arrow slits, crenellations, and thick walls of stone. In addition, while many monks may wander from town to town, others study and train at well-hidden monasteries and temples.

This chapter provides sample buildings that can easily serve as the home of a mid- to high-level fighter or monk—or the fortress of their enemies. Though typical for their size, no two castles are alike, so feel free to customize these designs and add your own details.

Border Tower

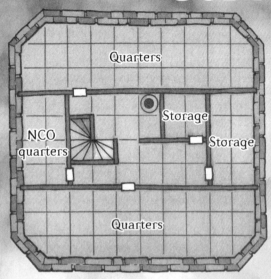

First floor (half below ground)

Quarters

NCO quarters

Storage

Storage

Quarters

Legend

- Arrow slit
- Barred window
- Fireplace
- Door
- Ballista
- Crenellation
- Spiral stairs
- Ladder
- Well
- Murder holes

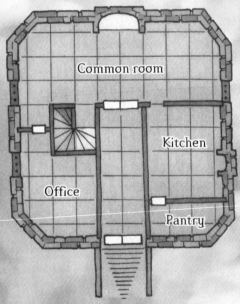

Second floor

Common room

Kitchen

Office

Pantry

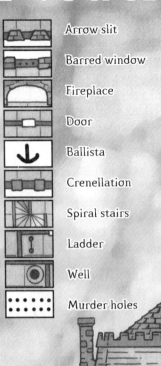

Exterior

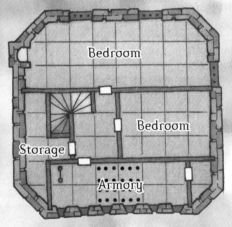

Third floor

Bedroom

Bedroom

Storage

Armory

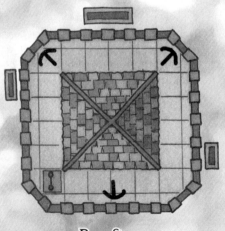

Rooftop

One Square = 5 Feet

The Border Tower

This tower is a typical outpost for soldiers guarding an important tollgate, crossroads, or shoreline. Though conditions are somewhat cramped, the border tower can accommodate more than forty soldiers in at least some measure of comfort—although they spend much of their time outside. In times of war, the stone structure proves a hard-to-capture redoubt with dozens of archers and the three ballistas on the roof. In addition, the tower can become a family-size dwelling without too much remodeling on the inside; many a noble's manor has a border tower at its heart.

The tower is a three-story building with foot-thick stone-and-mortar walls that slope gently inward. Inside, joists hold up wooden plank floors (which also serve as ceilings) and paneled walls set into the "shell" of the stone outer walls. A well in the basement provides fresh water, and three fireplaces provide warmth in colder climes. Waste disposal is by trash-bin and chamber-pot to a midden-heap that is too far away to notice from the tower, but close enough to walk to.

Most border towers have a few outbuildings: a small stable or barn, pit latrine, and (in warmer climes) a "summer kitchen" so the cooking fire does not heat the whole tower unbearably.

Soldiers regard the border tower as easy to defend. There is only one entrance, up a flight of stairs completely exposed to arrow-slits and ballistas above. The tower's few windows are high on the building, barred, and can be shuttered if need be. In addition, a crenellated walkway around the rooftop offers archers clear fields of fire in every direction.

First Floor

The floor is set 5 feet into the earth, so it is as much basement as anything else.

Quarters: Each of these two rooms is filled with simple cots or bunks and sleeps twenty soldiers. Accommodations are spartan, and in the winter, the soldiers complain about the lack of a fireplace on this level. If the tower has been converted to private use, these two rooms are either used as storage, servant's quarters, or extra bedrooms.

NCO Quarters: Four sergeants typically share this room. Their accommodations are rarely better than those of their men are, but they have some measure of privacy.

Staircase: This sturdy wooden staircase connects all three levels of the tower. On each level, a large closet lies beneath the stairway.

Storage: These two rooms typically hold sacks of staple food and a wide array of gear—anything this unit might have picked up during its assignment here. In a noble's tower, these rooms remain general storage or become the wine cellar.

Second Floor

Entryway: Two barred iron doors swing open to reveal a long hallway. The walls are generally bare. If the tower has been converted into a domicile, the entryway is an excellent place to display tapestries and paintings.

Common Room: A huge table and an equally large fireplace dominate this room. The soldiers take their meals in the common room and spend some off-duty time here too. The purpose of the common room remains the same in a private tower, although the furnishings are far more sumptuous.

Office: This is the headquarters of the unit, and the officer of the day is generally found here among the maps and paperwork that are part of military life. Nobles often convert this room into a library or drawing room.

Kitchen: It takes a lot of work to feed forty men, so this room is usually occupied. A large kitchen-hearth dominates one wall, and the rest of the room is an ocean of spilled ingredients, dirty cutlery, simmering pots, and vast washbasins. The soldiers take kitchen duty on a rotating basis, and they are always running downstairs to get water from the well.

Pantry: Extra food is stored here behind a huge padlock; only the sergeants have the key. If the tower is a private residence, the pantry is probably unlocked.

Third Floor

Storage: Much of the weaponry is stored here: braces of arrows, ammunition for the ballistas, extra polearms, and spare bows and bowstrings. Nobles generally store more prosaic items here.

Armory: This room boasts an array of arrow slits that overlook the field in front of the tower and machicolations (floor holes) designed to provide one last surprise to intruders who make it past the front door. Unless a threat is imminent, soldiers here busy themselves performing necessary tasks such as re-fletching arrows, sharpening blades, and waxing bowstrings. A ladder leads to a hatch, giving access to the roof.

Bedrooms: The officers generally split these two rooms up, with the commanding officer taking the larger and subordinates sharing the smaller room. In a civilian tower, these bedrooms are more lavishly furnished, and the room with the fireplace is considered the master bedroom.

Rooftop

Walkway: Between the crenellations along the edge of the outer wall and the sloped shingle roof

---

How Much Does It Cost?

This basic tower costs 40,000 gp to build (not including equipment for guards). Upgrading furnishings from basic to fancy costs an additional 25,000 gp. A force of 40 soldiers, 4 sergeants, and 2 officers demands 326 gp per month in pay, and their meals cost 138 gp per month (for poor meals) or 414 gp per month (for common meals). The soldiers take shifts cooking and cleaning, so no other staff is necessary.

The border tower takes four weeks to build.

in the center lies a walkway that encircles the tower, making it easy for archers to fire in any direction. Three ballistas are mounted just behind the crenellations.

Typical Border Tower Soldier: Human War1; CR 1; Medium-size humanoid; HD 1d8+2; hp 6; Init +2; Spd 20 ft.; AC 16 (touch 12, flat-footed 14); Atk +3 melee (1d8+1/×3, longspear) or +2 melee (1d6+1/19–20, short sword) or +3 ranged (1d8/×3, longbow); AL N; SV Fort +4, Ref +2, Will +0; Str 13, Dex 15, Con 14, Int 12, Wis 10, Cha 8.

Skills and Feats: Climb +1, Handle Animal +3, Jump +1, Ride (horse) +6; Point Blank Shot, Weapon Focus (longspear).

Possessions: Scale mail armor, longspear, short sword, longbow, 20 arrows.

Tactics: When possible, these soldiers fight in ranks. The soldiers in the first rank set their longspears against a charge while those in the second rank fire their bows. When the enemy charges, the soldiers in the first rank take their readied attacks (and probably attacks of opportunity) against their attackers, then drop their longspears in favor of short swords. The ones in the second rank switch to longspears, remaining out of the enemies' reach.

Typical Border Tower Sergeant: Human War2; CR 2; Medium-size humanoid; HD 2d8+4; hp 13; Init +2; Spd 20 ft.; AC 16 (touch 12, flat-footed 14); Atk +4 melee (1d8+1/×3, longspear), or +3 melee (1d8+1, light flail); or +4 ranged (1d8/×3, longbow); AL N; SV Fort +5, Ref +2, Will +0; Str 13, Dex 15, Con 14, Int 12, Wis 10, Cha 8.

Skills and Feats: Climb +2, Handle Animal +4, Jump +2, Ride (horse) +9; Point Blank Shot, Weapon Focus (longspear).

Possessions: Scale mail armor, longspear, light flail, longbow, 20 arrows.

Tactics: As above. Each sergeant typically commands ten soldiers.

Typical Border Tower Officer: Human Ftr3; CR 3; Medium-size humanoid; HD 3d10+3; hp 19; Init +6; Spd 20 ft.; AC 19 (touch 12, flat-footed 17); Atk +7 melee (1d8+2/19–20, masterwork longsword) or +5 ranged (1d8+2/×3, mighty [+2] composite longbow); AL N; SV Fort +4, Ref +3, Will +0; Str 14, Dex 15, Con 13, Int 12, Wis 8, Cha 10.

Skills and Feats: Climb +1, Handle Animal +6, Jump +1, Listen +1, Ride (horse) +10, Spot +1; Alertness, Improved Initiative, Point Blank Shot, Weapon Focus (longsword).

Possessions: Chainmail, masterwork longsword, large wooden shield, mighty (+2) composite longbow, 20 arrows.

Elven Canopy Tower

Few elves are talented stonemasons, but elven ability in woodcraft and in forestry is unparalleled. Defenders of the forest homelands often construct treehouselike canopy towers on the periphery of elven communities. Canopy towers house about twenty-five elven archers or a single extended family—though in times of war there is little difference between the two.

Elves use a combination of traditional construction techniques, elven forestry skills, and magic to build canopy towers. By coaxing branches of a massive tree to grow in just the right way, they grow a sturdy foundation and frame for the tower buildings, which are then built with planks and beams hewn from naturally fallen trees. The elves dig vertical channels in the bark of the massive tree trunk; furrows from above bring rainwater, while furrows leading down funnel away the waste that fertilizes the tree's roots. A large, flat stone in the center of each building serves as a hearth for a cook-fire.

Inside, the architecture emphasizes the nature of elven communal living. Few doors exist, with only tapestries hanging from doorways to provide a measure of privacy. Windows and balconies let in sunlight and offer views of the surrounding forest. In addition, those same windows and balconies provide platforms for elven archers when enemies attack the tower. On a nearby branch, elven gardeners have trimmed and trained two sturdy branches, twisting them until they form the spars of perfect catapults aimed at the forest floor beyond the tower.

Most visitors reach the canopy tower through a platform lowered some five stories by a rope-and-pulley system. In a pinch, rope ladders on any balcony provide more access—or a quick escape route.

Main Structure, Lower Level

Elevator: It takes two elves to work the winches and pulleys that lower this platform to the ground 50 feet below. The platform rises and falls at a rate of 5 feet per round. A ladder near the platform winches leads to the upper level of the main structure.

Storage: This room is typically home to whatever valuables the elves have, as it has the canopy tower's only locked door.

Living quarters: Eight elves typically live here, sleeping in vine-woven hammocks.

Storage: Extra food and drink are typically stored here.

Meditation Area: This room, with its panoramic view of the forest, is typically used for worship and quiet reflection.

Main Structure, Upper Level

Dayroom: Elves typically take their meals here, eating in shifts in this small room.

Elven Canopy Tower

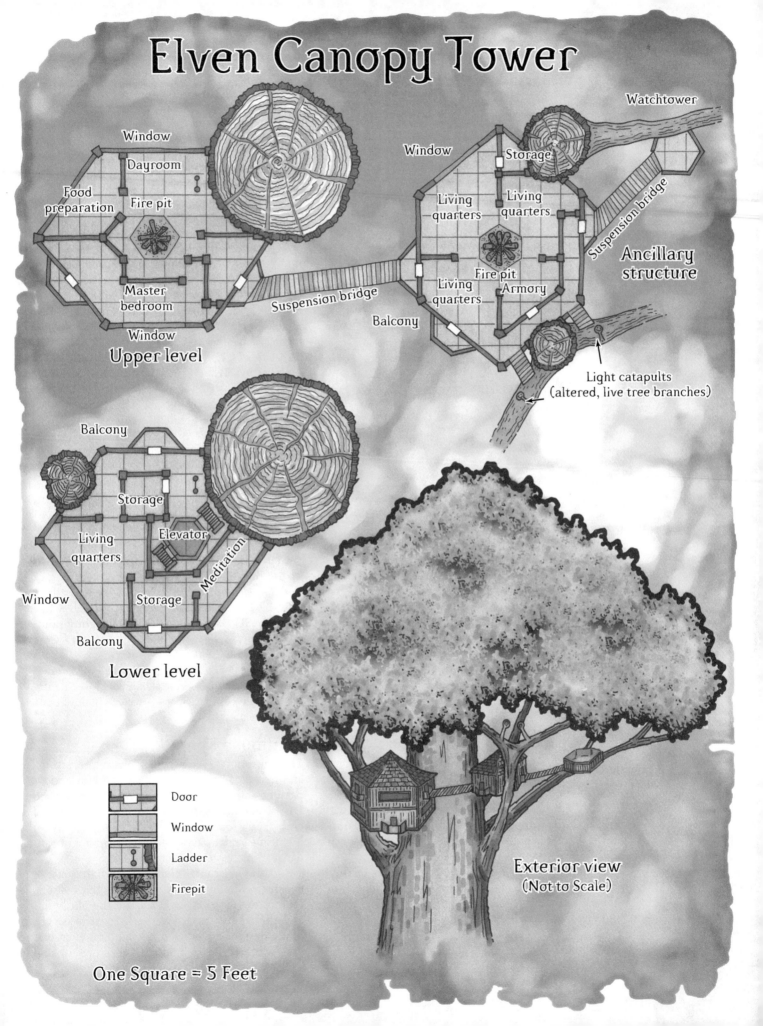

Watchtower

Window

Dayroom

Food preparation

Fire pit

Master bedroom

Window

Upper level

Suspension bridge

Window

Storage

Living quarters

Living quarters

Fire pit

Living quarters

Armory

Balcony

Suspension bridge

Ancillary structure

Light catapults
(altered, live tree branches)

Balcony

Storage

Living quarters

Elevator

Meditation

Window

Storage

Balcony

Lower level

Exterior view
(Not to Scale)

	Door
	Window
	Ladder
	Firepit

One Square = 5 Feet

Food Prep: Simple elven fare is prepared here, atop many cutting boards and amid jars of spices.

Master Bedroom: This room is reserved for the seniormost elf among the tower's inhabitants. Its furnishings are lavish, and the room features both a window and a balcony.

Suspension Bridge: This narrow walkway leads to the Ancillary Structure. It quickly detaches at either end in an emergency.

Ancillary Structure

Living Quarters: Up to six elves sleep in hammocks in each of these three rooms.

Armory: The elves keep spare weapons (including hundreds of arrows) here.

Light Catapults: Elven gardeners use a combination of magic and selective pruning to shape branches into organic catapults. Two are accessible from short suspension bridges and ladders.

Watchtower: A suspension bridge leads to this small tower, which has clear views of the forest floor in every direction. A giant owl befriended by the elves often roosts directly above this watchtower.

Typical Archer: Elf War1; CR 1; Medium-size humanoid; HD 1d8; hp 4; Init +2; Spd 30 ft.; AC 16 (touch 12, flat-footed 14); Atk +3 melee (1d8+2/19–20,

longsword); or +4 ranged (1d8/×3, longbow); SQ Elf traits; AL N; SV Fort +2, Ref +2, Will –1; Str 14, Dex 15, Con 10, Int 10, Wis 8, Cha 13.

Skills and Feats: Climb +4, Hide +2, Listen +1, Search +2, Spot +1; Weapon Focus (longbow).

Possessions: Studded leather armor, buckler, longsword, longbow, 20 arrows.

Typical Leader: Elf Div3; CR 3; Medium-size humanoid; HD 3d4+3; hp 12; Init +2; Spd 30 ft.; AC 12 (touch 12, flat-footed 10); Atk +1 melee (1d8/19–20, longsword); or +4 ranged (1d8/×3, masterwork longbow); SQ Cat familiar, elf traits, empathic link with familiar, scry on familiar, share spells with familiar, touch (via familiar); AL N; SV Fort +1, Ref +3, Will +2; Str 10, Dex 14, Con 10, Int 15, Wis 8, Cha 13.

Skills and Feats: Concentration +6, Knowledge (arcana) +8, Listen +3, Move Silently +4, Profession (gardener) +5, Search +4, Spellcraft +8, Spot +3; Alertness, Dodge, Scribe Scroll, Toughness.

Spells Prepared: (5/4/3; base DC = 12 + spell level): 0—*detect magic, detect poison, light, mending, read magic;* 1st—*mage armor, shield, sleep, true strike;* 2nd—*detect thoughts, protection from arrows, web.*

Possessions: Longsword, masterwork longbow, 20 arrows, *potion of cure moderate wounds,* scroll of *invisibility sphere,* scroll of *haste, wand of magic missile.*

Giant Owl: CR 3; Large magical beast; HD 4d10+4; hp 26; Init +3; Spd 10 ft., fly 70 ft. (average); AC 15 (touch 12, flat-footed 12); Atk +7 melee (1d6+4, 2 claws), +2 melee (1d8+2, bite); Face/Reach 5 ft. × 5 ft./10 ft.; SQ Darkvision (60 ft.), low-light vision; AL NG; SV Fort +5, Ref +7, Will +3; Str 18, Dex 17, Con 12, Int 10, Wis 14, Cha 10. 20-ft. wingspan.

Skills and Feats: Hide –1, Knowledge (nature) +6, Listen +16 (includes +8 racial bonus), Move Silently +9 (or +17 while flying), Spot +10 (or +14 in dusk or darkness); Alertness.

Lighthouse Keep

The lighthouse keep provides secure protection for an important navigation aid—a lighthouse to warn passing ships of a dangerous reef or rocky shore. Easy to defend, its sturdy construction is designed to withstand a force more powerful than an army—the hurricanes, tidal waves, and other storms and natural dangers that batter many coastlines.

As shipping routes change, new lighthouses are constructed, and nobles who favor the distinctive look of the tower quickly acquire the old building and the impressive view the keep affords. Lighthouse designs are popular enough that even inland castles sometimes mimic the keep's layout, simply replacing the lighthouse itself with an imposing central tower.

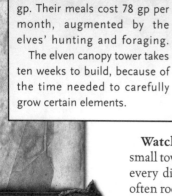

How Much Does It Cost?

This canopy tower costs 46,000 gp to build (not including equipment for guards). The monthly pay for a force of 25 elven archers and their leader is 177 gp. Their meals cost 78 gp per month, augmented by the elves' hunting and foraging.

The elven canopy tower takes ten weeks to build, because of the time needed to carefully grow certain elements.

Lighthouse Keep

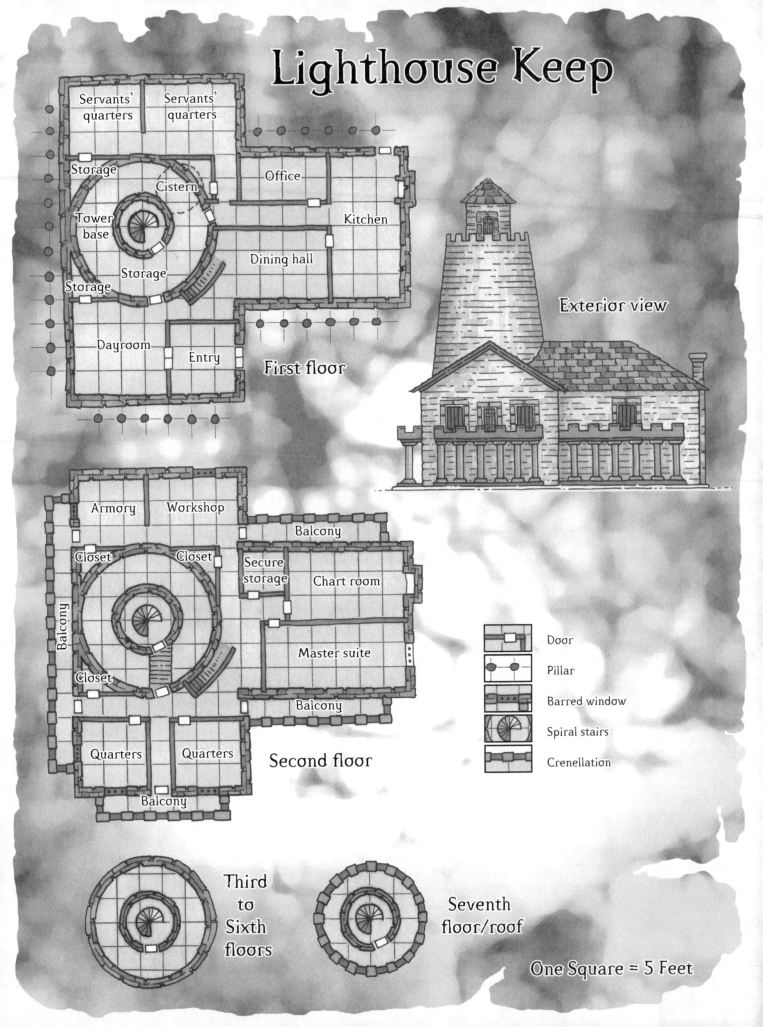

First floor

Servants' quarters
Servants' quarters
Storage
Cistern
Office
Tower base
Kitchen
Storage
Dining hall
Storage
Dayroom
Entry

Exterior view

Second floor

Armory
Workshop
Closet
Closet
Balcony
Secure storage
Chart room
Balcony
Closet
Master suite
Closet
Balcony
Quarters
Quarters
Balcony

Third to Sixth floors

Seventh floor/roof

Door
Pillar
Barred window
Spiral stairs
Crenellation

One Square = 5 Feet

The lighthouse tower rises five stories above the two-story living structure that surrounds it. Accommodations inside are rather comfortable for a keep, because the isolated location and harsh weather keep its inhabitants indoors much of the time. Gutters on the roof and the lighthouse channel rainwater into a cistern, and inhabitants typically take their trash to a compost heap nearby. A high promontory overlooking the ocean is an ideal location for a lighthouse keep, and if there is arable land nearby, the keep generally tends as large a garden as they can maintain.

When under attack, the keep's inhabitants defend themselves from crenellated balconies that face every direction, and the best archers generally take positions atop the lighthouse. If a storm is brewing, every window in the keep is shuttered from within.

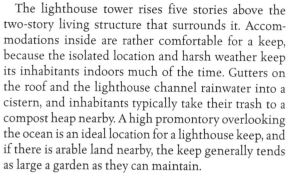

First Floor

Entry: This room is typically full of nautical bric-a-brac. Visitors wait here while the servants announce them to the inhabitants.

Dayroom: The keep's soldiers and servants spend much of their off-duty time here playing cards or reading. Chairs and tables clutter the room from wall to wall.

Dining Hall: This room is small enough that diners invariably overflow into the dayroom. A wooden stairway leads to the second floor.

Kitchen: The heat of the fireplace makes this a popular place in stormy weather. Shelves hang on every wall, and an array of washbasins and chopping blocks covers tables in the center of the room.

Office: This room is reserved for the lighthouse keeper, who is found here doing paperwork during quiet parts of the day.

Servants' Quarters: The cooks, janitors, and keeper's hands sleep in bunks here. A curtain separates the sexes, but little privacy exists here otherwise.

Tower Base: Two separate circular walls support the lighthouse, making it one of the sturdiest structures in common use. Each wall is made of reinforced masonry more than a foot thick, and giant spars connect the outer wall to the inner one. On the first floor, pipes from above connect to the cistern that serves as the keep's main water supply, and the rest of the space between the outer and inner wall is used to store the thousand items an isolated lighthouse might need. Inside the inner wall, a spiral staircase leads up seven stories to the lighthouse beacon.

Second Floor

Quarters: These two rooms are full of bunks for the soldiers that guard the keep. The rooms are small, so the soldiers spend little of their waking time here.

Balconies: These crenellated walkways are key to the defense of the keep. They provide one-half cover for archers behind them.

Master Suite: The bedroom for the lighthouse keeper is probably the most richly appointed room in the keep.

Secure Storage: This room is always locked, and only the lighthouse keeper has the key. The keep's paychest is kept here, as are any other valuables.

Chartroom: This room holds nautical charts, ship's logs, and other records on massive shelves along the walls.

Workshop: Keeper's hands are usually here mending rope or performing any of the countless maintenance tasks the lighthouse requires. This room is a tumble of workbenches, spools of rope, and tools leaning against every wall.

Armory: The keep's supply of weapons (mostly crossbows and spears) is kept here.

Tower: A catwalk leads from the spiral staircase to the hallway near the soldiers' quarters.

Lighthouse Top

Walkway: The spiral staircase ends at a door leading out to a crenellated walkway that provides a panoramic view of the surroundings. Like the balconies, the walkway provides one-half cover to those fighting from behind it.

Beacon: Magic keeps the beacon alight without requiring constant refueling. A ladder leads from the walkway to the beacon itself, which can be shuttered to protect it if the weather is severe. The shutter facing the ocean is made of slats that can be rapidly opened and closed, allowing the lighthouse to send coded messages to ships at sea via a series of flashes.

Typical Lighthouse Keep Guard: Human War1; CR 1; Medium-size humanoid; HD 1d8+2; hp 6; Init +2; Spd 30 ft.; AC 15 (touch 12, flat-footed 13); Atk +3 melee (1d10+1/×3, glaive) or +3 ranged (1d8/19–20, light crossbow); AL N; SV Fort +4, Ref +2, Will +0; Str 13, Dex 15, Con 14, Int 12, Wis 10, Cha 8.

Skills and Feats: Climb +4, Jump +4, Spot +2, Swim +5; Point Blank Shot, Weapon Focus (glaive).

Possessions: Studded leather armor, glaive, light crossbow, 10 crossbow bolts.

Typical Lighthouse Keeper: Human Exp3; CR 3; Medium-size humanoid; HD 3d6+3; hp 13; Init –1; Spd 30 ft.; AC 11 (touch 9, flat-footed 11); Atk +2 melee (1d6/×3, halfspear) or +1 ranged (1d8/19–20, light crossbow); AL N; SV Fort +2, Ref +0, Will +5; Str 10, Dex 8, Con 12, Int 15, Wis 14, Cha 13.

Skills and Feats: Craft (carpentry) +8, Craft (stonemasonry) +8, Knowledge (geography) +8, Knowledge (nature) +8, Listen +4, Profession (cartographer) +10,

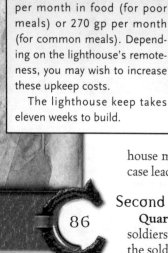

How Much Does It Cost?

The lighthouse keep costs 110,000 gp to build (not including equipment for guards). A staff of 20 soldiers and 10 servants and lackeys costs 150 gp per month in salary and 90 gp per month in food (for poor meals) or 270 gp per month (for common meals). Depending on the lighthouse's remoteness, you may wish to increase these upkeep costs.

The lighthouse keep takes eleven weeks to build.

Spot +12, Swim +6, Use Rope +5, Wilderness Lore +8; Alertness, Skill Focus (Spot), Skill Focus (Profession [cartographer]).

Possessions: Leather armor, halfspear, light crossbow, 10 crossbow bolts, spyglass.

Gnome Bridge Keep

Gnomes build bridge keeps to protect key entry points into their homelands and to earn revenue from tolls on the merchants and travelers that use the bridge. The keep combines a working drawbridge with a tollgate and well-protected fortification. In time of war, the bridge keep holds an important crossing for troops in the field—or denies such a crossing to the enemy.

Though gnomes pioneered the design of the bridge keep, it has since been copied by other races, which simply enlarge the doors, raise the ceilings, and increase the scale of the living space. However, newer gnome versions feature more elaborate bridge mechanisms and inventive traps for those who would seize or destroy the bridge.

The bridge keep consists of three stone buildings attached to a sturdy wooden bridge that crosses the river. A main keep houses the drawbridge mechanism and most of the living space, while an auxiliary keep on the same side of the river holds the kitchen and storage areas. A small gatehouse on the far side of the river collects tolls and guards the bridge itself.

The bridge is a wooden affair that retracts to allow any tall-masted ships past it. With the pull of a switch in the main keep, a water wheel under the bridge descends into the water. The force of its turning slides the center section of the bridge toward the main keep, where it remains until another switch sends a different water wheel into the river, pushing the bridge back into place.

The keep's inhabitants draw their water from the river itself and dispose of garbage in a midden-heap on the bank downriver. When under attack, arrow slits in the main keep and a crenellated roof on the auxiliary keep provides cover for archers. Anyone rushing across the bridge between the two main buildings is caught in a crossfire of by arrows launched from still more arrow slits.

Main Keep, First Floor

Keep in mind that the whole keep is sized for gnomes. This does not affect the square footage of the rooms much, but doors are only 5 feet tall and ceilings only 7 feet high. Furniture is built for Small users, too.

The bottom end of the bridge ramp is the same elevation as the floor here.

Patrol Entrance: This is the main entrance for the gnomes that live in the keep (visitors enter on the second floor). Most who come and go through here are the gatehouse guards and the soldiers who patrol the roads around the keep.

Office: The officer of the day has a small, spartan office here.

Armory: This locked room holds the keep's supply of weapons.

Workshop: This large room—full of tables and tools—is where most maintenance work is done. Accordingly, it is usually busy and noisy with the clang of hammers and rasp of saws.

Chapel: This room is used for various religious services. Those worshiping frequently admonish the gnomes in the workshop to keep the noise down.

Drawbridge Mechanism: This room houses all the levers, gears, and switches required to retract and extend the bridge. Two gnomes always man it, although a single set of hands can operate the bridge in a pinch.

Main Keep, Second Floor

The top of the bridge ramp (and the bridge itself) is the same elevation as the floor here.

Entry Hall: Visitors to the keep usually enter through this room, which has doors and chairs designed for Medium-size visitors.

Quarters: These two rooms house the keep's guards and soldiers in bunk beds.

Main Keep, Third Floor

Master Suite: The lord of the keep lives in this sumptuously appointed room.

Library: Books here include various engineering treatises and whatever books follow the lord of the keep's tastes.

Walkway to Auxiliary Keep: This crenellated walkway provides one-half cover to those heading toward the roof of the auxiliary keep. Because it is right over the bridge deck, it provides an excellent vantage point for scouting or archery fire.

Auxiliary Keep, First Floor

Quarters: This room houses the keep's bridge technicians and domestic servants.

Pantry: The keep's food supply is stored here.

Storage: Various cooking and cleaning implements are kept here.

Auxiliary Keep, Second Floor

Office: The bridge lieutenant or customs agent works from here, stopping every traveler until the toll is paid. If cargo inspections are part of the bridge keep's mandate, they are performed here, under the watchful eye of guards behind the arrow slits.

How Much Does It Cost?

The bridge keep costs 100,000 gp to build (not including equipment for guards). Upgrading furnishings to fancy costs an additional 40,000 gp. A staff of 20 guards, 5 technicians, and 10 servants costs 225 gp per month in salary and 105 gp per month in food (for poor meals) or 315 gp per month (for common meals). The bridge keep takes in approximately 1,000 gp per year in profits.

The bridge keep takes ten weeks to build.

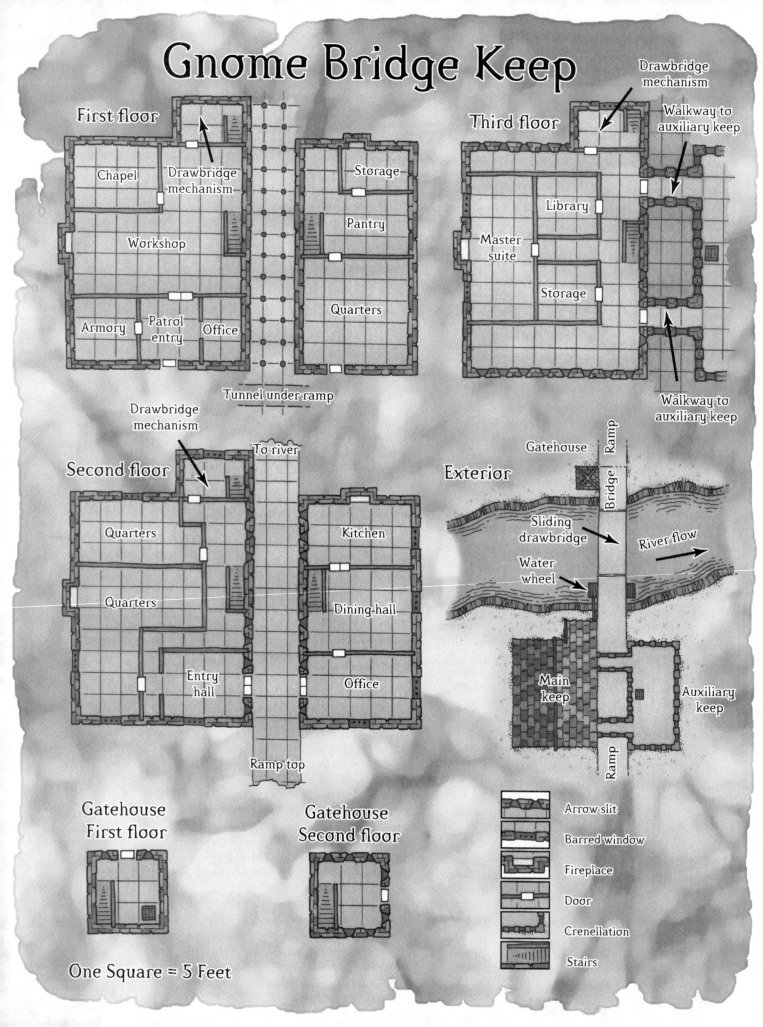

Gnome Bridge Keep

First floor

Chapel

Drawbridge mechanism

Workshop

Armory

Patrol entry

Office

Tunnel under ramp

Storage

Pantry

Quarters

Third floor

Drawbridge mechanism

Walkway to auxiliary keep

Master suite

Library

Storage

Walkway to auxiliary keep

Second floor

Drawbridge mechanism

To river

Quarters

Quarters

Kitchen

Dining hall

Entry hall

Office

Ramp top

Exterior

Gatehouse

Bridge

Ramp

Sliding drawbridge

Water wheel

River flow

Main keep

Auxiliary keep

Ramp

Gatehouse First floor

Gatehouse Second floor

Arrow slit

Barred window

Fireplace

Door

Crenellation

Stairs

One Square = 5 Feet

Dining Area: This room is small enough that the keep's inhabitants must eat in shifts. Accordingly, it is usually busy and always a mess.

Kitchen: This room is also a whirlwind of activity, with cook's assistants constantly rushing up and down the stairs that lead to the pantry.

Auxiliary Keep, Roof

Roof: Two walkways connect the wide, flat roof of the auxiliary keep to the third floor of the main keep. If the keep is under siege, much of its defense is directed from here.

Gatehouse

Gatehouse Interior: Each floor of the gatehouse is but a single room with perhaps a chair or two. The gatehouse is merely a defensible position on the far side of the river. A door connects the second floor to the bridge deck. In an emergency, gnomes trapped in the gatehouse climb out a trapdoor in the bottom of the gatehouse, then cross the river by climbing upside-down along rungs set into the bottom of the bridge. (This does not work if the bridge center has been retracted.)

▶**Typical Bridge Keep Guard:** Gnome War1; CR 1; Small humanoid; HD 1d8+3; hp 7; Init +2; Spd 15 ft.; AC 18 (touch 13, flat-footed 16); Atk +2 melee (1d6/×3, handaxe), or +4 ranged (1d8/19–20, light crossbow); SQ Gnome traits; AL N; SV Fort +5, Ref +2, Will +0; Str 11, Dex 15, Con 16, Int 12, Wis 10, Cha 8.

Skills and Feats: Climb –1, Hide +1, Jump –1, Listen +2, Spot +2; Point Blank Shot.

Possessions: Scale mail armor, buckler, handaxe, light crossbow, 10 crossbow bolts.

▶**Typical Bridge Technician:** Gnome Exp2; CR 2; Small humanoid; HD 2d6+4; hp 11; Init –1; Spd 20 ft.; AC 12 (touch 10, flat-footed 12); Atk –3 melee (1d6–1/×3, handaxe), or +0 ranged (1d8/19–20, light crossbow); SQ Gnome traits; AL N; SV Fort +2, Ref –1, Will +5; Str 8, Dex 8, Con 14, Int 15, Wis 14, Cha 13.

Skills and Feats: Alchemy +9, Craft (carpentry) +7, Craft (stonemasonry) +7, Disable Device +7, Hide +3, Knowledge (architecture and engineering) +9, Knowledge (geography) +7, Listen +4, Profession (boater) +7, Use Rope +4; Skill Focus (Knowledge [architecture and engineering]).

Possessions: Leather armor, handaxe, light crossbow, 10 crossbow bolts, various tools appropriate to current task.

Bailey Castle

This castle is typical of a landed noble whose job it is to provide for the defense of the lands around him. In times of peace, it is a gathering point for the residents of small farming communities that dot the nearby countryside, offering everything from horseshoes and beer to access to scribes and healers. In times of war, it is a place of refuge, able to withstand a concerted attack or outlast a siege.

Four stone towers dominate the main castle, the noble's residence and center of the castle complex. Reinforced walls 15 feet high branch out from the main castle, surrounding a wide array of wooden outbuildings that provide various services for the castle and the community at large; this area is the bailey that gives the castle type its name. Towers at the corners of the walls offer good vantage points for lookouts, and a barbican provides a well-guarded access point into the bailey.

Two wells (one in the main castle and another in the bailey) provide water, and the surrounding farms provide fresh food for the castle's denizens. Refuse is carted out of the keep and either dumped, burned, or used to fertilize surrounding fields.

If the surrounding area is attacked, civilians flee to the safety of the castle's outer walls, which form the first line of defense. If an enemy is successful in breaching the walls and takes the bailey, surviving defenders retreat to the main castle, where they make their last stand.

Main Castle

Four 40-foot crenellated towers anchor this three-story structure. The first floor is given over almost completely to a great-hall suitable for banquets and other important ceremonies. The second floor houses offices and libraries, and the third floor is given over to the lord's personal residence.

Each tower also has its function. This varies widely from castle to castle, but the northeast tower could be kitchen facilities, the southeast tower an armory, the southwest tower servants' quarters, and the northwest tower storage.

A huge set of barred wooden doors (hardness 5, 60 hp) guards the main entrance.

Outer Walls and Watchtowers

The walls are 15 feet tall and 10 feet thick and are made of stone and mortar (DC 15 to climb). A walkway runs along the top of the walls, connecting the watchtowers to each other and providing extra room for archers behind the crenellations. Watchtowers have narrow horizontal windows (providing three-quarters cover). Two soldiers typically stand watch at each tower, though many more fit if an attack is imminent. Simple wooden ladders provide access to the watchtowers and walls.

How Much Does It Cost?

The bailey castle costs 500,000 gp to build (not including equipment for guards). This includes a variety of fancy and luxury furnishings. A staff of 80 soldiers, 15 skilled crafts-people, and 15 servants costs 795 gp per month in salary and 990 gp per month in common meals. Services sold to area residents bring in an average yearly profit of 5,000 gp.

The bailey castle requires fifty weeks to build.

89

Barbican

This two-story stone-and-mortar building is the only peaceable way into the castle. The ground floor is merely a passageway wide enough for a wagon or cart to drive into the bailey; its only other feature is an iron portcullis (hardness 10, 60 hp) operated from a guard post on the second floor. The guard post has the same horizontal slits as the watchtowers, and it has machicolations leading downward into the passageway. Visitors to the bailey castle generally announce their name and business and then pass through the barbican, after a soldier in the guard post waves them through. The portcullis generally stays open from dawn until dusk.

In wartime, the flat roof of the barbican is a platform for ballistas and catapults.

Bailey

The walls of the bailey castle provide shelter for local commerce and the many services required by a castle.

Summer Kitchen: The heat of the cook-fire sometimes raises the temperature of the main castle to uncomfortable levels. In the summer, cooks use a separate wooden building, then carry the food inside.

Chapel: This small shrine is devoted to a deity favored by the lord of the keep, or one friendly to farmers (such as Pelor) or travelers (such as Fharlanghn).

Stables: Up to twenty horses can be stabled in this wooden building. A loft stores hay.

Brewery: This wooden building is popular enough that it stays locked. If the castle receives many travelers, the castle lord expands the brewery to include a small tavern.

Smithy: The blacksmith here does a booming business in horseshoes and plowshares, but she is capable of mending most weapons and armor.

Barracks: The soldiers who guard the bailey castle live in these simple wooden buildings.

Granary: This building stores extra food, which the castle inhabitants move into the main castle at the faintest rumor of war.

General Store: This small, wooden structure offers a variety of tools, spices for cooking, and the occasional luxury item from the big city. The local merchant has contacts elsewhere and can "special order" requested goods.

Typical Bailey Castle Soldier: Human War1; CR 1; Medium-size humanoid; HD 1d8+2; hp 6; Init +2; Spd 20 ft.; AC 16 (touch 12, flat-footed 14); Atk +3 melee (2d4+1/×3, ranseur) or +3 ranged (1d8/×3, longbow); AL N; SV Fort +4, Ref +2, Will +0; Str 13, Dex 15, Con 14, Int 12, Wis 10, Cha 8.

Skills and Feats: Climb +1, Handle Animal +3, Jump +1, Spot +2; Point Blank Shot, Weapon Focus (ranseur).

Possessions: Scale mail armor, ranseur, short sword, longbow, 20 arrows.

Typical Patrol Rider: Human Ftr1; CR 1; Medium-size humanoid; HD 1d10+1; hp 6; Init +2; Spd 20 ft.; AC 19 (touch 12, flat-footed 17); Atk +3 melee (1d8+2/×3, heavy lance) or +3 ranged (1d6/×3, shortbow); AL N; SV Fort +3, Ref +2, Will +0; Str 15, Dex 14, Con 13, Int 12, Wis 10, Cha 8.

Skills and Feats: Climb –1, Handle Animal +3, Ride (horse) +8, Spot +2; Mounted Combat, Ride-By Attack, Skill Focus (Ride [horse]).

Possessions: Chainmail, large wooden shield, heavy lance, longsword, shortbow, 20 arrows, light warhorse.

Dwarven Plateau Castle

Atop lonely mesas, dwarves build fortresses that are almost impervious to attacks from the surface world. They begin by building a quarry atop the plateau for all the stone they need. Then they construct the fortresses in the mined-out quarries themselves, leaving buttressed domes of solid stone as the only surface marker of their presence. A road runs through a notch carved into the plateau itself, depositing visitors at the only surface entrance to an impregnable castle.

The plateau castle consists of five cylindrical "halls" sunk into the ground so that only their domed roofs are visible. A crenellated platform sits atop each dome, providing room for dwarves to defend against surface attack. Underground tunnels connect the halls with each other and with single-story ballista towers that overlook the road leading to the castle. In addition, in larger plateau castles, these passageways lead to further underground labyrinths or the world-spanning Underdark itself.

Pipes lead from a series of cisterns to each hall, and enterprising dwarves even raise fish in some of the cisterns. Trash is burned in the forges or simply dumped into a natural fissure or other deep hole. Walls, floors, and ceilings are constructed of reinforced masonry or hewn stone, with wood and weaker materials only used when necessary.

Common Features of the Five Halls

Domes: These are constructed of magically treated, hewn stone (hardness 16, 1,080 hp) that has been polished to make it hard to climb (DC 24). Rain gutters surround the base of each dome and lead to the cisterns, but the dwarves are smart enough to plug the openings if an attack is imminent, to prevent foes poisoning the water supply.

Platforms: A flat platform surrounded by crenellations sits atop each dome. A chimney rises through the center of each platform, and a staircase spirals around the chimney, giving access to each floor of the hall below.

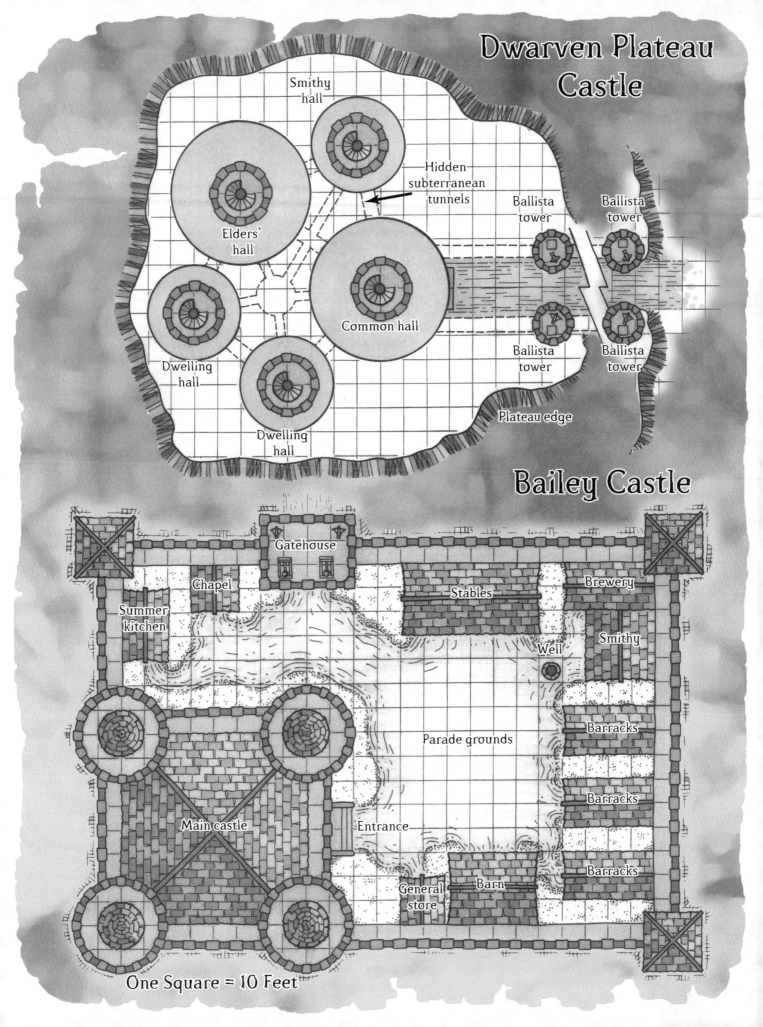

Dwarven Plateau Castle

Smithy hall

Hidden subterranean tunnels

Elders' hall

Ballista tower

Ballista tower

Common hall

Dwelling hall

Ballista tower

Ballista tower

Dwelling hall

Plateau edge

Bailey Castle

Gatehouse

Chapel

Stables

Brewery

Summer kitchen

Well

Smithy

Barracks

Parade grounds

Barracks

Main castle

Entrance

Barracks

General store

Barn

One Square = 10 Feet

Common Hall

This three-story structure (two stories underground) is the only part of the castle that visitors usually see. It includes a formal audience chamber, large kitchen, and a massive greathall where banquets and important meetings are held. In an effort to be accommodating to larger guests, doors and furniture are sized a little larger than necessary for dwarven frames. Most dwarves take at least their evening meal here, drawn by the bells of the massive clock in the greathall. Small temples and shrines to Moradin and other deities important to the dwarves can be found in this hall as well. A brewery and mushroom-farm share the lowest level. The large fireplaces of the kitchen lead upward to a chimney that pierces the center of the dome.

Dwelling Hall

A typical plateau castle has at least two dwelling halls, and some have as many as six or seven. Each includes living space for the soldiers who guard the castle, the servants and smiths who keep it running, and the families who live there. Smaller family kitchens provide meals for those seeking privacy, and sitting rooms are sprinkled around the hall where dwarves relax when they are not working. Each dwelling hall accommodates about 60 dwarves.

Elder Hall

The ruler of the castle lives here along with family and personal servants. Rooms in this hall are much more spacious and well appointed—any dwarf who can afford to build a plateau castle can afford fine stonework and furnishings. Art galleries are common in elder halls, as are libraries with histories of various dwarven clans. The lowest floor is devoted to a massive audience chamber, while the upper floors are the individual residences of the ruling family and their servants.

Smithy Hall

This hall is dominated by a massive smithy where the dwarves forge weapons, armor, and countless other metal implements. A crew of dwarves works here day and night on various items to be used either by the castle inhabitants or sold to the outside world. Given the dwarven love of fine craft, it is not surprising that the smithy and tools are first-rate. Other workshops for stonecutting, woodworking, etc., also have a home in this hall. A museumlike "chamber of craft" displays some of the castle's best work—which the lord of the castle is often eager to show off to knowledgeable guests.

How Much Does It Cost?

The dwarven plateau castle detailed here costs 550,000 gp, including a variety of fancy and luxury furnishings. Each additional dwelling hall (beyond the two shown on the map) costs 30,000 gp. A staff of 100 dwarf soldiers, 30 smiths and stonecutters, and 20 servants costs 900 gp per month in salary and 1,350 gp per month in common meals.

The plateau castle takes fifty-five weeks to build.

Outside the Castle

A long, sloping road cuts a notch in the plateau and leads to the common hall, ending at huge, iron doors. Two-story ballista towers overlook the road from both sides, but there is no access to the towers from the surface. The dwarves have built tunnels connecting the ballista towers to the common hall, so they need never expose themselves to the outside world. It is also common to have a well-disguised escape tunnel built for an emergency, but often only the lord of the castle knows of its existence.

Typical Dwarf Soldier: Dwarf War1; CR 1; Medium-size humanoid; HD 1d8+3; hp 7; Init +1; Spd 15 ft.; AC 17 (touch 11, flat-footed 16); Atk +3 melee (1d10+2/×3, dwarven waraxe) or +2 ranged (1d10/19–20, heavy crossbow); SQ Dwarf traits; AL N; SV Fort +5, Ref +1, Will +1; Str 15, Dex 13, Con 16, Int 10, Wis 12, Cha 6.

Skills and Feats: Climb +0, Craft (metalworking) +2, Craft (stoneworking) +2, Craft (weaponsmithing) +2; Exotic Weapon Proficiency (dwarven waraxe).

Possessions: Scale mail armor, large steel shield, dwarven waraxe, heavy crossbow, 10 crossbow bolts.

Typical Dwarf War-Healer: Dwarf Clr2; CR 2; Medium-size humanoid; HD 2d8+9; hp 18; Init –1; Spd 15 ft.; AC 17 (touch 9, flat-footed 17); Atk +2 melee (1d8+1, heavy mace) or +0 ranged (1d10/19–20, heavy crossbow); SA Turn undead (3/day); SQ Dwarf traits; AL N; SV Fort +6, Ref –1, Will +5; Str 13, Dex 8, Con 16, Int 10, Wis 15, Cha 10.

Skills and Feats: Concentration +8, Craft (metalworking) +2, Craft (stoneworking) +2, Heal +7; Toughness.

Spells Prepared: (4/4; base DC = 12 + spell level): 0—*detect magic, guidance, read magic, resistance;* 1st—*endure elements, magic weapon, sanctuary*, shield of faith.*

*Domain spell. *Deity:* None. *Domains:* Earth (turn air/rebuke earth, 3/day), Protection (protective ward, 1/day).

Possessions: Splint mail armor, large steel shield, heavy mace, heavy crossbow, 10 crossbow bolts.

Monks' Temple

While lords and soldiers rely on walls, towers, and battlements to protect them, monkish orders count on the isolation of their monasteries, their reputation for poverty—and their combat skills for protection.

A monks' temple consists of six to eight one- and two-story wooden buildings, connected by footpaths that wind through peaceful gardens and courtyards. However, sometimes a cadre of monks practicing their "mighty shouts" shatters the temple's serenity.

Temple architecture relies heavily on sliding panels for both interior and exterior walls. Exterior walls have many sliding panels that the monks open or close as the weather demands; these panels serve as both windows and doors. Interior walls consist entirely of sliding panels made of solid wood, latticework, or paper sheets supported by a thin wooden grille. Floors are typically raised on posts several feet from the ground, incorporating crawlspaces for storage beneath each building. Thatched or shingled roofs are steeply sloped, providing yet more storage space in the attics.

A sacred pool fed by a wellspring provides fresh water for the monks, who reuse or compost nearly all their waste. They grow their own food if the land nearby is arable, or purchase it with temple donations if not.

Temple Buildings

Public Shrines and Offices: This two-story building, somewhat more ornate than the others, contains various small shrines that both locals and pilgrims visit, leaving offerings behind for the monks. Shrines range from small cubbyholes filled with candles and statuettes to larger altars and statues surrounded by low benches. Those monks who have regular contact with the outside world (such as a monk purchasing agent, speaker, or recruiter) keep spartan offices here.

Hall of Inspiration: This single-story building is where the monks themselves worship, bowing before a series of statues of wise masters who have achieved at least a measure of enlightenment. Incense fills the candlelit air.

Hall of Learning: The monastery's scrolls and books rest here, along with desks and writing tools. Monks often spend long hours here studying calligraphy and seeking the "contemplative moment."

Hall of Prowess: This two-story building is where most of the order's athletic and martial-arts training takes place. At any one time, a handful of low-level recruits work to master basic stances and attacks, as well as more advanced monks sparring, training, or simply holding a single pose for hours on end. The attic and crawlspace hold the monastery's modest arsenal of weapons.

Hall of Veneration: This building is devoted to the memory of monks who have died in the service of the monastery. Hundreds of small shrines cover the walls, and shelves contain urns with the ashes of deceased brothers and sisters. The monks keep incense and candles burning here constantly.

Garden: This elaborate, immaculately trimmed garden is a favored spot for "walking meditations." The monks each take a turn pruning and planting to keep the garden in beautiful shape.

Hall of Contemplation: This building contains one large room for group meditations and any ceremonial meetings required by the order.

Living Quarters: Paper panels divide the first floor of this building into tiny cells where the monks sleep on mats. Upstairs, senior monks have larger rooms only slightly less austere. A doorway leads to the dining hall.

Dining Hall: A single long table is the dominant feature of this room, where monks take their meals in two shifts.

Kitchen: Kitchen duty rotates among the monks, with even the most senior taking their turn washing bowls and cutting vegetables. The fare is simple and often vegetarian.

Storage: The monk's supply of extra food is kept here.

Fountain: This fountain bubbles softly, the result of a natural wellspring that rises from the earth here. This is also a favorite meditation spot for the monks.

Typical Acolyte Monk: Human Mnk1; CR 1; Medium-size humanoid; HD 1d8+1; hp 5; Init +6; Spd 30 ft.; AC 14 (touch 14, flat-footed 12); Atk +1 melee (1d6+1, unarmed strike); SA Flurry of blows, stunning attack (1/day); SQ Evasion, fast movement; AL LN; SV Fort +3, Ref +4, Will +4; Str 13, Dex 15, Con 12, Int 10, Wis 14, Cha 8.

Skills and Feats: Balance +6, Hide +6, Jump +5, Move Silently +6, Tumble +6; Dodge, Improved Initiative.

Possessions: Robes.

Typical Master Monk: Human Adp3/Mnk3; CR 6; Medium-size humanoid; HD 3d6+3 plus 3d8+3; hp 17; Init +7; Spd 30 ft.; AC 15 (touch 15, flat-footed 12); Atk +6 melee (1d6+1, unarmed strike); SA Flurry of

How Much Does It Cost?

The monks' temple costs 60,000 gp to construct, though with free labor provided by the monks this reduces to 40,000 gp. The 100 monks who inhabit a typical monastery earn no pay and eat only 150 gp per month in meager meals, including food harvested from their own gardens.

The monks' temple takes six weeks to build.

Gladiatorial Arena

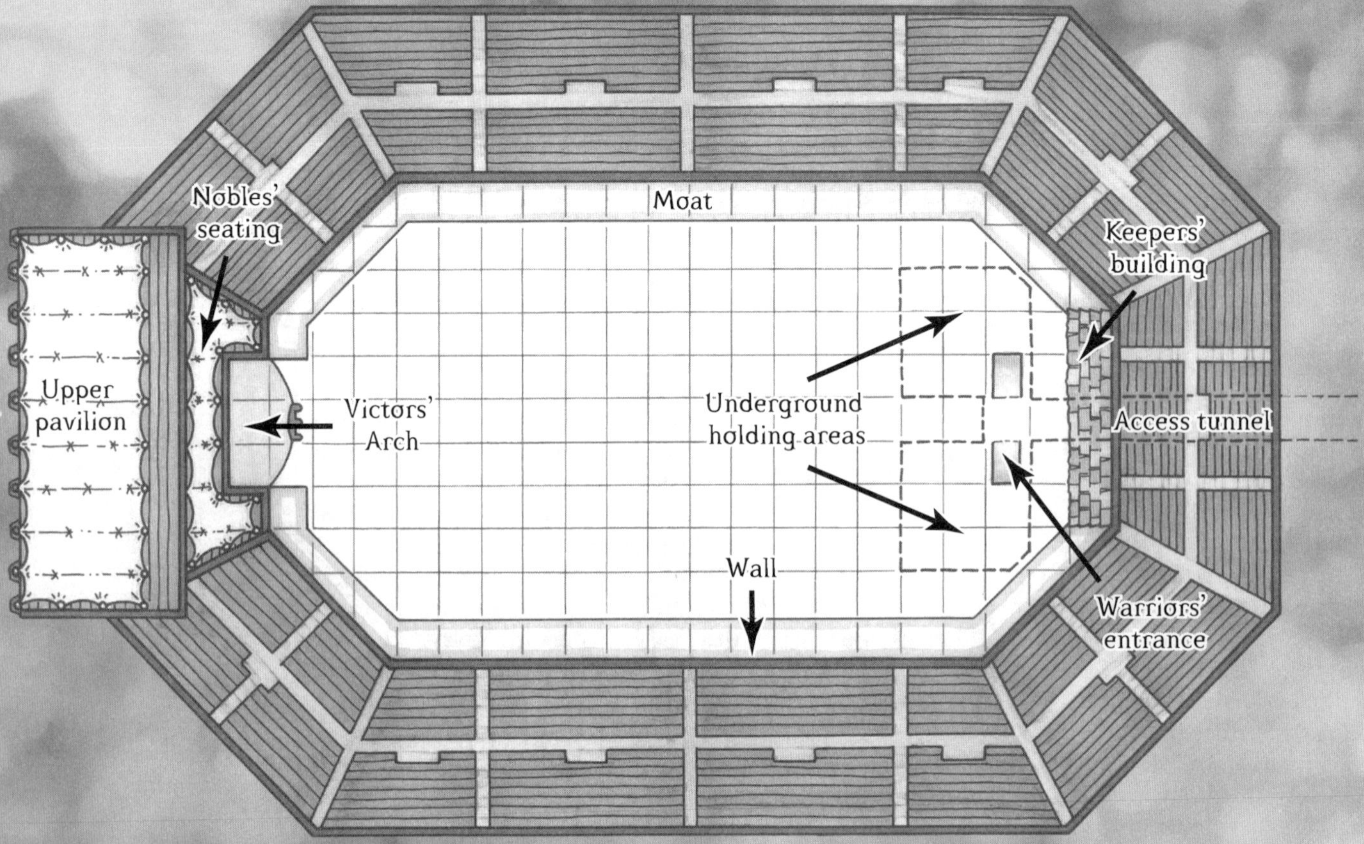

Nobles' seating

Moat

Keepers' building

Upper pavilion

Victors' Arch

Underground holding areas

Access tunnel

Wall

Warriors' entrance

Monks' Temple Compound

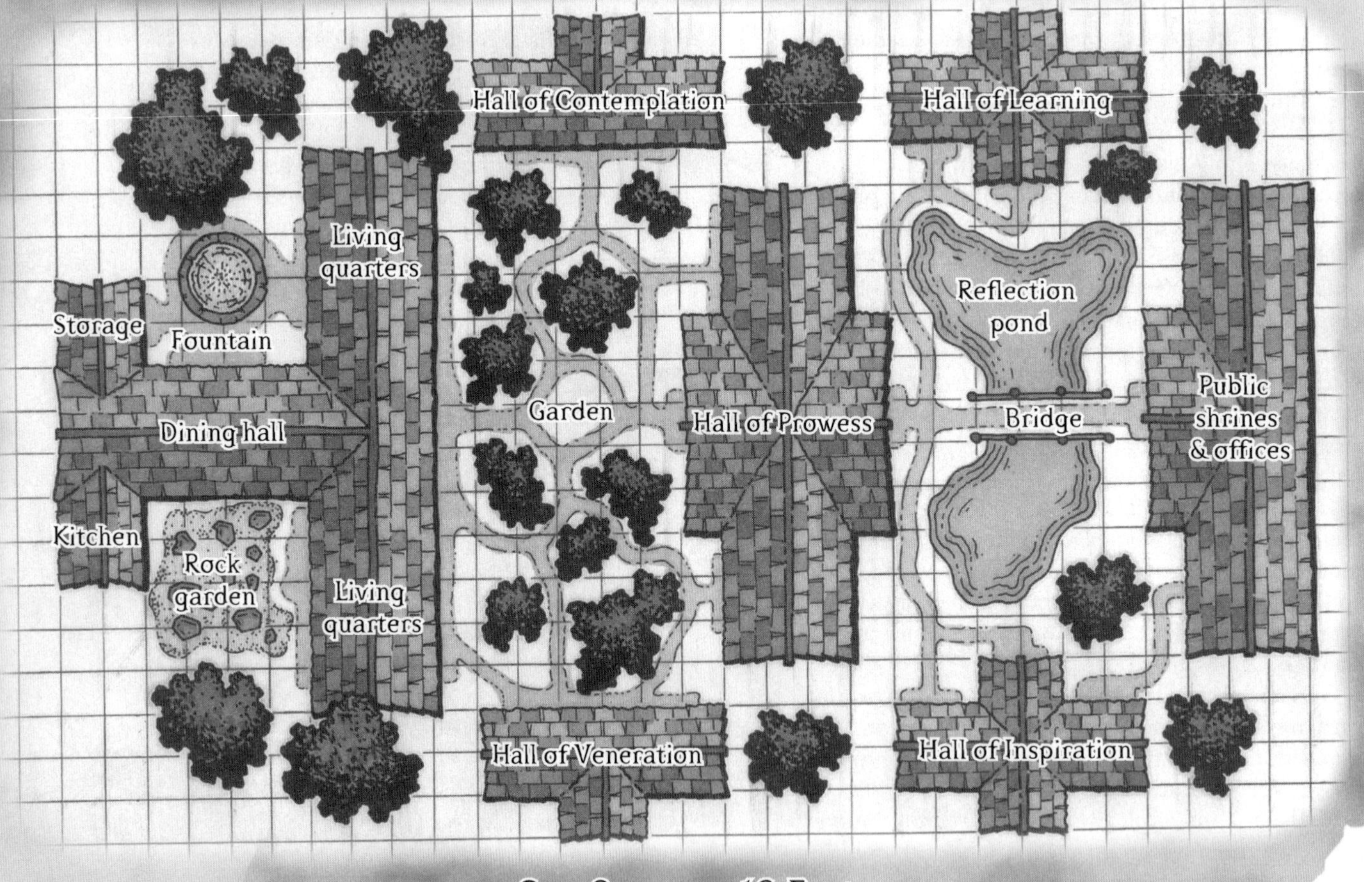

Hall of Contemplation

Hall of Learning

Living quarters

Storage

Fountain

Reflection pond

Dining hall

Garden

Hall of Prowess

Bridge

Public shrines & offices

Kitchen

Rock garden

Living quarters

Hall of Veneration

Hall of Inspiration

One Square = 10 Feet

blows, stunning attack (3/day); SQ Evasion, fast movement, still mind; AL LN; SV Fort +3, Ref +7, Will +8; Str 12, Dex 16, Con 8, Int 13, Wis 14, Cha 10.

Skills and Feats: Balance +5, Craft (calligraphy) +4, Diplomacy +6, Heal +8, Jump +3, Knowledge (arcana) +5, Knowledge (religion) +5, Listen +5, Perform (flute, drum, storytelling) +3, Profession (herbalist) +6, Tumble +9; Deflect Arrows, Dodge, Expertise, Improved Initiative, Weapon Finesse (unarmed strike).

Spells Prepared: (3/3; base DC = 12 + spell level): 0—*cure minor wounds, mending, read magic*; 1st—*bless, cure light wounds, endure elements.*

Possessions: Robes.

Gladiatorial Arena

Few public spectacles draw as much attention as a gladiatorial match does. Fans from across the city chant and shout from their seats as two combatants face off in a battle—sometimes to the death.

Gladiatorial arenas are designed to provide a good view of the battles below while keeping spectators and participants separated. Some gladiators are slaves who would love the chance to bolt over a wall to freedom. Other gladiators are monsters captured from the wilderness who have their own reasons to leap into the crowd.

Good reasons exist to keep the spectators under control, too. Fans sometime turn into angry mobs when a battle does not go their way, and unscrupulous gladiators sometimes plant associates in the crowd in an attempt to cheat by swaying the crowd's opinion.

Accordingly, this arena (typical of a small city arena) has a 40-foot wall of superior masonry (Climb DC 20) surrounding the arena on the outside edge of a 10-foot wide, 15-foot deep moat. Archers keep a close eye on both gladiators and fans, and a cadre of troops with halberds is ready to march into the arena and restore order if things get too unruly.

This arena seats about 2,500 spectators, including a large, shaded pavilion with individual seats set aside for richer fans. Most working-class fans sit in low benches on the east, west, or south sides of the building (when they are not standing and shouting, that is).

Arena Features

Keeper's Building: About a dozen or so heavily armored "keepers" watch the combats from this bunker-like structure. Keepers are responsible for setting up any props between battles, managing the animals and monsters used, goading unwilling combatants to fight, and dragging away the bodies afterward.

Moat and Wall: Referees with longbows man the top of the wall every 50 feet or so. They stand in pairs back to back: one watches the gladiators, the other watches the crowd.

Underground Holding Areas: Underground tunnels connect these two rooms to a nondescript building across the street from the arena (where the gladiators enter, out of the sight of rabid spectators). The quality of these rooms depends on the status of gladiators in the city. If they are slaves, these are simply well-guarded cages. However, if the combatants are professional athletes, these are warm-up rooms complete with coaches, weaponsmiths, and each gladiator's entourage.

Warriors' Entrance: This tent covers the stairway from the holding area and can be collapsed when a keeper pulls a single rope—a dramatic entrance sure to fire up the crowd. Gladiators generally enter one at a time, accepting the accolades of the crowd, then move north to await the start of the match.

Victor's Arch: Winning gladiators traditionally head through this arch, where they are showered with flower petals from the nobles, and from where the city's rulers get a good view of them. The arch leads only to a guarded series of waiting rooms, where the gladiators remain until the crowd disperses.

Typical New Gladiator: Human Ftr1; CR 1; Medium-size humanoid; HD 1d10+1; hp 6; Init +2; Spd 20 ft.; AC 17 (touch 12, flat-footed 15); Atk +3 melee (1d8+3/19–20, two-bladed sword) or +1 melee (1d8+2/19–20, two-bladed sword) and +1 melee (1d8/19–20, two-bladed sword); AL N; SV Fort +3, Ref +2, Will +0; Str 14, Dex 15, Con 13, Int 8, Wis 10, Cha 12.

Skills and Feats: Jump +2, Perform +3; Ambidexterity, Exotic Weapon Proficiency (two-bladed sword), Two-Weapon Fighting

Possessions: Breastplate, two-bladed sword.

Typical Experienced Gladiator: Human Rgr1/Ftr6/Gladiator 2; CR 9; Medium-size humanoid; HD 9d10+18; hp 69; Init +2; Spd 30 ft.; AC 18 (touch 12, flat-footed 18); Atk +14/+9 melee (1d8+7, *+1 dire flail*) or +10/ +5 melee (1d8+6, *+1 dire flail*) and +5 melee (1d8+4, *+1 dire flail*); SQ Favored enemy (humans), improved feint, study opponent +1; AL NE; SV Fort +12, Ref +4, Will +1; Str 16, Dex 14, Con 14, Int 13, Wis 8, Cha 14.

Skills and Feats: Bluff +7, Climb +13, Diplomacy +4, Handle Animal +8, Intimidate +4, Jump +13, Perform +7, Ride (horse) +12, Use Rope +8; Dodge, Exotic Weapon Proficiency (dire flail), Expertise, Improved Disarm, Improved Trip, Knock-Down, Mounted Combat, Track, Weapon Focus (dire flail), Weapon Specialization (dire flail).

Possessions: *+1 dire flail, +2 chain shirt.*

> ### How Much Does It Cost?
> An arena such as the one shown costs about 260,000 gp to build. Yearly profit amounts to about 2,600 gp.
>
> The gladiatorial arena takes about twenty-six weeks to build.

Unusual Gladiator Fights

Dwarf-and-Giant Battles: This many-on-one battle rarely pits actual giants against actual dwarves (although that has been known to happen). Usually a group of small, nimble opponents such as halfling rogues face off against a single hulking brute armed with an array of huge weapons. The small combatants must use group tactics to bring their big foe down, while the large gladiator tries to keep the quicker opponents at bay long enough to pick them off one by one.

Blind-Fight: This one is simple: Two well-armed but poorly-armored opponents are blindfolded before their fight. They are often festooned with bells that jingle whenever they move to give a clue to their position. The crowd typically finds comical the stumbles, missed charges, and wild swings these fights produce.

Hidden Weapons: The gladiators begin the fight unarmed and unarmored. Strewn about the field of battle are all manner of arms and armor—and enough low walls, barricades and other obstacles to make moving about the arena floor difficult. Gladiators must find weapons and armor to defend themselves before other gladiators find them.

Jousts and Mounted Battles: In societies that value equestrian prowess, arenas host as many horse races as gladiatorial bouts. Sometimes the two combine. Four mounted gladiators must ride an obstacle course to reach the three lances and shields at the end of the arena. Swinging low at full gallop to pick up their weapons, the gladiators turn on each other, spurring their tired horses into battle.

Chain Matches: These matches often use convicts, who are often promised freedom if they win. Pairs of gladiators are chained together, then released to do battle in a hand-to-hand free-for-all. Successful gladiator pairs coordinate their movements so the chain does not hamper them, and the best even manage to use the chain as a weapon.

Captured Monster: Some gladiatorial promoters are known to pay well for captured monsters from the wilderness—everything from bears and tigers to more exotic beasts such as hell hounds, dinosaurs, or minotaurs.

Race against Time: Two gladiators are placed on a dais suspended over a pool of acid, flaming oil, or poisoned water. Through magic or mechanical clock-works, the dais slowly sinks into the liquid. Only by winning the battle can a gladiator stop the dais.

The Siege: Arena managers build a wooden stockade in the middle of the stadium. A small team of gladiators must defend it with flaming arrows and vats of boiling oil, while a larger team armed with battering rams must seize the stockade (usually destroying it in the process).

Naval Battle: Only the largest arenas have the resources to pull this battle off, but it is always a spectacle that is talked about for years. The entire arena is flooded, then mock warships are constructed to give the spectators a taste of what real naval combat is like. Two rival navies ram each other, swing from ship to ship on ropes, repel boarders, and engage in swordfights in the rigging itself.

Spellcaster Duels: Arena organizers insist that all spells be suitably flashy and carefully targeted (area-effect spells such as fireball are prohibited). Creatures summoned with summon monster or summon nature's ally are particularly popular, as are rays and ranged touch attacks that do not have the certainty of a magic missile, for example.